THE RISEN SERIES BOOK FIVE
DEFIANCE
A ZOMBIE APOCALYPSE HORROR STORY

SOMETIMES
DEFIANCE
IS ALL WHICH
KEEPS ONE
GOING.

MARIE F CROW

Copyright

Defiance is a work of fiction. All names, characters, locations, and incidents are the products of the author's imagination or are used fictitiously. Any resemblance to actual events, locales, or persons, living or dead, is entirely coincidental.

DEFIANCE: A NOVEL
Copyright © 2020 by Marie F. Crow
All rights reserved.

Editing by KP Editing
Cover Design by KP Designs
- www.kpdesignshop.com
Published by Kingston Publishing Company
- www.kingstonpublishing.com

Table of Contents

THE RISEN SERIES BOOK FIVE

DEFIANCE

A ZOMBIE APOCALYPSE HORROR STORY

SOMETIMES
DEFIANCE
IS ALL WHICH
KEEPS ONE
GOING.

MARIE F CROW

"Dad?"

The man I never thought I would see again - the man I never thought I wanted to see again – stands before me highlighted like a phantom by my truck's headlights. The lights add an eerie glow to him, as if he is already dead, and gone, and this is just my mind tormenting me once again. But it's not. My father, Collin Hawthorn, is very much alive and well. At least, for now, he is.

Rhett and Lawless part, tense and waiting for me to either make peace or war with whom we have stumbled upon. I can almost hear Fate giggling with every step I take towards them. Her twin, Karma, is just waiting to see what I will do, as are those around me.

"Dad?" I repeat, as if fog will take the features I am seeing and twist them into a different man standing before me.

It doesn't.

"Helena?" I hear him ask.

Only for a moment, my father's eyes rest on me. He is already trying to peer through the burning lights of the truck for those he hopes might be inside. My father isn't looking at me. He was never even looking for me. He is looking for his Angels.

The same pit of nothing I have dwelled inside of slithers around me. It takes its cold grasp and leeches the tenderness from me that I had allowed to fool me. I was stupid to think this was about to become something more; something I used to once crave.

"They are dead," I tell him, and his hopeful eyes.

I watch the light shrink from his face. I watched the joy he was wearing shrivel to agony. I watch him transform and I feel nothing for him.

"I killed them," I tell him, further ripping the heart from his body. "I killed my mother. I killed Ashley. I killed Conroy."

The men around me shuffle the way people do when tension rises, but my men, they aren't normal men. They don't just shuffle. Knives are grasped and a gun is chambered. They are still too raw from what we have left behind to 'play nice'.

"Lilly?" my father asks me, noticing her name missing from my list.

His voice is breaking. The simple name caught in his throat before shredding its way free. A nicer person might be more tender with the bad news I have to share with him. A nicer person might care to ease this man through his suffering; a short, guided version of the tour that is waiting for him. I'm not that person. I'm the daughter he didn't want, and I have no comfort to offer this man.

"You can thank your wife for that death."

I watch as my words cripple him. I watch as they take the strength from his legs. He is reduced to nothing more than a pile of flesh in the arms of the two men beside him, as they guide him to the cold street beneath their feet.

David only used a little stone to kill Goliath. Such a simple weapon and it changed the world around them. Stones, like words, can do such horrible things to people. Truth, now that bitch, she can destroy people. I am Helena Hawthorn and the world has taught me well the damage Truth can do to a person's soul.

Chapter 1

I'm dreaming. It's the same dream I have had for as many nights as we have been on the run. We linger here or there until they find us. Somehow, despite our best efforts, the Risen always find us.

I'm four again. I'm standing in my new boots and my 'good dress' in the kitchen. A kitchen I will always remember being too white. It's too perfect, too clean, and everything I am not.

It's not white anymore. In my excitement to show my father the frog I have caught, I have trailed behind me the proof of the weather. The brown mud is smeared in child-sized prints trailing behind me.

I have been exploring every puddle, every overflowing ditch with the eyes of a child. They were worlds to me inside of my world and I dove deep into their waters, soaking my dress, my hair, and ruining my boots.

No one tells a kid the rules of suede. All I had known when I first saw them, was they were a deep red with gold stitching. They made me feel pretty, which was something I was starting to learn I didn't measure up to in my mother's eyes. After my little exploring adventure, they are almost black with the water soaking them and the mud encasing them.

"What have you done?" Carol screams at my former self.

She is not really looking at me. All she can see is the once perfect carpet of the living room I have marred. She sees the perfectly clean kitchen tiles I am dripping muddy water upon. In fact, I don't really remember her ever really looking at me until she wanted to eat me that morning in the hallway.

My father runs into the room hearing her screams. His eyes look from her to me and back as a smile slowly starts to form. Seeing his silent approval, I happily hold the wiggling reptile out to show him. Of course, it picks this time to slip free, bouncing across the tiles straight for Carol. It heads straight for the woman who has already filled the house with her pitch of distress. Her voice climbs octaves now.

My father rushes to save her. He is laughing as he chases the jumping creature across the floor, making a grand show of his heroics with his facial expression and remarks. I stand, my four-year-old self, laughing at the man I had placed all of my love and trust in, the way which little girls blindly do. I watch as the person who was once me, covers her mouth as sounds of childhood glee float from her.

I'm never really in the dream, but a soundless watcher knowing what waits for those I am watching, constantly unable to stop any of it. My point-of-view flips from the me then, to the me now, without reason or timing. It adds to the horror.

"I'm glad you two find this amusing," Carol wails. "I spend all day cleaning this place and for what? No one respects me."

My father almost snorts over her drama.

"It's just a frog, Car. It's not like she brought in the whole ark," he tells her, casting a wink my way.

"You always take her side. Ever since you brought her home," Carol cries, "I have not been able to do anything right."

I watch as the little girl who was myself cocks her head hearing what Carol has said. Even at that age, I knew it wasn't phrased right. The little girl with a wet dress, and even wetter braids, looks to the man she believes holds all the answers, but he won't meet her eyes.

"Not now," he says to the woman I thought of as a mother.

I watch as he reaches a hand out to Carol. I watch as she turns from him. Like someone underwater, I scream silently, trying to warn my dad about what is going to happen next. I try to tell my former self to run, to not look, but just like a person underwater, I'm choking on the sounds.

The true memory has Carol turning to shove my father away, but this isn't just a memory. It's the twisted effigy of what my mind holds as days meld with the past.

Carol turns as he reaches for her and she is as she was that morning I discovered what had become of our world. She stands, no longer in her A-line skirt with its matching blouse, but in the yellow nightgown, covered in the blood of my sister. Grabbing my father's arm, she pulls him to her sneering face, destroying him much as she destroyed Lilly.

She latches onto his neck where the tender flesh meets between the ear and shoulder. She pulls it between her teeth until the long cords of tissue sever. Spraying the white walls with his red blood in a mist, my father dies still staring at me with the slow smile of approval he came into the room wearing.

I'm screaming for me to run. I'm trapped behind the scenes unable to reach the cast of the play in front of me. Carol stalks towards the four-year-old who is staring at her with confusion. I close my eyes. I used to watch it like I could stop it. I used to stand, screaming into the space around me. Now I wait for it to end, but no matter how hard I close my eyes, I can still hear it all.

I hear the moment Carol finds me. I hear the sick, wet sounds of Carol destroying me. I know the moment I die, and I know I will die again tomorrow night. I die every night at the hands of a woman who was never really my mother.

It's always this memory my sleeping demons pick to twist. This is the moment in time when I first knew something was wrong. This is when I first caught the first of the clues I chose to ignore through the years.

She didn't eat my father and me then, but she killed us just the same. She drove the first wedge between us that day. He stood there, holding her as she cried while he stared at me.

"I love both my girls," he had said with worry engulfing him.

"If you ever loved me, you couldn't love her," Carol had said.

It was then the light in my father's eyes had started to dim for me. It was that day, in that very white kitchen, she had declared a war between her and I. A war a four-year-old would never win, and she never did.

"Hells," Lawless calls to me from the blackness that surrounds me. "Hells, it's just a dream."

My eyes flutter, opening to see the stars above me in their black landscape.

"Jesus woman, get some therapy so the rest of us can get some sleep," Rhett sleepily mutters from his spot beyond me.

"I could just kill him for you, Hells," Marxx offers, knowing fully of whom I constantly dream of now.

"Wouldn't be the first time you have offered," I say, remembering the many nights at the bar when I came in more defeated than just deflated.

"Won't be the last either," Marxx says, hinting at the long road ahead of us.

It's not just the miles we have to survive, or those we have survived. It's the blending of the two groups and it's not gone well. I haven't helped either. Surviving yet another near-death by a Risen, almost being hung, watching Chapel die, and escaping the burning school did not set the best of moods for a family reunion on the interstate so many nights ago. Not knowing I even had a family to reunion with also didn't exactly help with any heart-warming hellos. A greeting card writer, I was never meant to be.

For days I have felt like I'm living in madness trying to gently pull the truth from my father. Throw in the creatures wanting to dine on your flesh if you let your guard down and it almost feels like Christmas with the family again - one big passive-aggressive, death wish filled, holiday of fun.

"I don't even know why we are with them," Rhett continues to grumble. "They are just using the supplies we are already running short on. I swear if that boy asks to touch my bike one more time, I'm going to break his jaw."

"Rhett has a boyfriend," Aimes sings from her side of the fire.

"It's kind of cute, really," Dolph says, joining the conversation from where he is standing watch.

"Both of you, suck me," Rhett mutters and I can hear him pulling the nylon sleeping bag tighter around him.

The nights aren't as cold now, but winter keeps her fist clutched tightly around us. She refuses to give up as we refuse to give in. The slow shifting of the weather has allowed us to further space ourselves from the others. No longer are we confined to the random houses we have found deserted and depressing with their rotting dead, or worse, rotting undead. We haven't found anyone alive since leaving the burning high school. I think that is taking more of a toll on us than the many Risen we have been unfortunate to find.

"Don't worry, Rhett," Aimes says. "When I turn, you'll be the first one I come for."

"The sex that bad?" Lawless asks with a voice thick with sleep but unwilling to let a chance to tease them pass.

The silence from them both makes us all laugh.

"I'm up, Dolph. We can switch," I offer.

Dolph nods his time-tried, traditional head nod before heading to where his sleeping bag has been waiting for him. I watch as he slides into the fabric with an exhale a mattress company would envy for their commercials. A warm fire, a simple night's rest, and food consisting of something other than the canned questionable we have found are the only luxuries we now own. Needless to say, I think we are all missing the high school for one reason or another.

Slipping from the warmth of Lawless, I shiver when exposed to the night's air. I can see where the other group has their set-up similar to ours only a small space away. We keep just enough distance to keep the tension at bay, but not far enough space to prevent either group from quickly alerting the other should something go wrong.

Peyton gives a slight wave as I take watch. I return it, unsure of what else to do knowing he is watching me. Peyton has tried his best to bridge the gap between our two groups. I think it has only put him higher on Rhett's shit list.

Since Selma, Rhett has become a protective beast. He follows April like a dark shadow, daring Fate to come near her. Even now, the little girl is sleeping in his tight embrace and it's odd to see him acting as a father. His games have gone from veiled threats and innuendoes to tag and hide-and-seek. It's weird, and somehow still, all the more reassuring than any of the other many changes we have all been through. He makes me wonder if perhaps there is a chance for a 'normal' life still waiting for us.

Settling myself against the base of the tree Dolph had just left, I sigh when I recognize the shadow-like outline heading towards me. There are reasons I have stopped offering to help out. No one comes to talk to the men, but when Paula or I take watch, it's suddenly time for 'hey neighbor-like' chats around the campfire.

"How is everyone?" Peyton whispers.

Even with his attempt to stay quiet, I know from the sounds of the bags around me the men are aware he is here. After all, a deep sleep now could mean you're sleeping forever.

"Fine, I guess," I reply nonchalantly.

I don't try to hide the volume of my voice. If the men around me want to lay in the dark pretending to not be listening, I plan to call their bluff.

Peyton settles on the same tree trunk. His eyes are roaming the woods around us, watching the distant, dancing reflected lights. We have placed our little noisemakers, as Aimes calls them, around the thickest parts of trees. Everything from baby rattles to pots and pans hangs from various types of twine-styled material. They twinkle when the wind rolls them under the moon's light.

"I think we are a little road weary," Peyton shrugs as he says it, as if I asked about his group.

"What? Ginjer with a 'J' doesn't like our new life?"

I hadn't meant it to be so snarky. It just was. I guess I'm losing my touch of sarcasm.

Peyton makes a little sound of amusement anyway, before saying, "Yeah, I guess she is. I'm more worried about Genny."

I cringe when he says her name. It was one thing to discover my father was alive. It was another to discover most of my life was a lie. Not only was Carol not my mother, my siblings were only half, but I had a whole family I had never met. I had a mother who wanted me, while I grew up with one who didn't. It was bitter to hear and, in my mouth, still lingers its sour taste.

"Collin is worried about her, too. Losing her mother and her aunt like that, she's fading on us. He's trying his best, but the poor girl just keeps going deeper into herself," he says.

"Don't worry, Collin will grow bored soon enough and find something else to do."

I give Peyton big eyes of innocence when he looks at me after hearing my response. The men chuckle, daring Peyton to respond to me. He does anyway.

"I'm not going to pretend to understand everything between the two of you, or three of you, I guess," Peyton says. His lips almost frown trying to figure out exactly how we all tie together, before adding to his verbal downward spiral, "but I do know he feels a lot of shame over it. He watches you, trying to figure out what to say to you."

"You can tell him to stop," Lawless mumbles. "Anything he might have said, he should have said years ago."

"I don't think he has anything to say to you," Peyton says to the darkness behind him.

"Hell no, he doesn't," Rhett's voice answers. "He isn't that brave."

"But if his balls ever drop, he knows where we are," Lawless says with a yawn.

Our little camp comes fully awake when they hear Peyton's rustling of clothing, announcing he has not only come around the tree, but he's come to their side of the tree. I step from the direct line of glares when Rhett, Marxx, and Lawless sit up. I'm not interested in intervening in their little reindeer games, anymore. Dolph lifts his arm from over his eyes, but that is as far as he is invested in what is going on, at least for the moment.

"We don't have to like each other. We don't even have to really interact, but we all know there is safety in numbers. We have to get past whatever this is," Peyton tries to remind my group. It's cute and totally naïve.

Lawless pivots his head, looking to the other two men left to him now. Rhett's face is illuminated by the flames, making his shit-eating grin even more dangerous looking than normal. Marxx wears no expression. Trying to conceal the blade by his leg, he has already drawn his knife, hoping he knows where this is going to lead. Rhett might have become more docile since the high school, but Marxx has become more vicious.

"We are way past it," Lawless says, slowly bringing his eyes back to Peyton.

"Where is J.D. or Chapel?" Collin's voice asks when he appears beside the unfortunate tree. "Chapel finally gave up on your little deviant group? J.D. finally find a fight he couldn't win?"

The men stand at once hearing him and the names he has spoken. My head rolls back to stare up at the sky, wondering about my father's constant lack of the skill of timing.

"Ask the question again," Marxx taunts him.

His voice is so deep with his anger, and it pulls me to him. Touching Marxx's back, I try to ease some of the suffering I hear. I know Marxx is blaming himself for the loss of Chapel. He is convinced his injury has caused this somehow. Chapel gave himself over in the end so we could escape, knowing he would not survive the wound Travis gave him. There was nothing any of us could have done, but still, we each carry a 'what if' in our hearts. Marxx carries his on a platter draped with rage.

"You have your stories, we have ours. Everyone has lost someone now," Peyton steps further into our camp, trying to block the sight of my father. "Whatever lives we had before all of this; they are gone. Whatever we have done to one another, it doesn't matter anymore."

Peyton looks not only to our group, but the two men behind him as well. Terrence had also snuck into the circle, not risking his side to face whatever circumstance he thought they would, upon hearing his leader's almost pleading voice.

Whatever was to be said next, doesn't matter. The noisemakers are rattling by Peyton's camp and the screams bring even Dolph finally to standing as we rush over. I can almost hear Fate sighing with disappointment as Karma's little demons arrive around us, ruining her show. Somehow, the Risen always find us.

Chapter 2

Rhett places April between Aimes and Paula before following the rest of us. She doesn't call for him or cry out when hearing the panic around us. She has learned the lessons of this new life well. She is already following Paula to my large truck as Aimes is grabbing all the supplies, as is agreed upon when danger is near. You can't become scattered if you are already prepared to leave.

Risen are shambling through the line of trees. It's not the ones heading straight for us, though, who worry me. It's the ones creeping around the trees which makes my feet slow.

Their eyes seem to glow under the moonlight like an animal's eyes. The little oval orbs sway between the group running away from them and the group running towards them. This group is keeping to the trees, using the large bark-covered trunks to peek around at us. They seem to almost be plotting before sneaking in amid the chaos caused by the first group's appearance.

There wasn't even any noise from where they entered. There was no warning clang of the metal pots or the annoying plastic ratting from the baby toys hung around the area. My mouth grows dry realizing they figured out a way to untangle our alarms while letting the slower group distract us with theirs. They are learning, discovering new ways to defeat us as we are trying to learn new ways to survive them.

Lawless slows, feeling me missing from his side. He turns to see what I am looking at and I hear his exhale of the shared feelings. He shouts to those running ahead of us, causing them too to slow down.

We wait here, in this small space between both Risen groups. Ginjer and Genny run through our line, heading to the safety of Paula and Aimes. Kent, Terrence's son, slides to a stop by his father. The wound he had on his leg when our groups met has pretty much healed, but he still favors the hurt leg. When he smiles at Rhett with almost puppy eyes, even with the trouble before us, Lawless still snickers just loud enough to annoy Rhett.

"What are they doing?" Peyton asks.

He is watching the two different groups, trying to figure out which one to head towards first.

The five heading towards us are slow. Even with their voices at a pitch of excitement, their movements betray the stage of their decaying bodies. It's not to say they won't try to kill us. It's just these are not the main threat.

"They are waiting to rush us once we are busy with the first set," Terrence answers.

"No, watch them," Marxx argues. "They aren't planning to rush us. They are planning to sneak up on us. Look at how they are running from tree-to-tree to watch us."

"I think I would prefer if they were to rush," Dolph exhales his statement, exasperated with their constant evolution.

I watch as what Marxx had said is coming true. The other set are using the trees, and their casted shadows, to hide their movements. An occasional light-reflecting eye will peer around at us before vanishing back into the night. It's demonic. It's terrifying for my mind to watch.

"What's the deal with the other group then? What's making them so different now?" Kent asks.

Rhett leans into the teen boy's space, whispering darkly, "Why don't you go ask them? I got your back, promise."

"Why don't we just kill them and then ask Paula, should we live through this?" I ask, not risking Rhett throwing another layer of male agitation to the situation.

"Helena is right. This first. Whatever is going on, next," Collin says.

He smiles at me, trying to show his agreement with my idea. *Gee, thanks Dad, so happy to finally have your support,* is what my mind says. My face must have said something similar because his smile quickly melts, returning his attention to the monsters ahead of us and not to the monster he helped create – me.

"Great," I say, and as usual, I walk ahead of the men to taunt Death again.

"Hey!" Peyton shouts, but I don't turn to look at him.

"Get used to it." Marxx's voice silences Peyton's shouting. As he follows me, he says, "We have."

"Thanks, Dad," Lawless taunts Collin for the new motivation to my constant attempts of suicide, but I know without looking, he's running to be by my side.

I no longer flinch from the Risen. I no longer fear their sounds or their snarling, dripping mouths. There is almost a peace when I am killing. The noise stops. The pain stops. Not even my Angels play in my mind, anymore.

This is my life now, and when the white noise starts, all I can think about is how Chapel is missing from it. They took him from me, these now mutated creations from hell. I now spend every spare moment fighting the Risen. I fight in a way I couldn't fight them then, as if it might bring him back to me. It never does. Sometimes what doesn't kill you doesn't just make you stronger, it pisses you off. It's sealing my soul that much deeper in some darkness daring to rival even Marxx's.

The first kill is easy. The blade never hesitates. The puncture is paper-thin, already oozing blood and thicker fluid. I don't cringe when the dark blood splashes my face as I withdraw my knife. The murky drops are like red tears. Like the tears I seem to no longer be able to shed, they slide down my cheek to drip onto J.D.'s vest. He bathed the high school in the blood of his rage and sorrow. I keep his vest just as wet with mine.

Marxx is beside me, slashing at his own death-covered victim. He doesn't lodge his blade into the skull as much as he tries to punch his whole fist clutching the knife through it. The Risen has become so overtaken with decay, Marxx's attack concaves its head. The skull of the rotting woman seems to simply deflate, releasing so much more than just blood, but putrid gasses as well. Without the eye sockets, her eyes almost pop, smearing her face with the grease-like liquid when the corded muscle bounces them onto her cheeks. If any of this bothers Marxx, he doesn't show it. He is already moving to the next one when she falls under his feet and my body follows right behind him with his same white noise of a need to kill.

Law is watching our back. He is making sure that the other group of Risen doesn't see us as an opportunity. I imagine this is what the rest of the men are also doing. We've removed two already of the five that came from the tress, if there is to be a window of chance to be overtaken, it will come soon. When the window opens, the ones watching us from behind the trees will rush through it. With how they keep playing "peek-a-boo", I'm just not sure how many are going to fit through it.

A decaying teen reaches for me as her legs wobble under her. Her mouth, responding to the starving need to feed, is extended further than her decaying skin should stretch. She rips the thin skin around her jaw. The now tattered flesh bleeds black as sludge and the blood runs just as thick from her self-inflicted damage.

Using my shoulder, I push against her, watching her fall with her lack of coordination and gravity working against her. She falls to her side, clawing the ground to adjust her upper body to bite into my leg. As she lifts her head, I lift my foot. We collide against one another, but the force of my stomp plants her head back to the still winter-hard ground. Her head explodes like an overripe melon under my boot. It sprays brain matter and blood in a perfect semi-circle, and still her hand twitches, trying to reach for me.

Marxx has destroyed the last two. Their bodies are almost headless from his rage. He is standing with his eyes closed, head tilted skyward as he collects his breath. Lawless and I watch him. He seems to shudder with something so different than repulsion.

"Fun times," Lawless whispers into my ear.

I'm not the only one who has noticed the darker side of Marxx slowly escaping from its chains. Looking around, I see we're also not the only ones concerned about how to stop the man we have come to know from slipping away. Rhett is watching Marxx with his face mixed with emotions.

J.D. had taunted them so they would have to become something darker to survive. Ironically, it wasn't J.D. who had turned our humanity switch to pause. It was Chapel, causing a bigger hole in our souls than J.D. every could. Humanity is almost impossible to hold onto when we must become bigger monsters than the ones stalking us just to survive. It's a golden gate of a luxury none of us can afford.

"Heads up," Rhett's voice calls to our trio.

You don't turn your back to the monsters. You don't look away, but that's exactly what we have done. While we weren't watching, the real plan was set into action.

Seeing their original plan has failed, the group in the forest has come to stand beside the trees they were using to hide them. I count ten; ten sets of glowing eyes from the moon's reflective light watching us. Like the hunters they have been transformed into, they fade into the darkness with deliberate backward steps, and like the prey we have become, we watch them transfixed - not moving until they have slipped from our sight.

Even as we exhale, thinking it must be over, the sudden screaming shatters that hope. It breaks through the returning, streaming music of the night's creatures. It's Genny's voice, blending with April's, in a new song of panic. The gunshots are the drumbeats, setting the tempo of our running feet. Rhett's mumbled pleas are the chorus, framing the verses of our hard breathing as we rush to reach those who have started the second fight tonight for our lives.

Chapter 3

We had thought the group in the woods was using the five slow ones to distract us, hoping to rush us when our backs were turned. We were only half right. They were using both sets to distract us. There were never just fifteen. No, Fate would never be that kind. Watching the moving shapes among the vehicles, I count forty. There are forty ahead of us, easily.

They slam their hands against the windows of the vehicles from which our groups hide, trying to reach those who are screaming inside. Paula is using my truck's height from its elongated bed to fire into the ones who draw too close. The shotgun crackles with light, booming the sound of its barrels around us as she attempts to defend their group.

Aimes has thrown her body over April's, muffling the little girl's screams, but Rhett hears them just the same. His new life is trapped inside the truck and he runs as if hell is about to swallow them, stealing them from him forever. He is shouting their names, like a battle cry, desperately needing them to hear him so that they know he's on his way. When Aimes looks in our direction, Rhett somehow seems to run faster.

Genny and Ginjer are huddled in the backseat of the compact in which Peyton and my father travel. I can hear the teen's screams, but they don't reach me. They don't stir me the way Aimes' wide eyes do. My heart doesn't tighten over Genny at all. I should feel some guilt over this, I know, but I don't. Let my father worry over his new little family, the way he never worried over mine.

"There are too many," Dolph shouts.

"When has that ever mattered?" Lawless asks. His voice sets his intentions into motion.

"When we are this exposed! We gotta' go. We can't fight them," Dolph is panting his words, forcing them between his breaths, trying to bring logic to the emotion-fueled event unfolding before us.

The vehicles are already humming with their waiting engines. We learned long ago you can't really start a motorcycle and prep to evacuate. There are just too many of us now to orchestrate such an act. With all we have learned, tonight we will still be taught a new lesson.

Terrence and Kent shout from behind us where they have fallen behind. Their voices signal a new panic. Peyton and I turn to see the ones we had thought to vanish have finally found their window. Twice now, we have turned our back to the monsters and twice we fell into their trap.

Terrence is pushing his son, trying desperately to keep some distance between them and the group rushing towards them, but the gap is shrinking. Kent's leg is still weak from where he was injured. It seems like such a small space left ahead of us, but I know one of them won't make it.

"Rhett," I scream, turning his attention towards me, "get my truck."

Rhett is already far ahead of me, but he still sees behind me what is about to happen. He makes a motion for Aimes to see when he looks back at her, and whatever it was, seems to make sense to her. She slides to the driver's door, waiting for him. Marxx and Law clear his path, shooting into the Risen who attempt to reach for Rhett. Rhett never slows, trusting Marxx and Lawless with more than just his life. He is trusting them with the lives of those he is running towards, and when he almost collides with the truck, Aimes shoves the door open. Rhett uses it like a weapon, smashing the thick metal into the male who lunges for him. It bounces the Risen's skull against the glass, smearing it with almost burgundy-colored gore.

With Rhett in my truck, it's now my job to get to his Harley. Rhett spares me a smirk through the streaking gore when my truck whips around to cut off the second group. The ignition switch glows like a warning, asking me if this is something I really want to do. It's not, but I will. His Softail is wide through my hips and bucks underneath me as if it knows I am not its true rider as I ease the clutch, almost stalling her.

"Easy," Lawless says beside me. "Let her out easy. Swallow down the panic, Hells."

I do. Forgetting all that is around me, and all that is waiting for me should I drop this bike, I force my heart down into my chest and free from my throat. This time I walk out the clutch, straining for my toes to reach the ground. I don't fully lift my feet until the bike has gained a steady momentum. It still sputters, but it doesn't try to throw me like the wild beast I imagine them to be.

"A little more," Lawless coaxes.

Rhett is pushing my truck with his fast acceleration to reach Terrence and Kurt, mowing down the clumped groups of Risen like a southern teen aiming for mud puddles, and I can still feel his eyes on me and his bike. Embracing my middle finger of a mantra, I dare the bike, feeding it the throttle. When it roars under me, they all roar behind me, with Law, Marxx, and Dolph following me out.

Glancing in the side mirror, I watch as Law and Marxx smirk to each other, but it's my father and Peyton I'm following. They have split up, diving for the two vehicles left behind. Peyton has fought his way to the red Jeep while my father has forced his way through to the compact. With their headlights swinging towards us, they too are now following Rhett's charge.

Paula has lowered the truck's tailgate. Her hopes lie with Rhett bringing them just close enough for her to help pull the two men left to safety. Once again, such a small amount of space has grown into what looks like acres.

Rhett doesn't veer from his collision course. Terrence doesn't either. I inhale watching the two of them. Rhett is planning to sideswipe the two, not letting the Risen figure out where to move to block him. If either set of men mistimes this, the tragedy will echo louder than anything the Risen might have done so far tonight.

The small slice of space between Terrence and the truck causes me to gasp. Anything closer and Rhett would have taken the man's shoulder off. Knowing Rhett, I wonder how much of this was precision and how much was a dare. Watching through the back glass as Aimes hits his shoulder, I know I'm not alone in my thoughts.

Paula reaches for Terrence and Kent, leaning with her whole upper body to grasp their hands. They connect for a brief moment before everything goes horribly wrong. The truck strikes a Risen, bouncing the truck and slipping their hands apart. Terrence is shoving his son forward, but it's no use. Kent's leg is no longer absorbing the abuse, it's cramping. Terrence, seeing this, switches his strategy, lunging for the truck's tailgate, he lifts himself onto it with Paula steading him. Terrence turns, reaching for his son. Their fingers are just shy of the other's, causing Paula to shout for Rhett to slow down.

Rhett won't. Rhett is not going to risk our family for another's. We have played the hero before for a school that let us fall. Rhett won't fall again.

Humanity is so hard to hold onto. Compassion is even harder. We aren't the only monsters. We have just become more comfortable with being them since that blood-covered day in a snow-filled courtyard.

Terrence is screaming for Rhett to stop, to slow down, to do anything but what he currently is doing. Paula is slamming her fists against the back glass in anger and venom-filled threats. Even Aimes is shouting at him, motioning wildly with her hands in her agitation, but

Rhett ignores all of them. Like an empty void of concern, April is watching it all with her large, brown eyes from where she sits facing us.

I can hear Dolph cursing over the engines surrounding me. He knows as well as the rest of us what is about to happen. The truck is driving right through the center of the pack with Kurt running behind it.

Terrence is screaming for his son to jump, motioning with his hands to try. Kurt has no choice. He has only seconds until Rhett lures him right through Death's army. He jumps, bouncing his chest against the tailgate, and for a moment I exhale. One small moment, everything seems to be okay. Lawless throttles his bike ahead of me, leading our group towards the road before we too ride into them or the trees growing steadily thick ahead of us.

As I lean, praying Rhett's Harley doesn't test me again, I glance again to watch Terrence and Paula fighting to pull the male teen in. Their faces are adorned with their relief. I smile too; a brief 'thank you' to Life. She doesn't smile back.

Turning the truck to glance past the tree trunks, Rhett has no choice but to tilt the back-end right into the waiting arms of the Risen. They waste no time clutching Kent's legs, yanking him from his father's grasp with the help of the truck's forward speed. Time slows as Kent is hauled from their grasp. He slides backward from the very arms that were just holding him. His head bounces as it strikes the hard ground. He never screams when they overtake him. There is not a sound of his death from his lips, but it is being screamed just the same.

Paula is fighting to keep Terrence in the truck. He is clawing his way out, screaming for his son who has disappeared under the murdering mass. Kent's name is a wail behind me from Genny's lowered window. I recognize her tone. I held it in my voice for the man who refuses to look backward in front of me. Still, my heart doesn't constrict for her.

The few Risen that Rhett had missed fall to where the teen boy is bleeding as they tear him apart. They shove pieces of his body into their mouths with his clothes still attached to their blood-soaked hands. Kurt never made a sound. A part of me hopes he never felt his death. His father will feel it forever.

Terrence no longer fights to escape from Paula. He is broken, consumed, and may as well be dying on the ground by his son. One simple mistiming, and the world has stopped forever for him. Life didn't smile tonight. She merely shrugged as she watched, and she's already turned her back on us, yet again.

Having watched it all, still, we ride, heading towards another stretch of road with no destination in mind with headlights leading us in front and blanketing us from behind. The four of us don't talk about what just happened. We don't look to the one riding beside us. We keep our heads straight and eyes forward just as April had while watching it unfold. She never blinked. She never looked away. We don't either.

It's so hard to not become the monster. It's so hard to hold onto the last handful of compassion when compassion can cause such anguish. I don't miss my soul. I miss the man who had tried to save it. I'm not the only monster. I'm just okay with admitting that I am one.

Chapter 4

"We have to find somewhere secure, somewhere we can set up and stay," Dolph whispers to our huddled group.

We drove for as long as our bodies and minds could handle. I thought I knew this state with as many road trips the club would take to escape life. Honestly, I have no idea where we are anymore. We may have crossed into Georgia or another bordering state with as much as we have run, constantly moving to survive what seems to always find us. It's draining on more than just our supplies. It's draining to the small slips of souls we have left. The small glimpses that try to still stare out of our red-rimmed and tired eyes keep disappearing with each cost of an escape.

If there was a division with our groups before, now there is a gulf. Terrence is an empty shell. He stares into some distant time, unwilling to see into the current world. Peyton is peering out the weather-coated windows of our latest rest stop with the same blank face. In a way, I guess they both lost a son tonight.

Genny sits close to the red-haired Ginjer. Ginjer is murmuring into the teen girl's ear. I watch the two of them, further bonding in their grief, and for a moment a small flicker of sympathy threatens to flutter in the empty cavity of my chest.

Only my father either has the bravery, or a very cultivated death wish, to keep looking our way. I can feel his eyes on me, itching my shoulders with their intensity. We have been together for over a month now and I still don't know what the man wants from me.

"You don't think we all know that?" Lawless asks.

With their past histories, Dolph and Lawless are still walking on glass shards with each other. They tolerate the other because of the respect they have built as we have traveled, but a true friendship might never be in their cards. The fact Dolph is now riding J.D.'s bike does nothing to ease down the demons in Lawless.

"The only thing we have to really discuss is if we stay with them, or strike out on our own." Marxx mumbles. He is staring across the imaginary line watching their movements as the Risen watched ours last night.

The empty gas station makes it hard to hide conversation with how it echoes every sound. The way Peyton twitched, I don't think Marxx's question was hidden at all.

No one answers him. Instead, we all stare at the round spot made in front of us by our formation like it's some foretelling crystal ball. The floor is caked with spoiled food and other, darker stains. I could occupy my mind with guessing games over what each irregular pattern might be, but with as much as I have seen, my mind will only jump to the darkest of conclusions. It's never a good thing to do before bed.

The shelves are barren and disheveled. The place looks as if it was hit by a Black Friday sale during a hurricane warning. Luckily, someone had stashed a box of goods behind the ice chest. Someone who never came back for it, and once upon a time, I might have argued to leave something for them should they, but not now. It was divided and rationed with no thoughts to whoever might have put it there or might be expecting it to still be there. Finders keepers.

I glance to Aimes sitting across from me, as we always find ourselves. She is dozing in the protective shadow of Rhett. April is on his other side, hugging close to his warmth as she finishes the last of Rhett's jerky. She isn't the least bit troubled over Kurt's death or our lives. Watching her, I wonder if this is how my Angels would have turned out if I hadn't failed them. A part of me, watching the complete lack of empathy in such a small child, is guiltily happy I did fail them. Besides, Rhett would never have bonded with Ashley.

"As long as we are making do, I say we stick together," Rhett offers. "There is safety in numbers, or at least better victims than us."

Every set of eyes still awake in our circle slowly rolls to Rhett when hearing what he has said. Only Lawless dares to speak.

He says, "It wasn't your fault. Those things, they are changing. They are learning, getting better. They are figuring things out faster than we can invent things to keep them away."

Rhett shrugs, lifting only half his shoulder's height, but his blue eyes are frightening when he says, "If I have to choose between us or them, it's them every time. It's just how it's going to be."

"Chapel would be ashamed to hear you say that," Paula hisses with her whisper, trying to reach through the cold walls Rhett has constructed around his little family.

"Chapel is dead. He doesn't give a shit about anything I may or may not say," Rhett returns.

Lawless nods, sensing where Rhett is going with his dark thoughts, saying, "We tried it Chapel's way. We tried bending to the other's needs. J.D. would never have done that. He never would have allowed Travis to set up his little Kool-Aide brigade, but we did. Now, Chapel is gone and that is our fault."

Lawless pauses. He looks at each man staring at him, connecting their eyes and something deeper, making them each nod. Like always, I'm missing something again. When Lawless turns his dark brown eyes to Paula, he fills those of us lost into his little playground of mental games.

Lawless says, dark and menacing, "We won't bend anymore, and it won't be us to break. It's going to be us *doing* the breaking."

"That's not what Chapel wanted," I hear myself softly say, as I stare at my boots.

"Nope," Lawless agrees, as he slides down to sleep, "It's what J.D. told us to do in someplace similar to this. We didn't listen then and look where we are now."

"Right back in a rest stop sleeping on the ground?" Aimes asks.

"Not murdering small children to avenge our mourning?" I hear myself mutter.

I hadn't thought to say it. I didn't have any thought pattern to link Aimes' comment or mine together. Like a train of destruction, it slipped out, derailing with just as much force whether it was an accident or not. As if there were not enough 'daddy issues' already in this building, I went and opened another scab, sprinkling myself with kerosene before the heat of Lawless' anger ignites.

"What's the matter, Hells?" Lawless' voice comes from beside me. It's dangerously low, making me lower my head as I wait for his verbal blow. "You still upset about that? Kinda odd from someone who did nothing to stop it. You can run right into those things without a second thought, but you never have been very good at standing up to your fathers have you, Babe?"

Daddy issues - fun for the whole family!

"J.D. had his strengths, I get that," I cautiously say, still with my head low, trying not to smile over my most recent thought. "I do, but he had his demons, too. I know he wanted you to kill everyone the first night, Rhett. J.D.'s way was hit first, ask later, and never apologize. I'm not afraid to hit first. I just don't want to always be asking why later. There has to be some middle ground, or we will find ourselves fighting the living and the dead. We won't last."

No one around me is shocked by my little confession about J.D. and Rhett. Not even Dolph inhales or widens his eyes. As far as Rhett's reaction, I might as well have said I know what color shirt he is wearing. Maybe I was wrong over how far we have slipped. Maybe it's only me slipping.

"She has a point," Aimes' sleepy voice says from Rhett's casted shadow. "Besides, we didn't pack any tape to put on the ground again when we left the school. We know how you boys just love your little squares."

"I love it when you're silent," Rhett grumbles. He is pulling April into his lap as she begins to nod off to sleep.

"Then stop making her scream," Dolph taunts, as he too slips down into his bag.

Lawless, with all of his dislike of the man, chuckles hearing Dolph's jest. He says, "Don't worry, Aimes. Hells here will fall to sleep soon and she will cover your moaning."

"Yeah, pity for her, her screams are not from a man's touch anymore, though," Aimes says, with her signature smile.

Lawless chuckles again, before giving her a one-finger salute as his response.

Both of them missed Dolph's hand roaming my outer leg. They didn't see the way he looked at me when I turned to him. No one saw the question in his eyes. Dolph is staring at me the way I watch Marxx. His green eyes are filled with concern and they burn me. They slash at me deeper than anything J.D. had ever said, and open scars still raw, so much like my father's eyes still do.

I don't want his pity. I'm too tired to carry his fears or concerns over me or what Lawless may do. He and I both know Lawless will resurrect an old ghost of a buried man who tried to destroy us all if Law thinks it will keep us safe. There is no amount of begging that Dolph's eyes can do to change that fact.

Home. Safe. Survival. Such simple words. Such deadly, simple words in such a simply, deadly time.

Chapter 5

When dawn finds us, Peyton and Lawless are already debating over a road map they found. More than just the vehicles are running low on gas and one wrong turn could leave us stranded. It's a heavy burden for both men to bear.

Aimes and April are playing a game of chase with Rhett as their base. The large man takes it all in stride, watching the two with nothing more than his eyes as they run around him. It's comical in more ways than just the obvious.

The three of them are oblivious to how both groups watch them. We each are seeing something different. A mixture of amusement and agony is spread across the faces crowded together. Some of us are dwelling in the memories they are innocently recreating. Others sit on the surface of now, happy to just have a distraction. Take one picture, pass it around, and everyone will see something different because we all want to see something else.

"She reminds me of Lilly."

I jump hearing my father so close to me. Collin Hawthorn, in all his Greek God glory, rests his body on the truck beside me as we watch the game. My throat clogs with the taste of my panic dripping from my tongue. Lawless was right. Risen, demons, nightmarish gore-dripping children - check. Fathers? Nope.

"Lilly wasn't so cold."

I force my tongue to move, refusing to so easily fold under my anxiety over him.

He smiles before saying, "No, she was the sun and you were always my moon."

Something on my face must have called his bluff. He squirms, adjusting his body as if suddenly uncomfortable. His head tilts back-and-forth as he searches for what to say to me.

"We weren't close, I know," he starts, "but I think you are starting to put it all together."

"The fact you weren't just a horrible father? You were a horrible husband, too."

Collin sighs, searching for his words again. "I was a lot of things I wish I wasn't."

We both can agree on that one. Our silence does.

"You can ask me anything," my father whispers when I don't offer anything more to the conversation.

"Maybe one day. I have enough information to hate you with as it stands."

"Your mother loved you. She was so like you," he says, almost in a pained whisper.

"Maybe. One. Day." My teeth are clenched, adding, "Not today."

I don't want to travel this road. I don't want to bond over it or repair it. I don't want to mourn for a woman I never met when my eyes burn from crying over those I knew. She didn't want me then and I don't want her now.

"Helena," he whispers again, and I know by his tone what he is going to ask me, "where are they?"

"Right where you left them, Daddy," I reply, coating what they used to call him with bitterness.

I look at his face. It's contorted with confusion. His eyes sway, trying to read my face for some hint. I don't make him search for long.

I say to him, wearing a smile Aimes would be proud of, "Haunting me."

The hint registers. It hits home, concaving his chest with the blow. I listen as he fights to inhale his breath. It doesn't bring me any satisfaction. Sometimes the truth does that. It just is, and it weighs nothing.

Sometimes the truth is scalding. It burns with the pain and the guilt it causes. For my father, the latter is true. For me, it doesn't bring me anything at all. It's weightless and smothering all the same.

"You can ask me anything," I whisper back to him, watching as his pain clouds his eyes.

"Maybe one day," he returns, and I wait to see if he will go all the way. "Right now, I have enough information to hate myself with as it stands."

A simple twist of my words and I can feel the blade slide into my heart for a small flash of an instant. I startle when Marxx drops a new collection of noisemakers into the bed of my truck with more force than needed. The various objects rattle and clang against one another, and the solid metal of the truck, as well. Loud noises and hushed conversations tend to make people jumpy these days. If anyone had missed my father and I having our little chat, they are aware of it now. I let my eyes express how thankful I am to Marxx over interrupting it.

"And here you thought we had nothing in common," Collin tells me, reminding me of the conversation and its moment that has slipped away.

He pushes himself from my truck when the sounds of the many forms of transportation fire to life around us. Since becoming the center of everyone's attention, my father doesn't avoid the clump of Harleys. He walks right through them and their riders who stare at him with unmasked annoyance.

Lawless looks to me with his eyebrows arched over his dark sunglasses. I give him the same smile I gifted my father as Aimes, Paula, and April climb into my truck. He tries to hold his face neutral, but a smile creeps across those lips. When he fully gives in to his mirth, my smile changes from sarcastic to a teasing of a playful curve. If there were a more bipolar couple than he and I, I have yet to meet them.

"Feel better?" I ask Marxx, as he too walks away from me.

Marxx shrugs with his back to me. He calls over his shoulder, "I'd rather hear that shit than his shit. At least one of the two are actually useful when they are making noise."

I have to smile as he tells me this. There is something warm and fuzzy feeling when you're not the only one who hates someone.

"You do so love to prove him wrong," Aimes says over my father's and my chat when I finally climb in the truck beside her.

"Every girl needs a hobby," I return, still blessing those around me with my smile.

Slipping my sunglasses over my amused eyes, I start the truck and follow the leaning forms out of yet another parking lot, of yet another building, on yet another attempt to find some form of a life for us. The sun is dancing behind the trees, peeking out with a strobe light of flashing as it rises in the sky. The weather isn't as biting with winter admitting its defeat, but still, we only crack the windows. As I've learned, nothing dares Karma like fully opened windows.

I'm following behind everyone. I'm lost in the peace of our trip, not really having to focus on the road ahead of me. Traffic is a thing of the past. Even the guys are enjoying the freedom of being able to spread out as they follow behind the Jeep. They lean, tilting their bikes into lazy formations. Rhett continues to harass Dolph, edging closer than needed with dramatic maneuvering just to see if he can spook him. When Dolph finally steers J.D.'s large monster into Rhett's latest attempt at bumper bikes, it's Rhett who jerks first, and the three of us in the truck laugh louder than we have in a long time.

"You think they will ever really get along?" Paula asks me.

"Well, Rhett hasn't shot him, yet," Aimes offers. "It's a pretty good sign."

"If Dolph were in real danger, Rhett wouldn't be dicking with him. Teasing is a good sign in their world. It's when they ignore you, you have to worry," I tell her.

"You think he was serious about what he said last night?" Paula's voice says with more curiosity than worry.

"Rhett or Laws?" Aimes asks. "Or are we back to Dolph?"

"Both. Rhett and Lawless," Paula answers.

"As much as Law idolizes J.D.," I add to help direct the conversation, "he also hates him. J.D. was supposed to be this hero; someone who could control the world and keep it under his thumb. What J.D. did, Law can't figure out how to deal with it. It's like when kids learn their favorite hero is just a man in spandex with all of the same flaws and faults as their real parents. They still want to believe in the hero, but somehow it just feels a little less."

"Who was it for Conroy?" Aimes asks.

She has been doing little pushes like this since the day in the neighborhood when we discovered Travis' hanging tree. She hasn't asked outright, but she wiggles her finger into the wound to see if the bleeding is still rampant, or if it's slowing. The blood she pools depends on the day and my mood. So, she keeps testing and I keep avoiding giving her what she's after.

"The Flash," I answer. "He was one of the slowest kids on his baseball team. He so wanted to run like The Flash. I bought him shoes with the character on them for one of his birthdays. He was convinced he ran faster when he wore them. Law even 'lost' a race with him wearing the shoes because they made him so fast."

The truck is silent with the mood swing. Glancing at the women sitting beside me, I stare into the eyes of April. She is watching me like a doll, unmoving and uninterested. There is something dark in those brown eyes that disturb me. If an abyss could stare back at me, it is.

"Helena!"

Aimes' scream jerks my head forward to the windshield, but it's not what is ahead of us that has her screaming. A man is running full speed at the side of my truck. He throws himself at my door, standing on the foot rail and clutching the thin space between the glass of the rolled down window to support him.

His eyes are wild, with constricted pupils staring at me from a bloody ruin of a face. He is balancing on the runners of my truck with one hand desperately pulling on the old-styled handle to open the door. I went from staring at an empty abyss to a pool of fear.

He keeps shouting, "Let me in!" at me in my dazed state.

Without any real idea of what to do, I press the brakes hard, jerking the wheel to spin the large beast. She squeals with the abuse to the tires. She shimmies to a stop, blocking the crazy man from the rest of the group. The random act slung the rest in the truck to the far passenger side, leaving only myself close to the deranged stranger who has fallen to the street.

Before I can open my door to demand answers, the answers appear. Through the same overly thick tree line he had suddenly appeared from pours the very things we keep running from. In every stage of decay, they rush from the trees after the man they were chasing. Their combined sounds bring the hair on my arms to attention and my knees to something weaker than water. I won't be able to block the men on their bikes if they reach us before we are ready.

"My name is Jeremy," he tells me. "You can't let me die! You can't! My name is Jeremy. I'm a person. I have a family. Let me in, damn it! You can't just let me die!"

The man is pounding on my window again with my indecision of what to do. His hands are leaving bloody prints where they pressed against the glass and his desperation turns into something more when he sees I am not opening the door.

Balling his fist, he slams it into the glass. The skin of his knuckles breaks, leaving more gore to the already streaked glass like a mosaic of punishments. The thick glass just vibrates, mocking his attempts. He glares at me through the mess he has made. For a moment, I see a glimpse of the real person behind those eyes and it's not fear peering out at me anymore.

When the man rears his fist back again, he crumples with the sound of a gunshot ringing through the air. Marxx is already turning away from where he was standing to shoot the man in the leg. Jeremy is screaming on the ground, clutching where his kneecap used to sit.

Aimes puts it together faster than I do. "Shit," she says in a long exhale of a breath.

"Let's go!" Marxx shouts, setting a bait for the Risen who are rushing towards the scent of blood. Marxx knows, as well as we do, the scent will rip them to pure animals.

"Hells?" Aimes whispers, as if the men could somehow hear her over their already retreating Harleys.

I say nothing. My eyes are lost as they bounce from the man on the ground to the already blood-caked crowd rushing towards him. Once upon a time, like some dark fairy tale, I would have jumped from my seat to try to save this stranger. I would have risked my life and potentially those around me for him like some lost heroine looking to prove her worth. Shelia learned with her life the lesson of what happens when you help strangers. I almost learned with mine what happens when you let strangers help you. Neither she nor I will ever receive a happily ever after.

"Hells?" she whispers again, stressing my one syllable name a little harder than needed.

There is already a gap forming between my truck and our group. It's in reverse proportion to the space between the demonic army and us. I close my eyes, praying for forgiveness for what I am about to do.

"My name is Jeremy! You can't just let me die!" He keeps screaming over and over at me, hoping me knowing his name will taunt my morality into action.

He is watching me with his wide eyes of terror and pain. He can't believe what I am about to do, or what has been done to him. I know

Jeremy will join Carol tonight in tormenting me. They will dance with my past sins and I will be awed by their cruelty.

"April," Aimes sadly whispers, "hide and seek."

The little girl closes her eyes with the hidden code expressed. I wish I could join her. I wish I had thought to close my eyes many times, on many things, I can never now unsee.

Turning the wheel as tightly as I can, I maneuver my warhorse to catch up with those who have already left. The screams grow more hysterical as I pull away. His pitch only slightly changes when the Risen starts to descend upon him.

They tear into whatever flesh they can reach first like hounds from hell. They don't try to kill him. His suffering is of no thought to them. They are only there to feast. Pulling and severing his legs and arms like a stuffed doll, they almost fight among themselves for any scrap of dripping meat their fingers touch.

He is not screaming anymore. The sound is one long wail of suffering; a pitch of sound that tears at your soul as if it, too, had fingers to scoop your body clean. It calls my bluff before I am even aware of it. Pressing the brakes hard, the truck lurches as if confused why I am commanding it to stop.

"Hide and seek," I whisper to very silent women beside me.

Aimes mutters under her breath, slinking down where she sits. Paula wraps the already blind April in her arms, bending her head over the child to further protect her in some way from what I am about to do.

I keep my eyes on the grinning skulls staring back at me with the men stopped and confused. Aimes and I once had a conversation about the skull. We had wished for Chapel's Arch Angel, but this is not a world for angels anymore. This is a world for skulls with their silver tear and empty, black eyes.

I don't check the mirrors. I don't think at all as I push the truck too quickly into reverse. My action causes the large tires to skip a beat as if to ask me if I'm sure about this. I'm not, but when has that ever stopped me before?

It's a confusion of collisions when the truck finds them. The metal bumper decapitates the ones bent over the body as if they were birds of carrion. The sound of their skulls hitting the truck sounds like large pieces of hail raining down on a tin roof. The tires bounce, almost slipping in the trail of carnage they leave. I don't ease the pressure from the gas pedal until I have mowed my way completely through the crowd as if I were parting a sea. It's a very red sea with what I have done.

The man no longer wails. Jeremy is nothing more than wide-flung pieces of thick meat between what the Risen started and what I ended. My tires found his head, silencing him forever with a simple feel of a bump as if he were nothing more than a log in the road, but he was once so much more. He was a person like us; trying to find a life in a world built around death. His name was Jeremy and I killed him.

I pay no attention to the few Risen who are left. They are broken, or paralyzed, with their unfeeling, immortality-like bodies. They can't stand. They can't move. They aren't my problem. Pushing the drenched tires back through the many shades of my red sea, I head towards those waiting for us.

Conroy loved The Flash with his bright red suit and wit-filled banter. He loved how he could run, always there to save the day with his speed. The Flash was the hero Conroy always wanted to become. I'm glad Conroy never saw this world as it stands because there are no heroes anymore, you can't outrun death, and the color red is getting a bit overused. We are all just people with flaws and faults trying to outlive the memories of our parents and those we have lost.

Chapter 6

I was right about Carol and Jeremy. Standing here, staring out another set of windows as the sun rises, in yet another house that isn't ours, I had volunteered to take back-to-back watches to avoid them. They make me almost miss Margaret and her schoolyard of murder-covered best friends forever. Even Ashley with her destroyed flesh, pink pajamas, and her taunting of my failures would have been better than watching what Carol had done to Jeremy and what both have done to my few hours of sleep.

She tore him into mutilated pieces as he screamed his name, begging me to help him. I didn't. He kept reminding me he was a person just like myself, and just like myself, Carol destroyed him for her pleasure while I watched. I'm sure a therapist would have an award-winning novel built around the many hidden revelations I could bring. Their replaying of my many deep-rooted issues has left my knees weak and my stomach sour. I can still smell his copper-like blood and feel its warmth on my body as it splashed me with Carol's brutality.

I sensed him before his arms slipped around my waist. I relax into his heat, enjoying the feel of his lips against my neck. These little moments are all Lawless and I are allowed anymore. Somehow his silence and his arms are more comforting than any words or anything else we could exchange.

Lawless adjusts his body to support us both on the bench seat of the bay window. I don't resist his gentle urging to relax, letting him become an anchor to hold me steady amid the ravaging sea of my dreams. By the way he tenses for a brief second, I think it is as much as a shock to him as it is to me when I nestle into the length of his body.

He rests his face on the top of my head, whispering, "You should try to sleep while we can. No idea what today will hold for us."

"The same thing it holds for us every day, Pinky. Risen taking over the world," I whisper back.

He does a short exhale of a laugh with the memory of old childhood cartoons.

Lawless says to me, "I'd be happy to be the sidekick for a while."

"You don't have to call all the shots alone. Not even J.D. did that."

I can feel his shoulder shrug from where I am resting on his chest with what I have said.

"And who should I ask?" his voice rumbles.

It's my turn to shrug. I'm not really the one to give advice, considering how very little I listen to it. If you want me to kill something, fine. If you want me to help guide you through to the light, nope. Darkness doesn't come with a roadmap. It's a touch and feel your way out of this type of situation and my touchy-feely is running dry.

"Do you remember when I fell out of my bedroom window?" I ask him.

I can feel his body adjust to my question. He's wondering where this is going. Am I such a time bomb?

"Yes," he answers stiffly. "You were leaning out to help sneak me in."

"Me and windows, never the best of friends," I tease, wishing to ease down his apprehension. "You jumped right down after me. You didn't even think about it."

He shrugs, still tense and nervous, saying, "Wasn't that far if you didn't go headfirst."

"You snuck me to my car to take me to the hospital. We were both too nervous to tell my parents I was hurt."

"Mr. Hawthorn, hi, yeah, I'm going to need to take Hells to the hospital. You see, Sir, she slipped out of her window as I was trying to sneak in to get me some," Lawless teases. "Yeah, can't imagine why I didn't knock on the door."

"Anyway," I say, with a gentle nudge of my elbow to his ribs, "It wasn't J.D. who sat with you all night. It wasn't Rhett, or Aimes, or even Chapel."

"It was Marxx," he says, silently.

"It was Marxx," I repeat.

His body goes still as his thoughts overtake him. I sit, just as silent in his embrace, letting him work through the very touchy-feely darkness.

"I'm worried about Marxx," he confesses.

"He was never the teddy bear type," I offer from the warmth of his chest.

"He was never the enjoy killing type, either."

"I don't think he enjoyed what he did to Jeremy."

"Jeremy?" Law asks, mentally running through the laundry list of names we have developed.

"The guy today. His name was Jeremy."

Lawless sighs, letting the air out as slowly as possible. It's amazing the weight a name can give to a victim. Until you have a name, it's just another dead body. Once you place a name to the face, everything changes. They become human and that is something becoming rarer by the day.

Lawless murmurs after a moment of thought, "No, maybe he didn't enjoy it, but he didn't even think about it. That's more of Rhett's deal. Marxx was always there, but he never swung first."

"Isn't that what you wanted?"

I can feel his body stiffen hearing my question. His thumb has started keeping a tempo with whatever thoughts he is having as it taps against my arm where he holds me. I know he is trying to avoid saying what is on the tip of his tongue.

"I want to stop losing the people I love," he finally says, with a tone like a cold shadow over a grave.

I know what he is saying. Death is not only stealing those around us. Life is doing her fair share of damage, too. When Death takes someone from you, he leaves you with only the memories of what they were. When Life takes someone, she lets you keep the shell. She leaves you with not only the memories, but also the pain of those memories, as she forces you to watch their decay.

"There was never any guarantee about that before any of this started," I tell him.

"No, I guess not," he says, with a sigh again. "There just seems to be less of everything now, including any guarantees."

"Things will even out once we find somewhere to call home again. When we can finally let our guard down some, Marxx will settle whatever is eating him."

"Maybe," Law shrugs again. "Any ideas of where that might be?'

"Somewhere far out from any towns or residences with lots of space. If there is anybody left, they won't be clumped up in their townhomes. Too much risk. Too much paranoia."

His thumb slows as his thoughts do, but he says nothing.

"We could try what Peyton's group did with the crypts. Rhett will love that," I say.

I can feel his smile as his mind runs with similar thoughts. His thumb is caressing my arm now, running little patterns of circles and ovals instead of the drum-like tempo. Still, he says nothing.

"They said they had supplies they left behind. Not sure why they are running with us if they have stuff stored away, but it's a thought," I keep offering to the suddenly one-sided conversation.

Lawless still says nothing and I fall into silence as well.

"What if it doesn't?" he finally asks me.

When I say nothing, he asks me again.

"What if there is no settling? No safety? What if this is really all that is left for us now?"

"I can't believe that," I tell him. I sound as fragile as porcelain with the thoughts he has caused.

"But what if it's true?"

It's my turn to sigh. It fills my lungs as full as they can with the ache his words cause me. In less than a year, my flirt of a man with his boy-like charm has become so much more darker as Life steals pieces of him from me. I'm just happy it's only Life who is slicing us with her dagger. Once Truth joins in, her sisters Karma and Fate teach us real lessons of suffering.

"Then we keep going. We get up, we move, we keep going. Giving up is not an option, because once we give up, then there is no hope," I whisper.

"You still have hope?" he asks.

"I still have you."

His arms tighten around me hearing my response and it might have turned into something more if Rhett had been asleep.

"So cute," Rhett's voice calls from the semi-circle of where our group sleeps. "Really, it gets me right here."

Rhett's voice is mocking with the sound of false tears. He is pointing to his stomach, not his heart, and the many who were faking being asleep begin to try to hide their laughter.

"Yeah, somewhere with lots of space," Lawless says, pausing to recount what I had said moments ago, "and maybe no windows."

"And miss my graceful exits? Never," I say, with full sarcasm blooming.

"So, what's the plan?" Rhett asks.

"Don't know," Lawless tells us honestly. "We are low on food, low on gas, and nothing is currently panning out. If you have a suggestion…?"

Lawless leaves his question open, letting whoever wants to answer him do so. We are just as lost as he is, though.

"So, let's go scavenge?" Rhett says, almost with a sigh.

Marxx has come to stand by the window. He leans his body, watching the front lawn to avoid having to see us. It's something he has done a lot of lately.

"What about her?" Marxx asks Rhett.

Rhett doesn't need to ask whom Marxx is asking about. Nor do any of the rest of us.

Looking down at the sleeping April, Rhett says, "Guess having the other group is a good thing."

"You trust them that much?" Marxx asks, still avoiding us.

"Not all of them," Rhett answers honestly.

"Only takes one," Marxx does finally turn to look at Rhett with what he has said.

"Look, Sunshine," Rhett starts, "not sure what is going on in that head of yours, but enough with the who's-more-grumpier-than-me routine. I get it. We lost J.D. We lost Chapel, and it was our job to see shit like that doesn't happen. We can't change it. So, start to live with it and stop pouting. If you can't, then go put a skirt on, and let's all just call it what it is."

"Damn it," Lawless whispers under his breath so softly, only I can hear him.

He taps my arm, letting me know to move. He doesn't want me too close to them should he have to separate erupting male egos.

"Maybe if you weren't so worried about a kid that's not even yours, instead of your family, we wouldn't have lost Chapel," Marxx replies.

There was no anger in Marxx's voice when he said it. His tone was cold, collected, and so much more brutal, in a way, than if he had shouted it.

"Is that what you think?" Rhett asks him.

Rhett stands and stretches as if what has been said to him is not the cause, or the effect, for his need to suddenly get up. I hadn't moved when Law had first signaled for me to. Now, I'm not only moving-- I'm moving quickly.

Marxx doesn't reply to Rhett's question. He just stares, keeping his eyes level with the taller man's. Paula, remembering what I had said yesterday, moves further from their path. She pulls April and Aimes with her. After all, it's when they start to ignore you that you have to worry.

Lawless is waiting, standing, but waiting. I know from past G.R.I.T. altercations, if this is something Marxx and Rhett want, he will let them have it, but only to a degree. His hands are already resting on his belt buckle in his normal mockery of relaxation.

Dolph waits, still lounging in his sleeping bag with an arm tucked under his head with a pose of disinterest. This isn't his fight. He won't become involved unless he must.

"I asked you a question," Rhett says and there is no subterfuge now as to his mood.

Rhett's eyes are melting to their color of danger. His body relaxes to absorb the first blow or to be ready to deliver it. I don't think he completely cares about which one happens first, just as long as something happens. If Marxx wants to push these buttons, Rhett will make sure the ride is worth it.

"I heard you," Marxx replies, keeping with this calm tone. "I just don't care. If it were up to me, I'd drop her with those upstairs and never look back at any of them. I guess playing daddy has made you a little weak."

Rhett looks away from Marxx. He is not avoiding the man across from him. He looks as if Marxx's words haven't hit him, yet. It's almost like Rhett is hearing someone talking near him. It makes me wonder just how many of us J.D. is haunting. When Rhett's eyes return, they are completely cold, completely void of any of his dark humor.

"I was watching Law's back. I did my job," Marxx says. "I didn't lose anyone, Sunshine."

Marxx pulls every vowel he can from the nickname. He returns Rhett's insult with just as much sarcasm as when the name was originally said. When Rhett's head rises, I know just where Marxx is taking this.

I had thought his slow seclusion was due to his guilt over Chapel. It wasn't. Just like every other time I had wished for my own shiny, leather vest to help me figure things out, I could have once again used one these past few days. Marxx doesn't blame himself. He blames Rhett.

Rhett steps towards Marxx, reducing some of the space between them. Lawless mirrors the action, keeping himself at the same distance from the two men. Neither of them is acknowledging the younger man at all.

"Why don't you just say what you want to, Princess. Unless you are just waiting for Hells to come to save you again?" Rhett almost whispers his question with a hiss.

I feel myself roll my eyes at the mention of my name and the memory of Marxx and I in the courtyard. His job was to get me to safety. I had turned us around, forcing his hand and ending us both in the middle of the very danger he was supposed to keep me from. It was me who pushed him when we first thought there was no hope. It was me who almost killed us both, too.

"At least Marxx never walked away when it got too heavy," my voice says.

I don't know when my mouth moved. It just did. Lawless' head sinks, shaking slowly back and forth when hearing me. Aimes' little snark of a laugh doesn't help me either.

"Hells saved you, too, if I remember," Aimes says, never the one to let me walk through the shadow of male egos alone. "It was her who kept telling them to keep faith in you and Marxx; it was you who went to help find April. So, I guess Rhett isn't the only one trying to play daddy."

At least she didn't say sunshine.

"I went to keep you and Helena safe. It didn't have anything to do with some bastard kid Rhett decided to claim like some little bitch," Marxx says, and he knew exactly what would happen next.

I think every male in the room knew. They just didn't know how far it was going to go. Something about the word bitch tends to rake the ego.

Lawless slides backward, stretching his arms wide to try to keep the chaos contained. Dolph is up, doing something similar to Law, but on his side of the room where the rest of our group is standing. There is nothing either of them can do to really contain it completely, but they hope to help divide the potential damage.

Rhett didn't exchange any verbal warning or change the look upon his face. He went from still to running, using his shoulder to push Marxx through the window behind them. The resulting sound is shattering, sharper than the shards of glass they create. It's sharper than even the scream from Aimes as the two men sail through the ruined window.

Footsteps are running to us when hearing the commotion. My father's group is heading down from the upstairs rooms they claimed last night to help keep the tension down. Obviously, we didn't need them to help stir the pot of rage. Marxx Betty-Crockered that all on his own.

Lawless and I waste no time running out the front door to where the two men are rolling, exchanging blows as fast they are receiving them. There is no thought or form in this style of fighting. They are just trying to hurt the other as fast as they can, with anything they can reach.

I can hear the glass crunching under them. The wooden porch moans with the force of the two of them. The rocking chairs and other once well-maintained furniture is slid and pushed awry with the fighting. They will kill each other. I have no doubts about it.

Lawless grabs me when I try to run past him. Struggling in his arms, he lifts me from the ground. It removes my ability to try to outmaneuver from his grasp. He crushes me to him, shocking me some and fully gaining my attention.

Lawless whispers into my ear, "They need this."

"They are going to kill each other," I shout, not even attempting to keep my thoughts between us.

"No, they won't," he tells me. "Let it play out."

"What the hell is going on?" Peyton shouts over the turmoil of the fighting.

Dolph has come outside as well, using his body to block the men from the other group from interfering. He looks to the men behind him as if they are completely stupid for not knowing, but he says, "Therapy."

"This is how yours handles things?" Collin asks.

"We could just abandon our responsibilities, but we prefer to be more hands-on with our problems," Lawless tells my father, setting my feet back on the porch.

"I remember hearing that about you," my father taunts Law. "In fact, I believe your hands have been on just about every woman in our town."

"*Seriously?*" is what my mind says. My mouth says, "Well, they do say girls always end up with men like their fathers."

"You have no idea what you are talking about," Collin says, but his excuses still don't matter to me.

"You're right, maybe I don't, but I don't care! This is stupid," I shout. "We have those things out there, anywhere, hell everywhere. We have no supplies, no plans, and no idea how we are going to make it through this, but this is what you think is best to be doing right now? When you guys want to start acting like this is real, great. When you get over your damn selves, wonderful. Let me know. Until then, Aimes and I will go out to try to find us something to live on while the rest of you compare dick sizes."

My shouting has stalled the fighting on the porch. Peyton and my father, Collin, look as if they have broken jaws the way their mouths hang from hearing my outburst. Dolph is smiling his lopsided smirk. The men of G.R.I.T., they just stare, completely used to me and my ranting. I'm legendary, remember?

Looking to where Aimes has come outside when hearing my voice, I say to her, "Get in the truck."

I don't wait for her answer. I don't need to. She already has one of the black duffels in her hand and is following me down the porch steps.

"Hey Rhett," she calls over her shoulder, "it looks like Hells has saved you both, again."

Yea, though I walk through the darkest valley of male egos, I will fear no anger, for Aimes is with me. Her wit and smile, they comfort me. Surely amusement and snark shall follow me all the days left of my life; until I dwell in the house of Death, forever.

Chapter 7

"So, what is the plan?" Aimes asks me, when she feels it's safe enough to talk again.

I don't have one. I never did. I just had to escape. My quick eye shift from her and back to the road expresses it.

"Greeaaatt," she exhales. "Well, let's think like girls. Going from store-to-store is pretty male and mind-numbing. Everyone still alive has done that already. We need somewhere most wouldn't go to look for stuff."

"Dad said my aunt raided a pet place for food and water," I offer.

I don't know if the idea of eating pet food has her eyebrow so high, or the fact that I mentioned my true mother's side of my family. Maybe it was because I called him 'dad' and not by the many other pet names we have created for him through the years.

"Yeah, that's great and all, but no," she answers, wearing her eyebrow still arched as if I will answer her unasked question.

"Daycares?" I ask.

Both her eyebrows match now. They are raised so high she looks almost cartoonish.

"They had to feed large numbers of kids. There should be food and first aid supplies for any injuries. Prescription pills for any of the kids who needed them since they were there so many hours a week. If nothing, at least some basic pain relievers for the teachers," I say, as I keep rattling off reasons, waiting for her to either agree with me or call me crazy.

"Maybe some Midol for the guys?" she asks.

I smile and I guess her joke is the only agreement I'm going to get.

"Not much for ammo, or the likes, but it's a start."

"Maybe there will be cars in the parking lot to siphon gas from," she says.

"Do you know how to?"

"I watched a YouTube video once."

"Why did you watch a video on how to siphon gas?"

I shouldn't ask this. I know better than to ask Aimes questions. I did anyway, though.

She extends her hands, palms up, saying, "I typed in how to give good head. That's what came up."

See, you don't ask Aimes stuff.

"Now we just have to find one," I say, skipping over her latest round of confessions.

"I think there was one back before we found the house-of-the-hour."

"Completely in the opposite direction we are heading?"

Aimes only smiles, fully appreciating my annoyance.

I spin my beast, making her scream under the feel of my escalating mood. Bracing herself, Aimes' smile widens. I can almost hear her thinking. Setting my face, I wait for her thoughts to become words with as much trepidation as I have left to gather.

"It's nice to see your fire back, even if it is directed at the club," Aimes says after the truck completes its rotation. "I've missed you."

"Which part of me? The one where I keep getting people killed or the part where I keep trying to get myself killed?" I ask her with open honesty.

"The part that keeps fighting no matter the cost. The part of you that keeps *us* fighting with pure defiance to life's constant fisting."

I feel her hand on my arm, but I keep my focus on the road with its empty miles ahead of me.

"If you give up, they will give up," she tells me.

I blink past the sudden pitch in her voice, fighting my emotions as well.

"I'm not their keeper. I never wanted to be. What they do or don't do, I can't control," I whisper.

"Are we still talking about the club?"

Her question lacerates me. I inhale with it, clamping my jaw and losing the battle with my eyes to keep from crying.

"It shouldn't have been me. They shouldn't have been left for me to protect. I failed them and it cost them everything. I don't want to make that same mistake twice."

Aimes doesn't say a word. She sits like a picture on a wall, staring and frozen, but watching just the same.

"I keep trying to do the right thing. I think to myself if I'm the one out there, then someone else won't have to be, but I just keep losing them all the same. I keep killing them." My breath catches and the words tumble out, finally free from their dark chest of imprisonment. "When I came home, Carol was being odd. I thought someone had killed Lilly and she was mourning, in shock. She wasn't. She killed Lilly like we all know how by now. So, I killed her. I killed my mother. Aimes, I killed my mother."

The last part is nothing but a whisper with my strength escaping my words. Still, she is a picture of interest and nothing more.

"I took Ashley and Conroy," I say. "I didn't know what to do or where to go. I couldn't think of anything logical at all but to follow our normal routine, to get them to a safe place they knew. All the kids were turned, Aimes. Every last kid who was left alive was turned and they came for us. Ashley just stood there. I didn't save her. I didn't fight for her. I watched my little sister die. Aimes, I let her die right in front of me and I did nothing but run."

I have to stop to breathe. I might as well have fire in my lungs with how they are burning. I feel as if I am suffocating from their smoky flames, but the words keep falling forward as I smother.

"I threw Conroy to them. I thought I was saving him. I swear I did, but I was murdering him. I could hear his screams. Just like Jeremy, I just stood there and listened to him screaming for my help. I didn't help him, either. I killed all those kids. With my bare hands, I killed them all. Now, they are in every dream. They are in every scent, every moment, and every passing hour. I killed Kira. I killed Shelia. I killed J.D. I killed Simon, Ross, and Chapel. I killed them all because I thought I was doing the right thing. I thought if it were me taking the pain, I could save them. I didn't. I killed them."

"And now you are trying to kill yourself."

Her voice is as soft and tender as mine. I can hardly see the road ahead of me through the haze of my tears. I'm panting, trying to find any air left to my lungs. There is nothing but the flames, scalding me the way the truth always does.

"I want it to end." I whisper my last confession, like she is a priest who could save my soul, saying, "I want to die."

"Chapel died so you could live. He gave his life for us. How is you giving up now any way to repay that debt?"

"I would take his place if I could."

Aimes is no longer whispering. She is hissing her words between her teeth, "You can't. You can't bring any of them back and killing yourself won't change that fact. Haven't we all lost enough? Haven't we hurt enough? What do you think your death would do to us? If we had to lose you, too, what do you think that would do?"

I turn my head to her so she may see my answer. I want her to really hear my answer.

"I don't care," I tell her. "I have nothing left to care."

Her eyes darken to a shade between anger and betrayal before saying, "Poor Helena. Always poor Helena with her messed-up family and empty life. Suck it up, Zombie Barbie. Here is a newsflash for you - all of our families were messed up. Why do you think we all click so well? Each of us has that piece of us that is missing, and we fill it for each other. Your scars are no worse, or better than ours. You just want to tell yourself that so when you finally off yourself, or do something stupid getting yourself offed, you won't feel like a pussy for letting it happen."

My foot finds the brake before my mind does. My truck jerks with the force of the command when we come to a sudden stop in the middle of the road and I can't help but wonder how annoyed she is with the constant changing of our demands of her.

"What did you say?" I ask, looking to Aimes.

"I said you are a pussy."

Aimes doesn't sugarcoat her words or try to hide her feelings. The same *I dare you* smile she has worn for the men to taunt them she is wearing it now for me.

"All this time," she says, "I thought you were so brave. You're not brave. You're just as scared as the rest of us. The only difference is we admit to our truths while you would rather drown in yours. All of this is a pity party for one, rolled into some guilt trip you have created for yourself. Now I understood what Rhett meant when he said you weren't interested in using a gun. He said you would use us."

I stare at her, confused by what she is saying to me. I'm confused not because of how accurate it all is. I'm confused because of the why. Inhaling sharply against the words riding my tongue, I turn to see the road again.

It stretches long and two-lanes ahead of me. I can't see the ending any more than if I looked in the rearview and tried to see its beginning. Like Aimes and I, like the club and us, it's hard to really pinpoint anymore where it all began. It's even harder to see where it might all be ending.

I know what she is doing. It's the same thing the men are doing. Everything we have kept bottled up, we are releasing like evil genies as people begin to rub us the wrong way. All the things we wouldn't normally say to each other, we are now, because we are all so incredibly angry.

We are angry with ourselves. We are angry with each other. We are angry with this life. You can only yell at the mirror for so long before you run out of words to be used and this life doesn't care for our feelings anymore. That only leaves us each other to scream at.

"I guess we aren't past our little high school stay, either?" I ask her, reminding us both of a time we have glossed over.

Her face softens for a second before falling stiff, and unreadable. She looks almost puzzled when she says to me, "I guess not."

"So, what? You want to start exchanging hits?" I ask her.

"No. It might not be much of a face, but it's all God gave me, and besides, we both know you'd win."

"Then what?"

Aimes shrugs. It's not only the men who are unsure of what to do anymore. There has been too much between all of us, and like a racoon with his fist in a trap, we are all defiantly holding on to it all.

I'm staring at the road again as my mind wanders, taking us both along for the ride.

"Do you see the road?" I ask her.

"Is this where you start to insult my intelligence by asking the obvious?"

"If I wanted to insult your I.Q., I would have brought up you and Rhett."

Aimes shrugs, but smirks as well before saying, "Yeah, I see the road, my brilliant leader."

"That's all we have now. There are no turn-offs, no resting, just long roads for miles and miles."

"You going somewhere with this? Or, just miles and miles of rambling?"

I roll my eyes with a sideways glance, telling her, "Yeah, I want to give up. I desperately just want it all to end when I think about where we were and where we are heading, but I won't. It's not me. It's not us. It's not what we do. We keep going. Mile after mile, we just keep going. Once we all get past whatever this is festering, we will be back on our road. So, stop worrying about me. It's like J.D. said years ago," I begin, as I put the impatiently waiting truck into gear, "no matter what happens, you just keep grinning."

"And riding," she finishes.

"No matter how life torments you," I start, with a mocking rendition of his quote.

Aimes quickly falls into a pattern. "You keep grinning and you keep riding, even in constant torment, you just keep riding."

"Because riding is the only real escape they can't take from you."

Aimes puts her hand over her heart and with a false mockery of being moved to tears, she says, "Good ole G.R.I.T."

Like a Band-Aid applied over an opened scab, we smile at each other.

"Do me a favor though, Aimes?" I ask, as the truck begins to roll forward.

"Hmm?" she answers, her smile a bit tenser now than a mere moment ago.

"Leave me out of your pillow talk with Rhett?"

"Actually, we don't talk much about pillows. Normally one of us is-"

"No. No ma'am. We are not going there!" I loudly exclaim, talking over her.

She laughs when my dark warhorse pulls us forward, past the many dashes of yellow lines. They are put there to keep the two sides safe and divided. They let us know where our space is and where the other person's starts.

Our yellow lines are gone now. We have no personal space, or personal thoughts, or even personal scars. Everything is one giant cauldron of shared pain. Everything is exposed for anyone to watch or prod. Like a wound, bleeding, and seeping from the viciousness of its cause, we are all leaving a trail to be followed. For miles and miles, we have been bleeding out and only our defiance over surrendering and our stolen moments like this has kept us riding on, in torment but still grinning.

Chapter 8

"Oh look, it's our merry little band of personal madmen," Aimes says, upon hearing their engines. They haven't even crested the hill ahead of us before she asks, "Think we can ditch the truck and make a run for it?"

I lift an eyebrow with the thought, and if there was not a good chance of what lurks in the woods around us also hoping we would do that, I might take her offer seriously. If I must choose which demons to face, I'll choose the dark beasts of G.R.I.T. every time.

"No, but I can scatter them again, if you want?" I ask her.

Her amused smile is almost as frightening as her taunting one. She braces her knees against the dash when the truck roars its matching pitch with my encouragement of her gas pedal.

"Just don't kill them," she tells me. "We might actually need them one day."

"Oh, ye of little faith," I whisper, earning me another bold smile.

Our two groups sound like trains racing towards our destination and still I don't let off the gas. The annoying responsible side of me knows this is a waste of resources, but the side of me who so enjoys seeing the men reminded of who I am, only whispers dark praises.

Truth be told, as of late, I don't feel the day is complete unless one of them is staring at me as if they are just meeting me for the first time. Men's minds are easy to twist, and I've made a hobby out of it just to avoid the constant self-twisting of my own.

"Remember when I said, just don't kill them?" Aimes asks me.

She is slinking further down, bracing tightly as the truck's engine gains pitches with the speeds being forced upon her. Her smile is tight, not sure if she should be still filled with glee or evacuation plans. It's more than just the men I enjoy tormenting.

Knowing how they ride, I know their pattern. I know where each bike will be in reference to the other. If their engine noises weren't so thundering, I would be more cautious, but the full throttle of their pace tells me they are riding close and not spread out along the road. Even with maybe being the last people in the area, old habits are hard to break. They are even harder to break for bikers.

I crest the hill, almost airborne with the speed and slope of the road. Hidden behind their dark glasses, I can still see the raised arches of their eyebrows when the large grill of my truck is aimed right for their tight little ball of male compensation. They do exactly what I had expected them to do. Riding so close, they can't brake. They are forced to slide to one side of the road, hugging its line, as their side-by-side becomes one single file of arched eyebrows and set lips. Like the bitch I am, I forced them out of my way with no regrets or apologies.

Marxx shakes his head as we soar past them, bouncing the truck's tires with the impact. I don't slow. I don't wait for them when they turn around to follow me. I don't chase after them anymore or after their respect. In fact, I think they only chase after me to see what I will do next.

"How did they even find us?" I ask her.

She is slowly unfolding from where she had become something of a human accordion. She says, "You mean other than the wonderful skid marks you left while traveling down a straight road with no turn-offs? Must be a miracle."

"Want me to sling you against the door, again?" I ask her, reminding her of my wonderful driving skills.

"Not really. If I am to be tenderized for the Risen to munch on, I prefer it done in more pleasurable ways," Aimes says, daring my bluff.

I don't. It's disturbing enough to think of her and Rhett, or even hear her and Rhett. I won't ask her any questions because she would answer them without hesitation or shame. Some things I do not want rolling around in my mind with so much already tearing it apart.

"I guess we aren't shopping alone," I tell her.

The men, Law, Rhett, Marxx, and Dolph have already closed the distance and are hugging the truck. I'm not sure if we are being escorted or followed by the look on Lawless' face. Maybe he's just not happy with my attempt to turn a half-ton truck into the General Lee.

"You could always slam it into reverse and try your luck again?" Aimes asks me.

When I hesitate to answer, she cautiously arches an eyebrow.

Smiling, I tell her, "Been done. The shock value is only good once." I bounce my eyebrows, letting her relax before asking her, "Where was this place you saw?"

"We passed the street with our new squatter rights, so it should be up here soon."

It is. I pump my brakes to let the red lights signal I am slowing to make the turn. I figured it's the nice thing to do since I keep trying to run them over for pure enjoyment.

It's a long driveway and it's in as good a condition as anything else in this forgotten section of town. My tires bounce along the neglected road while those behind me must slow and negotiate the many landmines waiting for their tires like gaping jaws along the asphalt. It allows me to place some distance between us and our constant, hovering shadows.

The daycare, or small private school, is a basic brick building with the red and cream colors intermingling with its stonework. The windows' trim was once bright white when it was built, but time and abandonment has crackled the paint and dimmed it in wattage to a cream. The wide, cement porch has also seen better days, as well as the painted mural displaying the name of the building. A matching themed artwork of clowns frames the whimsical lettering, as their many, differently colored balloons appear to be floating off the mural. It has a sad, forsaken feeling to it, but when Aimes points at the moving curtain, it takes on a different heartbeat.

"Remember that whole comment about why you shouldn't kill them?" Aimes asks me.

I can hear her nervousness as memories of the many things we have already encountered overcome her. To this day, neither one of us can see a dead child, or see the many dark crows lined along a wide branch of a tree, without shivering as Travis' insanity still lingers long after his death. Just like with Chapel, and the others we have left to the darker pits of our uncharted hearts, they still walk with us long after we can no longer walk with them.

"My truck has a higher kill count than some of the ones you don't want me to kill," I answer her.

"Well, yeah with how you drive!" Aimes shouts to me as I'm exiting.

I'm not waiting on them. I'm not hiding in the shadows, waiting for some man to come to hold my quivering hand. I don't need them to whisper reassurances into my ear or shove fables down my throat with promises of happy-ever-afters. There are no more happy-ever-afters, and if Prince Charming was a lie before all of this started, I sure as hell don't need him now. I never cheered for Snow White, anyway. I have always been more 'Team Wicked Witch'.

"Hells!" Aimes calls to with me a hiss when she sees I am going in alone. "Really?"

I hear her frustrated sigh. The way she slams the truck door expresses even more of what she is not saying.

"You have a plan here, or just like always, run in with more ego than IQ?" Aimes sarcastically asks me.

Ignoring her, I test the knob on the front door. It seems to scream like an alarm as I twist it. Aimes and I both wince with each decibel it climbs. We brace ourselves for any sudden rush from a tribe of rotting, cannibal people to run out at us when the door swings open. The only thing that hits us is the smell.

It's as strong as a punch to the gut. It almost doubles us over with its strength. There is something about the smell of death and decay, and how it swirls with stale air to remove any bravery or sense of pride from your thoughts. Now more than ever, because we know what the smell is attached to - the dead. The main problem is the dead are no longer aware they should be dead.

The men's arrival buys my nerves and stomach some time. I'm not stalling. Like well-armed back up, I'm just waiting on them, as they have asked of me a thousand times. A little smudge of the truth for male pride is something women do all the time.

"Here are our Prince Charmings now," I say, with my previous thoughts coloring my greeting when their Harleys go silent.

It's cute how they ride in a formation, park in a formation, and even cut the engines in the same boring, and predictable formation, I think to myself with acidic sarcasm.

It used to never bother me before, but as of late, their little world with their little rules and unspoken meanings strips me raw. I used to be envious, even proud of it. The sight of their patch passing me on our town's roads would bring a smile to my face. The only thing that smiles anymore is their skull and it seems to be taunting me more every day.

Rhett is the first to the porch, as expected. His stride is his normal relaxed smoothness, but there is a bit more of a hurry to it than normal. Either his fight with Marxx has stirred another demon or it's the sight of Aimes so close to the unknown. Either way, the last thing any of us need is more of Rhett's personal demons motivating him into action.

"Never was much of a fan of Cinderella," he says to me, and a part of me wonders if he even remembers that was the nickname J.D. held for me as he is talking. "More of an Ariel fan."

"Why?" Aimes asks him before any of us can stop her.

"At least she'd be more honest about her smell," Rhett answers, keeping his eyes open for the first movement from inside the school.

Rhett doesn't shrug or smirk with his answer. It's just Rhett's logic, but the rest of us shake our heads or roll our eyes, glaring at Aimes for making it so easy for him. If Rhett notices, or cares about our responses, he doesn't show it. He is peering into the darkened building with anticipation.

"What am I? A urinal?" Aimes asks him, trying to mock him with what she perceives as a concealed insult.

I'm pretty sure she means one thing, hinting at Rhett's jokes of feminine scents Too bad everyone, but her, is already bracing for where Rhett is going to take us now that she has opened the way.

"Don't know," he says, still with his empty voice of lackluster emotions, "how many men have you let use you?"

Rhett doesn't wait for her answer before he takes the first fear-filled step into the unknown. He didn't ask her for one. He asked her to shut her up. That Rhett, always the charmer.

"Do you even know?" Lawless whispers to Aimes, resulting in her and I both jumping from his voice so close to us.

"Do you?" I ask him.

My question and my tone bring his friendly jest to a different level. I watch the friendly spark in his eyes ignite to a different pool of brown.

Lawless says, dropping his voice to the same emptiness as the man who slipped ahead of us, "Men? None. Some of the girls I wish I could forget at times."

Just like Rhett, he doesn't wait for any comeback. He slips into the darkness as he too was aiming to just shut me up. It does the job, but unlike Aimes, I'm not about to just stand here with my jaw hanging.

At first, the things around me are nothing but dimmed shadows hovering along the walls as I wait for my eyes to adjust to the lack of light. Rhett and Lawless are already easing their way through the abyss. Their guns are pointed to the ground with their well-trained finger resting and waiting to pull the trigger should there be a need. They move without sound over the layers of papers, which were once neatly amassed on the reception desk or waiting in the many cubbies with their crayon-like colored names scrawled above them. With my eyes still fighting to really see, I still sense something is very wrong.

Papers wouldn't hold such a heavy smell. The depth of the scent is too thick; too many layers to it to be just from the many scattered sheets about us. When my eyes finally adjust, I see how correct I am.

The same papers I had thought were only scattered randomly are actually stuck to the floors and walls like large pieces of confetti in the dark, dried blood smears. Some of the papers have slid, dragging its glue-like bonder with it. It mimics the outlines the bodies would have left - if there were any. There is just blood and wordless echoes of chaos. Even if we can't hear the screams, we can see what has happened because we have become so familiar with it ourselves.

Watching those around me, I can see their individual reactions. Their minds are making private hells into movie reels starring whom they imagine once belonged here. I let my eyes wander too, as we wait for any noises to hint that we are not alone.

There are pastels cards on the desk. Picking one up, I pulled it apart from the one which was once only its neighbor until the splashed blood made them conjoined twins. Written in a cartoon chat bubble is a rhyme about growing older. It's signed by many different names in many different scripts with just as many private jokes. Whoever once sat here, it was her birthday when this happened. Touching the wilted and brittle skeletons of the roses that were left on her desk, I watch as their petals fall, so resembling the dried blood all around us. I wonder if she died that day, too.

"It was her birthday."

The voice from the darkest pit of a hallway spins every male around me. Their various sizes of guns lift with the same unison to the spot where it came from. Aimes instinctively takes a step backward. I, being the sadist that I am, takes one step forward.

"Who are you?" I call back to the voice.

It earns me quick, side-glances of confusion as I take the 'leader' role from the men's club around me.

"Pinky," he calls back, still hiding in the shadows.

"Seriously?" Rhett asks. "Someone named you, Pinky?"

"No, that's just what they called me," he says. "I used to blush a lot."

The irony of the name isn't lost on me from Law's and my earlier conversation. Looking at this teen though, I doubt any part of him is capable of helping to take over the world. I can hear the sadness in his voice, but before I can question him, Marxx does first.

"And they are who?" Marxx asks.

The voice doesn't call back. Pinky doesn't answer Marxx's question. When he strolls out of the darkness, he is staring at only the roses with their damning memories and not the men with their guns pointed directly at his head.

He isn't anything more than a teen, but his shoulders sag with the weight of a fully burdened adult. His clothes look worse than ours, as if he hasn't changed out of them since the beginning. The shading of the stains is obvious, and seeing the wraith of a male teen in front of us, the men relax their aim. They don't completely lower their weapons, but they are no longer pointed at Pinky's head.

"It was her birthday. I came in to surprise her with the flowers," Pinky says, touching the fallen petals. Only his fingertips caress them, shuffling them more than handling them.

"Are you here alone?" Aimes asks him.

Her arched eyebrow is more curious about who, or what might be lingering in the back rooms from where he came than whatever story this teen is stumbling upon to share. Like a skipping record of times gone by, I'm more interested in the story. Whatever is waiting for us to discover it, can wait. Glancing around the open room again, I have a feeling I already know what we are going to discover.

"The older ones left for the day to see a movie at a theater in a town over. It's just the littlest ones here," Pinky tells the petals.

We all glance at each other hearing what he has said. Rhett's gun rises again. He is no longer looking at Pinky. His eyes are only for the hallway and the dark secrets it is holding.

"Where is your mother?" I ask Pinky.

His eyes lift from the memorial on the desk to me. There is a quivering of his lower lip. It doesn't match the shock in his eyes I have left with my question.

"With them," he whispers to me.

It's all Rhett needed to hear. He doesn't wait for any of their little signals. Rhett is already down the hall, swallowed by its darkness before Pinky can stop him.

The teen transforms into something of pure rage watching Rhett walk past him. Before Pinky can take more than just a few steps, Lawless has him by the hair, kicking the back of the teen's knees. They unhinge and come undone by the force from Lawless' boot. Lawless follows the advantage of gravity and puts the teen to the ground completely. As Pinky screams into the collection of confetti, he never stops struggling under Lawless' strength.

With a head nod, Law motions for Marxx to back up Rhett and I follow with my curiosity as if it's a noose around my throat. Lawless reaches for me, but with him being the main keeper of the possessed teen, he is easy to avoid. With nothing more than his cursing over my decision following me, I follow the two who have already been swallowed by the darkness ahead of me.

I follow their sounds, refusing to wait for my eyes to adjust. It's something we have learned to do. Waiting around to be able to see what is in the dark only allows the things already in the dark a better chance to see you, and worse.

Rhett and Marxx wander slowly into each room we find. I wait by the door, keeping a watch for anything to slither from the darkness, but I can't keep my eyes from seeing what is around me. The rooms are large caverns of age-appropriate items. Everything from miniature desks to large plastic bins of toys sit silently unused and forgotten. Each room seems to adjust to a younger age group, unsettling Rhett with the discoveries, as their silent picture grows more shocking.

The rooms before were easy to figure out. They were basic school-like rooms where the children seemed to have just left and should return at any moment. Each room now is slowly becoming grislier. It started so slow, it was almost easy to miss if you weren't already searching for any simple clue, which could cost you your life. Toys weren't put perfectly away. Cartoon themed bags weren't stacked perfectly. Now, as we are standing in a room filled with cribs and such, there is nothing simple or easy to ignore and the smell is growing thicker as well.

The sheets are crumpled in the cribs, stained with so much more than anything a small child could provide. Matching colors of unease are spread in wide, sprayed patterns behind the cribs on the walls around them. The small explosion of dried blood paints a perfect explanation of what has happened to the small toddlers who once belonged in those cribs.

Marxx's eyes have glazed over. He is only registering what his brain needs to see. The rest he is blocking out as he fights to hold onto any small piece of sanity. I'm already half crazy. I'm already haunted. I see it all.

I see every spot where someone stood pointing a gun into the many cribs. I see the spots where the babies were laid, soaking the carpet with their deaths. I am seeing another fragment of hell on earth. The only supplies here are the nightmares and the missing pieces of someone's soul.

"One more door," I call out into the room, when both men seem to stand mute and disoriented.

"Yeah," Marxx answers, less than thrilled with the fact.

I don't know if he is agreeing with me or acknowledging me because he doesn't move. Neither he nor Rhett takes any steps towards the hallway where I am waiting for them by the last door. The men J.D. molded to break the world are now breaking because of this world, but not me. One day, maybe one day, I will learn to fear what these men with hearts as black as theirs have come to fear. Life would be so much easier if I would.

The door opens without a sound, but the room isn't silent. The blinds are open in this room. The sunlight is as cruel as the bloodstains within it, showing everything and nothing at the same time as it filters through the room. The sounds and the smells tell everything the sun doesn't want me to know.

Glazed, almost colorless eyes, stare at me from between the many wooden bars of the cribs sitting around the room. Sweet, chubby faces of babies are sending my spine to vibrations of weakness instead of my heart with the sounds coming from their stained and ruined mouths. Lips, which were once milk-stained, and gurgling with their innocence are crimson streaked. They growl at me, craving me for reasons they never held any grasp of only a few short months ago. It's not the feel of my arms around them or the sound of my heartbeat they want close to them. It's the taste of my flesh and the blood my heart is pumping they now desire.

I hear Rhett's sharp inhale from behind me. He pulls me behind him, attempting to block the room from my memory. I let him. I lean into his dark, leather vest and inhale the scent of it to escape from the scents around me. I press my forehead between the framing bones of his shoulders as my breath rips my body with its rapid pattern, but the sounds, the sounds he can't protect me from.

The soft growling has become something louder, something more primitive and feral with Rhett standing in the doorway. Not even the teen screaming under the strength of Lawless can fully remove the chorus ahead of me. By his screams, I know what has happened here. I know now what I had only imagined I knew before.

I don't know the exact moment I turned to head back to the teen. I don't know what I really had planned to do, but when I find myself pressing my boot to the side of his face, something as dark as the demonic children I left behind me takes over.

"Why?" I ask him. "Why did you do this?"

"They are just babies. They don't know what they are doing," Pinky tells me, fully understanding what I am asking him even if the others don't yet.

"Your mom?" I ask.

I already know his answer. I just want to hear it before I become his judge and jury.

"She didn't understand. She was killing them. She was shooting them. "

Lawless stands slowly as if he was kneeling in something disgusting when he hears Pinky's confession. He keeps one boot planted in the teen's back while the fingers on his hands twitch, as if they too are covered with some dreadful substance. He doesn't look at me. He, like myself, has put the pieces together. We can do that now. Life has granted us this bow-graced gift.

"So, you killed her?" I ask Pinky.

"She didn't understand," Pinky almost whispers. "They're just sick. They don't know what they are doing. They can be cured!"

"Your mother, and a few others, were left here alone when some of the teachers took the older kids away. She did what she thought was best when they turned," I shout at him, still lost in the depravity of his sins.

"No, she was killing them! All of them!" Pinky shouts, but his eyes aren't seeing us. "I asked her to stop. I begged her, but she wouldn't. So, I stopped her. I took the gun from her and I stopped her. Then I fed her to them. I fed all the teachers who were left to them. I keep them safe now. They are safe until I figure it all out."

"You fed your mother to those things?" Aimes asks, her disbelief proportionate between each of his confessions.

Her voice is high pitched and outraged with just a touch of disgust.

"They're just babies. They have to eat. They're just sick and don't understand. She was a murderer. They all were," Pinky tells us.

I guess it wasn't just Mommy Dearest and her friends he offered to his new charges.

"No, *you're* sick and don't understand. *You're* the twisted little freak," Aimes tells him.

Before Pinky can answer her, Lawless has already skipped ahead or he is stuck behind because he asks, "Figure out what?"

Pinky is now limp, wanting to melt into the stained floor if he could with Law and I standing over him.

"For us to go to the fort," Pinky whispers into the stained papers.

Pinky wasn't seeing us when he said it. He wasn't seeing the room with his sins sprayed across the walls. Pinky is seeing someplace else; someplace he has deemed in his mind as a haven for himself and his new responsibilities.

"What fort?" Aimes asks from her corner of the front room.

"The fort. The one the woman was setting up for everyone. It's supposed to be safe. I just have to figure out how to get us all there," Pinky says, as if he really believes the monsters in the back room would be accepted there.

His voice is as far away as his sight. He is daydreaming, planning, and plotting. I just wasn't prepared for what he had in mind.

Lawless, lost in his thoughts, has let complete pressure escape from Pinky, freeing him from his forced imprisonment. Pinky's voice was so soft when speaking, so out of touch with what was going on, he had made himself appear non-threatening. Even I, the one so angry just slips of a second ago, have forgotten about him when hearing the explanation of somewhere safe nearby.

I didn't hear Pinky stand. I didn't hear the gunshot. I didn't feel the blade slide into the flesh of my thigh. All I can feel is the red, hot ruin of Pinky's face sprayed across my own. My sight is even tinted red as if I am looking through a rose glass-stained window. A window so red in color the dried memory on the desk beside me would have once been envious.

Dolph is trying to pull the revolver from Aimes' hand with more force than needed while Lawless is cleaning my face with his shirt and inspecting me with his eyes. Dolph jerks it from her tiny fists so hard she stumbles, almost falling beside the body of the headless teen. In my shock, I have no voice to argue with Dolph's treatment of her, but neither is anyone else. Not even Rhett says a word to stop Dolph as he shoves Aimes back into the corner she had been using as a cloak to hide in its darkness.

"What were you thinking?" Dolph shouts at Aimes.

"You could have hit Hells," Lawless says.

Lawless isn't shouting. His voice is calm, neutral, and so much more frightening than any volume Dolph's voice might harbor. It robs our pixie from any courage to argue with him. Her mouth just hangs open, but her voice isn't brave enough to lend it any help. When she looks to Rhett for support, he turns, giving her his back as he and Marxx return to the back room to do what they have to do.

Lawless is kneeling before me, and with one look of apology, he pulls the small knife from my thigh. Like the heat from a fire and the searing of a flame, I feel every inch of it as it is removed. It tears a sob from my mouth. The sound melts Law's eyes to his amber pools when he presses his bandana to the bleeding slash of my flesh.

"What is your obsession with stitches?" he whispers to me.

"It's much like my obsession with trouble," I reply.

"What's back there?" Dolph asks me.

His voice might say he doesn't know, but the furrowed lines around his eyes as he braces for my answer says he does.

"The babies. They turned. Pinky has been feeding them and keeping them in their cribs," I explain.

I let the tone in my voice carry the emotions over what I saw. Sometimes just words are meaningless with the many horrible things we keep discovering. Dolph lowers his head. He understands completely.

Lawless keeps his gaze straight and even with mine. He'll stay with me in every horror we stumble upon. He won't look away if I don't. He won't hide if I don't. I'm not hiding now, and he's letting me silently know he is right here beside me. Words, they are sometimes such meaningless things.

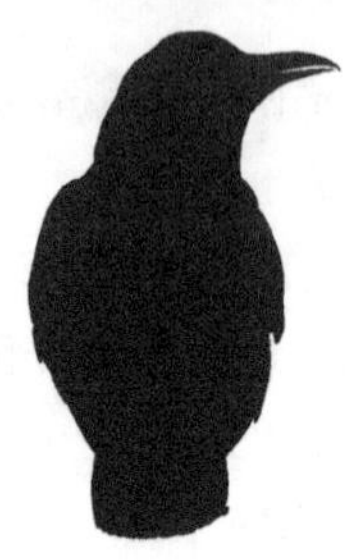

Chapter 9

"He said there was a fort?" Aimes whispers to me.

She and I are waiting outside as the men once again take charge. This should ruffle every single one of my hard-headed tinted feathers, but it doesn't. I don't want to force my way into the room filled with the dead babies Rhett and Marxx put to rest. I already have the smell of death caking me with the horror story that once had happened in the building. I don't want any more side effects from what was allowed to take place.

"He didn't tell us where it was. You shot him."

She rolls her eyes, much like the teen princess mode of which she seems to be stuck in, saying, "He had a knife!"

"That he put into my leg. Lawless could have handled him."

"Okay, so next time I will wait until one of our vested crusaders comes to the rescue when I think someone is about to kill you. Happy?" Aimes asks.

Her tone is anything but happy and her sarcasm isn't hiding that fact.

I look at her, arching an eyebrow, and tell her, "If someone is truly about to kill me, then please, feel free to shoot."

"Even if it's you?"

"Cute," I reply.

She shrugs, saying plenty before actually asking, "Do you think there really is a fort somewhere? I mean, let's be honest, he was not at the top of the sanity food chain."

"Who is?"

Aimes shrugs again, but this time it's more of an agreement than a concession.

"If there was," I say, when she doesn't take up the banter again, "there has to be some mention of it somewhere in there. Someone like Pinky doesn't come up with bright ideas on his own. Someone had to have told him about the place and he most likely wrote it all down."

"What? Like a dear diary of depression?" Aimes asks.

"Something."

Aimes is silent, chewing on her bottom lip with her thoughts. She finally says, "I know where it would be."

I groan when she pushes from the truck and heads into the very place I was content to avoid.

"Can't you just tell them where it is?" I shout my question and it turns Marxx towards us when he hears me.

"I could, but I thought you were tired of our Prince Charmings?" Aimes shouts back.

She knows how to push my buttons so well.

"At least they don't think of me smelling worse than a urinal," I say to her as I pass her.

She blows me a kiss with more sound effects than needed. She once again sparks the curiosity of the men around us. Marxx watches our approach with complete distrust. I guess I've earned that.

"Hey, pookie bear," I mockingly call to him, trying to ease down the storm building in his eyes.

He only arches an eyebrow. He is waiting to see what I am plotting before siding with either side of my plan. Seeing the jagged scar on his arm, I guess I've earned this from him, too.

"Our Pinky thinks she might know where psycho Pinky might have kept a clue to where this fort is, or whatever he was talking about," I offer him.

See, no tricks up my sleeves, is what I try to make my face say. With his eyes scanning its every curve and line, I don't think it's saying it at all.

"You don't want to go in there," Marxx says, shifting his body to block my entrance. "We had to put those things and what they were living off of down."

"Things they were living off of?" Aimes asks, repeating Marxx's choice of words.

"Not all of the kids turned, and not all of the adults were killed," he tells us softly, like a parent breaking bad news to a child.

My mind puts the pieces together again just as it had when Pinky was dropping hints, but I don't believe it. I can't believe it and that must have shown on the very curves and lines Marxx was staring at. Marxx reaches out, grabbing my upper arm while shaking his head.

"Not this time, Hells," he tells me. "Don't do it."

His grip is tight. It squeezes my arm and I'm sure I will have bruises to remind me I had a chance to avoid all of this. He gave me an out, but he and I both know I won't take it. Marxx tilts his head seeing the truth on my face. I watch as his eyes dim to pity where storms had been just moments ago. Dropping his hand, he sighs fully knowing I'm going in.

"Where?" Marxx asks.

"He thought of them as his. His twisted little head made him believe he was in charge of some saintly duty. If he were keeping notes, they would be in the boss' room," Aimes tells him.

"Side room; off from the lobby," Marxx tells us.

"What? Don't want to come to play with us?" Aimes asks him.

She meant it as a jest, a simple little taunt, and tickle. It doesn't have that effect.

"I'm tired of your idea of games," Marxx tells her. "One day, your luck is going to run out and there might not be anyone there to play hero."

"Well good thing I have Suicide Barbie with me!" Aimes calls out as she walks past Marxx.

Her tone sets both him and I to wince, but for different reasons. Of course, in typical Aimes fashion, she leaves me to deal with his wince.

"I'm serious, Helena," Marxx whispers. "One day, you might just find yourself all alone. I made a promise to myself a long time ago to keep you safe but promises have a way of failing the ones you love."

I close the gap between us, embracing this man who I once thought of as colder than a winter's frost. He stiffens when feeling my arms around him, but slowly he lets himself relax. He returns the hug. Cradling the back of my head with his hand to his chest, I can hear him exhale some of the tension he has let his shoulders carry. He winces when I tighten my hold on him and I remember the reason Aimes and I had set out alone.

"Guess Rhett landed a few good ones?" I ask Marxx.

He smiles at me, a halfhearted smile, but it is a smile and I haven't seen one on his lips since we lost Chapel.

"I think we both did," Marxx tells me.

"This makes you two back to the 'I love you man' stage?"

Marxx widens his smile. I think I can *actually* see teeth.

"Good," I tell him. "I'd hate to see you kill the crazy bastard."

I can feel his chuckle, but I don't hear it. Even so, it's wonderful. He and I have both locked our souls away in such a deep cavern and the sensation of his laughter loosens the shadows clinging to me. I may have found my figurative father, and some form of the word in a blood relative, but this man is more family to me than either of them.

"Hey, Barbie, you get lost between the porch and the lobby?" Aimes shouts to me from where she is waiting inside.

She has no problem trying to shoot me in the head, but walking into a room alone is giving her pause. Good to be needed, I suppose.

Marxx does one of the trademark pats on my back to let me know he is okay. I want to tell him the hug was more for me than it was for him, but you don't tell a man such things. Instead, I let him slip from me and his smile eases away in time with his arms. Like a trick of the light, one head nod pointing inside, and our moment is gone.

Aimes gives me a wide-eyed look of *it's about time* when I enter the lobby. Even with the door having been propped open, the smells are just as heavy. It feels as if you are breathing in death and not just walking in it.

The men have flipped the place in every sense of the word. Old plastic milk crates with their bright colors are lined along the hallway. Whereas once their purpose was to hold the many cartons of milk or juice for the children, now they are being used to hold the items deemed by the men as keep worthy. Looking at the completely random collection, Rhett must be the one picking the items.

Aimes is waiting at the door to what was once the office of the manager. Her eyebrows are almost arched into her hairline with her frustrated expression. In her mind, it's been hours since she hatched this plan. In reality, her mind is a little lack at keeping time.

"If you are in such a hurry," I tell her as I pass her into the darkened office, "you could have gone in without me."

"We kind of have this thing of doing stupid stuff together," she tells me, still perched against the doorframe. "Why break up a good thing now?"

I shrug with my face, spinning the blind's lever to open the dust-covered plastic blinds. The sunlight slowly peeks into the room. Even it is a little hesitant to see what these rooms hold now.

I won't say it out loud, but Aimes was right. This room has been kept how it was the day before everything happened. There is no murder scene or frantic rush of an escape here. The room is almost a time capsule of before things went wrong; when the nine-to-five was the mundane, and before Death took to the streets. There is almost a soft scent of perfume as if the woman who once called this office hers just walked out and will be back any moment.

"Why is it when we find someplace untouched, it makes it that much creepier?" Aimes asks me.

Her fingers trail along the pictures in their frames from different times in a woman's life. The many degrees the woman has earned are also framed and hung in a modern pattern of blocking. It's the picture on the desk, though, that is the most telling of who the woman might have been.

There, in a yellow bikini, she stands with her arm draped over the teen who called himself Pinky. The deep red lip prints covering his face match the red of the woman's lips and the flush upon his cheeks and chest. They are standing on a riverbank with matching grins over a shared joke that must have taken place only moments before the camera found them. Pinky's mother might have worked behind the front desk, but the woman who was in here looks to have been a different type of mentor.

The top of the desk has been kept stacked and neat, making it obvious to see what has been of use recently. The rest of the building stands like a stain of a memory, but this room has been kept like a monument of love. Pinky never even bothered to secure the last of the roses or birthday cards for his mother. In here, he has kept this woman's office pristine.

Aimes has already started going through the tall, metal filing cabinets. She doesn't hold the same sainthood for the woman as the teen did. Aimes is discarding the thick files on the floor; scattering the papers like leaves from a tree as they fall and blanket it. I know what we are looking for won't be in there. No, those files aren't personal enough to have interested Pinky.

Sitting in the plush, leather chair, I rock as my eyes roam the room. I'm trying not to see what is in front of me, but to see what isn't. I scan past the walls holding their many frames and their time-earned haze. I ignore Aimes with her paper party of files. Spinning the chair some, I glance behind me to where the office plants are just now starting to droop on their wooden shelving unit. Looking lower, I see the many different long boxes used to hold whatever paperwork the woman needed to keep close at hand. The last box, the one closest to the wall behind the desk, this is the one which speaks to me.

It's slightly slanted; just enough to touch its one corner to its neighbor, when the rest of the boxes sit stiff and separated. I touch it with the toe of my boot. It scoots with the gentle pressure and continues to whisper to me as if I were a child for it to taunt. It works.

The box opens easily, but all that is within it is many different sizes of receipts. Not exactly the buried treasure I was hoping for, to say the least. My disappointment is creased on my face. I purse my lips, tilting my head to see around the box. What I find is a different stash of buried treasure.

The first box wasn't taunting me to find out what was inside it, but what is behind it. A small black box tied with deep, purple ribbon sits in the shadows made from the larger boxes. Pulling it to the light, the ribbons come undone in my hand with how loosely they were tied. I can smell the soft wave of perfume drifting from it. Inside are photos of Pinky and the woman in many different poses and holidays. Nothing about the pictures scream anything other than these two people spent a lot of time together, but they still send shivers of loathing through my fingers as I shift through them.

"Pssst," I call to my partner in pink.

"Find something?"

"Yeah. Why Pinky was a little creepy," I tell Aimes.

Handing her the ribbon-wrapped box, I let her play through the innuendoes as I start my search again. Right under where the secret box was left, there is a black notebook. Its edges are torn and shredded. Many different patterns have been swirled across its cover with just as many colored pens.

Flipping through it, I read the many entries about the teen and the woman who worked here in his thoughts. He loved her, or at least as much as any teenager thinks they love someone. It's filled with thoughts about their meetings and how he felt being around her. There is nothing proving anything ever happened between the two, but there is enough to roll my stomach with my assumptions.

The thoughts become darker as the pages slide away. What was once puppy adoration has turned into a thing of obsession. Like in a timeline, Pinky has dictated every act the woman ever did, every date she had, every man she smiled at, down to the very clothing she wore each day. It's all described in great detail here in his thick block lettering of fixation.

In bold ink, he has written about his plan to make her his. He heard about a new drug. A drug that was created by an accident and how it turns people into mindless versions of themselves. If she were to receive this drug, he muses in ink, she would be his forever. He would take care of her. He would keep her safe and she would forget about all the other men in her life. There is a drawing that sets my blood to ice and I now know just how dark Pinky really was.

"Found something," Aimes says, pulling me from the assumptions my mind is racing with. "Look. It's a map."

She hands me the many folded and creased sheets of paper. I don't have to read it. I recognize the name from the notebook of delusion.

"Think this is it?" she asks me.

I nod as my stomach turns to knots. Aimes thinks she has found some missing piece to our possible future. What she doesn't know is she actually found a missing piece to a forgotten past.

Chapter 10

"Lookie what we found!" Aimes is bouncing towards Rhett with her excitement.

The men are loading the back of my truck with the crates when we exit into the fresh air. For a brief flash, Rhett's cold eyes brighten to match the lift of a smirk on his lips when he hears her voice. It fades though, just as quickly as it arrived, when a shadow of a memory clouds his face. If Aimes noticed either occurrence, she doesn't show it.

"It's a map to that fort thing Pinky Murdering Brewster was rambling about," Aimes explains.

She clutches the piece of paper much like the children with their golden tickets to the chocolate factory. I guess, in a way, she just might be holding ours. That is, if we can all get along long enough to find the place.

Lawless holds the thin paper much in the same way as she had. I watch his eyes follow along the marked routes, as he mentally tries to find the place. If you really want honest directions to a place, don't ask the gas station attendant. You ask a biker, a real biker. Back roads and unmarked short cuts are their thing, and watching the eyes light up on our bikers, I know finding this place won't be a problem.

"This isn't too far from here," Marxx says.

His eyes have traced the same route as Law's had moments before. They are both nodding as if some silent conversation has been passed between them. Rhett stands silently. He was watching the map with a different look of possibilities than Aimes and Lawless had held. All three of them seem to have a different flavor to their hope.

"What do they have?" Dolph asks my back.

I jump a little when I hear Dolph behind me. I must have made a noise to match since Law is suddenly so interested in Dolph and I. His hands are still holding the paper, but his eyes are only tracing the man beside me.

"Sorry," Dolph says, but his smirk doesn't convey the emotion. "So, what are they looking at?"

"Aimes maybe found a map to the fort the teen was talking about."

"Think it's legit?"

"The guys seem to think so."

"Do you?"

I pause in our exchange with his question. Do I?

"If Pinky really thought it was, there would be proof. All we found was a notebook of his ramblings."

I don't explain any more of my riddle. I know what the notebook held. I have matched all of Pinky's little secrets together like a rubix cube of dementia. People don't fall into crazy. They are born into it and then pushed or led into their levels of madness. Like a science experiment, Pinky wasn't just pushed; he was prodded and caressed. The owner of his descent is still waiting for him.

Turning to head back inside the blood-caked madhouse, I slide my blade from where it rests in its holder on my thigh. The wound from the teen is still searing me, mocking my attempt to be brave. Inhaling from my wince, I can feel Dolph waiting for me to ask him for help. He's learned to not offer, and just like Law, he'll wait right beside me until I ask, or his own conscience forces him into action.

"Want to come play?" I ask him, finally easing down his unrest.

He smiles at me with his half-smile of amusement. He knows how hard it is for me to admit I need help and he is just as amused by my style of asking.

He shrugs and his eyebrow seems to be connected to his shoulders as he says to me, "Since you asked so nicely, sure."

I can't help it. Something about his smugness ignites the battered girl inside of me, and before I can stop my tongue, I hear myself say to him, "Oh goody, I'm getting tired of being the only one brave enough to do the killing around here. Might be refreshing to see you do more than just watch my back."

His smile doesn't fade. It doesn't even flinch. I'm becoming just that predictable. My ego and my tongue are known for their courtship.

"Whatever you say," Dolph tells me, still wearing his smirk like a war badge.

With my temperament as of late, or as of always, he doesn't ask any questions when I pivot from him. He doesn't make one sound of curiosity as to where I am leading us when we enter into the thick darkness of the once laughter-filled building. I think he is even whistling under his breath as he follows me. There is a sick twist of irony that it's "Mary had a little lamb".

"Why that song?" I ask him, before I can stop myself.

"Dunno. Nervous I guess," he honestly answers. "I keep thinking I'd get used to it. Always finding this kind of stuff, I should be used to it."

"But you're not," I answer for him when he pauses.

His silence stretches. It seems to elongate the hall even more than it naturally is. The blinds have been opened in each room. It lessens the shadows some, but still, it's a hallway from hell and all of hell's victims are splashed against its walls.

"It's not a bad thing," I say, filling the void.

"What isn't?"

I shrug, much as he did on the porch of the place, before saying, "Not being used to it. It's not a bad thing. Who knows, one day maybe we won't have to see it anymore."

I hear his chuckle of disbelief and its mixture of sorrow. "Wouldn't that be nice?" he asks me with a lowered voice and a southern drawl.

"What? And not constantly smell like a slaughterhouse?" I ask with a smile. "You know you just can't bottle this."

"I think a few blonde celebrities tried."

I laugh. I can't help it. We are both stalling before going through this final doorway I have brought us to. He is stalling because he doesn't know what is on the other side. I'm stalling because I do.

"You don't really have to do it," I whisper. "I can."

"I don't even know what "it" is," he whispers back.

"The teen, Pinky, it was his idea for the kids to get the shot. He set it up to have it done here before the kids left to go on the field trip since it was technically a school. It wasn't the first round. The gossip had already started about the shot being what was causing the madness in people. Pinky wanted it. He wanted her to change into what was being said people were becoming. He wanted it because he wanted her. So, he did it and now he has her, forever."

Dolph is staring at me as I try to explain what happened here. His face takes on the different angles of his emotions as he listens, but he doesn't stop me.

"He waited here. It was his idea for the older kids to be taken to the movies after their round. He didn't want them or the extra teachers in the way. He encouraged the director to take the shot first. It was a way to settle the kid's nerves. He really just wanted to be sure she'd take it. Then it happened. They turned. Most likely it was his mother who began to fight them. When she began to kill the turned, thinking only to save her son from whatever was happening, Pinky killed her. He killed his mother to keep his obsession safe."

Dolph does make a noise of disgust now, but he still doesn't ask me anything.

"He kept the babies. They were her favorite. They were the reason she started this place. She couldn't have kids. This was her chance to be surrounded by them. To keep them 'alive', he stored the extra staff in a closet. He would feed pieces of the staff to the babies. He was studying how to amputate limbs without killing the victim through practice and perfecting his theories. He was perfect for this world, as so few of us are, but Pinky was perfect."

"Why?" Dolph finally breaks my monologue. "Why would someone do something like this?"

"You never really fall out of love with your first," is all I offer him to help him understand what is happening here.

"You don't kidnap her and keep her in a closet."

"You don't turn her into a flesh-eating monster and feed her coworkers and friends to her either. But hey, what do I know about romance and love? You've seen Law and me."

"You're telling me you think she is still here?"

"I'm telling you she *is* still here. That's the real reason he was trying to find the fort," I tell him, sending him an even stare to further accent my words. "How many are left of the staff? That I don't know."

"I guess we are about to find out," Dolph mutters, more to himself than to me.

He's right. We are. If the notebook is correct, Pinky has kept his pet and her food in this back room.

He was worried the screaming would upset the babies. He didn't want them to hear what he was doing to the staff in order to keep the babies 'alive'. In his mind, they were still human, and it was now his duty to protect them and his true love.

"You sure you want to do this?" I ask, repeating the same question Marxx held for me.

"No, but I understand you're tired of me just watching your back," Dolph answers.

There is no heat to his reply. There is a smirk on his lips similar to the one he wore when we started this little tour of depravity. He's just trying to use my anger to bolster my nerves. I did mention I'm just that predictable, right?

Rolling my eyes, I open the door that has stood like a barrier to protect us. I never was really good at just walking away and letting barriers do their job. I don't need to kill her. There is nothing that is forcing me to do this but my sense of self. It's the very same thing that seems to always drag me right back into the fire. When the ashes are nothing but cooling embers, this is when I always have to throw oil to the flames just to watch it all burn brighter around me.

This fire is a room filled with plastic tarps and buzzing flies. There is more blood on the walls around us than on the white sheets of plastic under our feet. It soars high in an almost black arch of patterns. What were once puddles on the sheets are now congealed into gel-like, shoe stealing spots. The smell brings up what little I have had to eat to burn my throat. Not even Dolph is immune to the gagging stench around us. He covers his face with the bandana the men keep in their back pockets. I'm not sure how much of the odor the thin fabric blocks, but he clutches it to his face with desperation etched around his eyes.

Like the guys had done with the map, I let my eyes roam the road-like patterns of where bodies have been dragged through the massacre scene. The heaviest of the lines leads to one door hidden behind a standing mattress. Swallowing past my fear and rolling acid-filled stomach, I walk to where the mattress stands like a giant beacon of a hint.

This rectangle of cloth is just as blood-soaked as the walls around it. When it falls from my push, the perfect outline of where it had stood during the bloodletting is almost shocking. The noise heard after the fall is even more shocking.

"Hello?"

It's a small voice. Something destroyed by fear and pain to the point of being unrecognizable as either male or female. Dolph and I exchange looks when hearing it. I know he, just like myself, is wondering how many more nightmares we are about to add to our already amassed fortunes of them.

"Hello?" it calls again.

One deep breath to steady my shaking hand before I open the door. One last breath of clotted blood and bowels before I face what is calling to me from behind yet another barrier I am about to ignore. One last second before my sense of self will scar me again. Tossing the oil to the flames, I can almost hear what's left of my sanity begging for help.

Chapter 11

The closet's walls have been lined with small crib mattresses. Thin lines of inner material are escaping from the lengths of a few. Someone has tried to claw their way past the man-made barrier of walls.

The someone, or one of the many who were once stashed in this converted closet turned hostage room, is staring at us from the furthest corners with arms wrapped tight against jean-clad legs. The state of her long, black hair and the bruised, delicate features scream of hints about the possible abuse she has endured. The way she watches us, gives even more information.

"Look at me," Dolph whispers to her.

He shines the light from his flashlight against the gaunt and bruised face of hers. Being in the dark for so long, she almost whimpers from the pain the focused beam causes her. It's her eyes Dolph wanted to be sure of. He wanted to be sure her eyes didn't glow like a wild beast's and lack any life, like the statues remodeled from demonic visions.

"What's your name?" I ask her.

I kneel down to her, as she tries to scurry even deeper against the thin mattress blocking her escape. Her eyes are wide and wild as she watches Dolph and I. Her clothes bear testimony to the many things she has survived. Mentally, she's little more than a beast being driven by instinct to survive. Her mind is trying to prepare for fight or flight, and I don't really have the energy to deal with either.

"I'm not going to hurt you," I tell her, trying to keep this as peaceful as possible.

I guess when you have been locked in a closet while listening to your friends being prepared for cannibalistic dinner, there is nothing about peace left in your dictionary. She charges at me, almost flying through the air with the force of her attack. There is no time to do anything but to brace for it. With a slow exhale I prepare myself for what every part of me knows is coming.

There is no plan of skill with her attack. All she sees is me between her and the door to her freedom. It's not even me she wants to fight. I'm just the one who happens to be in her way at this moment. If I didn't understand this, I would just shoot her. What's one more soul to my book of the damned?

Instead, I roll her with my weight, as another fight flashes in my mind. With her thrashing body pinning me, Carol's face flickers between the woman's above me and the pictures of my mind. It paralyzes me as I am torn in time between the day in the hallway and the little girl who has died as many times, as many nights, as there has been since we left the burning high school. I can't fight. I can't breathe. My body is locked by my mind and both have given up. As this woman tries to defy her believed future, fighting to survive, I have surrendered.

Dolph has placed his arm around the throat of the woman. He is trying to use her need for oxygen as a motivator for her to release her hands from my throat, but she's not relenting. Her long, dark hair has become a curtain around her and I. I can see Dolph through waves of her stringy curls, and whatever he is seeing on my face, is setting him higher to desperation.

"We aren't going to hurt you!" Dolph is shouting, as he wrestles with the woman.

Every tug he places upon her only tightens her grip around my throat. He is at a loss as how to get her off me without further hurting me, or worse. Personally, I've had enough.

Whatever cloud had settled around me, paralyzing me, has lifted. A much darker cloud, my anger, replaces it. Using my elbow like a wake-up call, I collide it across her cheekbone. The sudden blow rocks her. Stunned, her grip loosens for that pivotal second Dolph needed to peel her from me. I'm not waiting for the peeling.

I thrust my palms into her chest. My added force helps Dolph lift her from me with enough speed to land the woman on her back. Dolph, not wanting a repeat of any sudden impulses, follows her body down. He pins her with his legs on her shoulders. He doesn't really sit on her. He uses his weight as a warning of what may happen if she doesn't stop her attacks.

"I'm not going to hurt you," Dolph says again, hoping to reach through whatever barrier of crazy in which the woman is clinging.

Her wild eyes jerk to me before looking back to the man above her.

"*She* might hurt you, yes," Dolph answers her silently asked question. "So, don't do that again."

The sound of our commotion has reached the group outside. Lawless, Rhett, and Marxx rush into the room and stare at me and the other woman on our backs. Only Rhett smiles.

"Making new friends?" Rhett asks us, hinting to where his mind normally stays.

Sending him my one finger answer, I stand. Once again, I am blood-covered, but at least this time it's not mine. Well, not completely. Pinky's parting gift has seeped through the bandana Lawless tied around my leg. Just once I'd like to make it back to wherever it is we are staying without having to listen to Paula's scolding, or to be the subject of her cold eyes.

"How did you miss a woman being kept prisoner in a closet, oh smart-assed one?" I ask Rhett.

He shrugs before saying, "I already have enough crazy women. I guess I wasn't looking for another."

"I'm sure Aimes will be happy to hear that," I reply.

I'm buying myself time to collect myself and the ghosts who are still draped over me like familiar quilts. They have wrapped themselves around my mind and I am filled with their familiar emotions just as long-worn quilts contain scents that stroke our memories. Carol was not the last I have killed. She was not even the most inhumane, but she is the one who follows me down every dark hallway of my life.

"Who is this?" Lawless asks.

Dolph and I both shrug. We never had time to really exchange pleasantries with her. Bruises, yes. Hellos, no.

"Leigh."

The same small voice I had heard from behind the door speaks again. There is no confusion this time as to whom it belongs. It's still just as small and just as soft, but the eyes boring into me are neither.

"How long have you been in there?" Dolph asks Leigh.

"There isn't exactly a calendar or a clock," she replies. When no one shrinks from her attempt to be cocky, she admits, "There were four of us. The first two he took quickly. Rita, he took his time with. He would cut pieces from her before burning the wound closed. Then he just never brought her back."

The emotions are easy to read on her face and in how she instantly braces her body to move if she needs to. Dolph releases her. Either he doesn't see her or is refusing to see her shift of mood. Dolph is not G.R.I.T., though. They have read her language to perfection. Already, they have spread out like a net of preparation, just waiting for her next move to ensnare her.

Seeming to be completely unaware of what the men around him are doing, or even what the woman below him is capable of, Dolph asks her, "Did you used to work here?"

Leigh slides to a sitting position. She is very aware of the men standing around her. It's almost cute how she is no longer glaring at me, but at Dolph, who is nothing more than a tiny bundle of nerves and second thoughts.

"No," is all she offers.

She stands with such slow ease; it almost looks like a perfected dance move. The way her eyes bounce to each man around her, says nothing of the graceful world of dance. She's poised for something a little different, a little more violent.

Wetting her lips with her tongue, she asks, "You said you wouldn't hurt me?"

"Wrong," I answered for the room. "He said he wouldn't hurt you. The rest of us are a bit different with our thoughts."

"Meaning?" Leigh asks.

She still is not glancing towards me. Her eyes are still for the men around her who pretend to be almost bored with the tapping of their fingers on their belts or a slight tilt of their head. I'm not insulted. I'm amused with how it seems to be Marxx who is the one giving her the biggest case of the jitters.

"Meaning we haven't figured out what to do with you, yet," Marxx answers her.

"More worried about what Pinky was going to do with her," I say, and Marxx looks towards me with a questioning look. "Pinky wasn't feeding her friends to just the babies. There's more."

There is only one door left to this room. It holds no barriers or any style of a lock. The stains that once seeped from under the room's door are now dried and dark; the only memory left of whom to which they once belonged. Unlike a purple door at a gym long ago, which held the first truths to what my future would become, I know what secrets are waiting behind this door.

Chapter 12

I'm not a fan of words or long explanations. If someone has to explain something to you, it's because you didn't want to understand it. People pretend to be blind or dumb, but in truth, we all see more than we ever really want to know. We just ignore it. I apply the same lackluster for conversations now.

The men just watch me. They too have grown used to my show and not tell routine. It's a lot like that special hour set aside in elementary school, but with more middle fingers and eye-rolling as its main theme.

I swallow down the fear I am hiding. I don't let it weaken my legs or place shivers along my skin. I ignore the burning of my leg and the warmth my blood is lending to the cloth tied around it. It's unsettling how many different temperatures blood can hold. The blood around me is dried and cold. Its color is reflecting the fact of how lifeless it now sits with the darkest of the shades. It's as if when life is leaving the substance, so does the brightly colored hues. I wonder how many shades she will be wearing.

I don't know why I paused in front of the door. I don't know why I let these few moments slip from me because I know once the motion forward is stopped, your mind starts. All the possible worst situations begin to play out in front of your mental eyes, while your body stalls with the fear it provides for you. I know this. I have seen this cost people their lives or the lives of those around them. So why am I falling into the same deathtrap?

"Hells?" Law's voice sneaks into my mental cage.

I can feel the heat of him before he touches my shoulder. It lends me some sense of self; some feeling of strength my mind had stolen from me. My hand moves in the same mindless fashion I had thought I had trained my body to do before it betrayed me. I can almost feel my mind being swallowed by the white noise of serenity when it understands, once again, I'm not going to heed its warnings despite the blaring colors it's displaying them in before me.

The dead have a smell. It's a twist between dread and mourning. The undead, they have a smell, too. It finds me like a lost memory when the door opens. The crossover between the two states of her body is a bouquet of rot and murder. Neither smell does anything to help my slipping courage.

The woman sitting before me is no longer the sultry beauty of her photos. As she stares at me, I can see into the very darkness that has become her mind. There is a moment of confusion across her bloodstained face, but it fades quickly to the stalking perfection of what she has become. She is waiting for me. Like the spider to the fly, she is waiting for me to enter into her little cavern of slaughter. Who am I to disappoint her?

The chain around her neck begins to vibrate like the tail of a rattlesnake with her cautious movements. She matches my every move like a waltz. I step forward. She glides backward. I shift to the left. She rotates to the right. She is as much testing me as I am testing the chain and collar keeping her secured to the wall behind her. Neither one of us is holding a lot of trust for the other.

Lawless inhales behind me. He isn't in shock or even shocked. Mildly surprised at best.

"Meet Pinky's first real love," I tell the room behind me.

Rhett is the only one who moves towards me. His curiosity is something between morbid and amused. This same twisted sense of curiosity is what allows him to be the man we need him to be. Even as he kneels down and throws some discarded trash from the room at her, who am I to knock it now?

The woman who once directed this place is watching us. Her glazed eyes roll from me to Rhett and rests only for a few moments on Lawless. Her fingers drum on the stained carpeted floor, telling of the person Pinky had dissolved her into. She appears almost bored, but I know differently. The Risen are better hunters than their human counterparts might have ever been. They have no emotions to slow or deter their motives. She's not bored. She's waiting. She knows well the length of her chain and the logic of the three of us to her one. Her little finger game is meant to distract us; to pull our eyes to something other than herself so when she does attack, she might have a small edge over us. She might have had it too if she had been behind door number one instead of door number two. Door number one has a score to settle.

I didn't sense Leigh rushing towards us. I saw Rhett's casual sidestep. With a shoulder block turned into a whole-body shove, he pushes me. Our height difference alone with such a move is enough to rock me off balance, but add a deliberate shove, and it's all Lawless can do to keep me from ending up back on the floor. Before my feet have the time to catch me Lawless already has me behind him, as the two men brace for whatever brand of crazy Leigh is exposing to the room.

Where Leigh found the slim replica of a knife, I don't know. Its blade is no longer than my finger, but she charges forward with it as if it's a weapon of mass destruction. There is no hesitation, no fear as she rushes the chained remnants of a woman.

My instinct is to rush in with her, to not let her face this moment alone. Law's is to block me. Rhett just watches it all with the same smirk as always, as Marxx stands silent and cold beside him. They both form a wall in front of Lawless, as if doubting his ability to really keep my self-destruction at bay. That's not Law's fault. That's mine.

Leigh is screaming; filling the room with her high-pitched anger as she rides what is left of the director to the ground, as they both fight the other. Her voice is banshee-like with nothing on her mind but the utter destruction of the walking demon underneath her. She doesn't just want to end whatever form of life is staring back at her, but to destroy the shell of which it lingers.

Everyone in the room knows her anger. We know with each stab Leigh is no longer seeing the muted eyes underneath her. We know with each attack she doesn't register the damage she is doing, but the damage that has been done. She isn't thinking of what she is killing, but of who has been killed by it. She isn't concerned with the pain the fight is causing her body as the monster underneath her struggles to win, but with the pain the monster has already caused her. So, we don't move. We don't offer to help her. We watch, silently, as Leigh does what her soul needs her to do to survive what has been done to her. The battle ends as all wars do - with one side screaming and forever changed with what they have done to the other side. Only then does Rhett move to lift Leigh from the carnage she has caused.

She doesn't fight him. With everything poured from her, she is empty and almost limp with the void it causes her. The director stares now with completely vacant eyes locked in some last expression of shock at the room decorated with the black shades of her blood. It's as if in her last moments some piece of her tried to return to the surface, but just like her blood, all her beautiful hues are gone. Just like Leigh, there is no life left to her now. Leigh watches me as she exits the room with eyes as dark as her last memories of what she's survived.

Chapter 13

"Who is that?"

Aimes doesn't like the woman who Rhett is placing on the back of his warhorse. She isn't even trying to hide it with the locked scowl and unhidden gestures. Rhett doesn't hide the fact he sees her, either. He smiles across the war zone, winking before slipping his dark glasses over his eyes. I used to think they wore them to protect their eyes from the road. Now, I think they wear them to protect them from their mistakes.

"Leigh," Dolph says, as he places the last crate of supplies into the bed of the truck. "Helena and I found her locked in one of the rooms in there."

Thanks, Dolph, is what I allow my glare to sarcastically tell him. I can feel the heat of Aimes' eyes already swinging towards me. I don't have sunglasses to hide behind to protect me from the damage from which Rhett has escaped. I shrug, hoping the little gesture will save me. It doesn't.

"You couldn't have just killed her like you do everything else in your path?" she asks me.

"No. Despite the rumors, I don't make it a habit of shooting at the head of living people," I reply.

I shouldn't have. I should have just ducked and covered. Never said I was the brains of this survival team.

"Let's define the word 'habit'," Aimes says, and I can already feel my skin being raked with the sarcasm she is aiming towards me. "Habit is when someone does something often, as they often plan to shoot at people. Now if you really want me to develop this habit, I can."

"Hey," I offer, sliding into the truck as if it could be used as dark glasses, "I'm not the one with her on my bike. I'm just the one who didn't shoot her."

"Good to know that option is still open for taking," Aimes says, sliding in from the other side.

I cringed. I did. I let her last little swing connect and bit my tongue against the return pitch. Maybe I am learning after all.

"Did you find out any more about the fort?" Aimes asks.

She can't handle silence. It doesn't matter how angry she is with someone. She would rather fill the silence with meaningless conversation than sit in defiant anger. Which, for a normal person wouldn't be a bad thing, but for someone as gifted in verbal manslaughter as she is, there are times I'd just prefer silence.

"We have the notebook. Once we get back to the group, we can all discuss what we want to do," I tell her, keeping my eyes on the road ahead of me.

"You mean if we want to keep hopping like squatters from home-to-home or maybe find an actual place with actual people to actually live?"

Her tone is so sugary sweet with false concern my teeth hurt.

"Yeah, that's what I mean."

Aimes says nothing. She is watching the men behind us and I remember not so many months ago, when I, too, was watching something similar. Law was just playing a different game than the one Rhett is smirking over.

"You remember how when we first hooked up with these monkeys how we didn't know how to ride? We pretty much kept our eyes closed the first few turns where they tried to out spark the other?" she asks me.

 I nod. I'm not risking another swing.

"So, why is it that every bimbo seems to know just how to ride once the apocalypse hits? Tits are perkier, boots are easier to find, and every come-save-me-slack-gina knows how to ride a Harley."

"But not a stick," I hear myself say.

I almost sink further down in the seat when I feel the ice of her eyes swing my way. I can't hide the smirk, though.

"I guess I'm just not a slack-gina," Aimes replies.

"Nope, just a urinal," I say, with a smile slowly growing larger across my face.

I can't help it. I should learn to, but I just can't help it with the roles reversed.

"What really happened in there?" Aimes asks me, unwilling to further make way for my sarcastic enjoyment of the situation.

"Remember the pictures of Pinky with the older woman?" I ask, waiting for her mind to switch gears and follow along with our new direction.

"Yeah. Okay no, not really."

"Well, let's just say that Pinky didn't take too well to his version of cougarville finding men her own age."

"The boss lady was with the teen crazy?"

"Yeah, with his mom working as the secretary for the place."

"So, what does Rhett's new seat warmer have to do with it?"

"Pinky was feeding people to the babies and his lady love. In his mind, she was just a little out of touch with reality and he could keep her forever as his own."

"He was a little out of touch."

"Leigh said she didn't work there. Pinky must have been finding people to feed to the things. She said she was held hostage in a closet with four others he used as a snack break for his little secret."

"Stop, just stop. You're making it hard to hate her and I really want to hate her."

Clicking my tongue, I tell her, "You don't even know her."

Aimes looks at me with one of her arched eyebrows and matching smirk before saying, "Since when did that little fact ever matter before?"

I shrug again, not really having the words to explain why I find myself defending the woman other than for the obvious reasons. "She is going to have one hell of a long road ahead of her," I offer, as some type of answer.

"You could have at least tried to clean her up some," Aimes says. It's the closest thing to an agreement with me, with her brand of blame that she's going to offer.

I shrug again. It hadn't occurred to me. I'm not sure what that says about my mindset when seeing someone covered in gore and death doesn't bother me anymore. I'm even starting to see it as normal.

"What are we going to tell the other group as to why we have another stowaway?" Aimes asks.

"Murderella had a bad week?" I offer, trying to bring a little more humor and less death into our conversation.

"Are there good weeks?" she asks me.

"Are you dead yet?" I ask in return, growing tired of the constant emotional babysitting our days are filled with.

"I'm not sure who the lucky ones are anymore," she says. "Are they those of us who are left, or those of us who've escaped?"

She repeats the same question I have asked myself many times, and hearing it formed on the lips of another other than my own, it steals my breath. My heart clamps, forcing me to breathe through the pain as my mind recalls each person we have lost, either as a group, or from our personal collection of souls. Are we the lucky ones? Or, are they for no longer having to debate such questions?

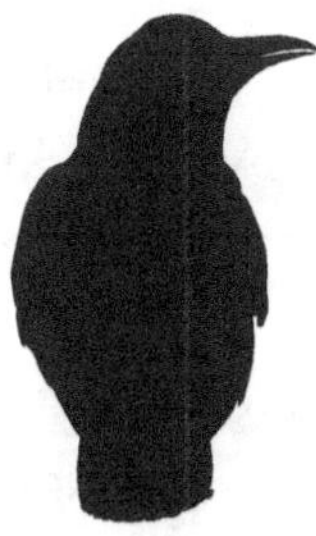

Chapter 14

The pouting male egos Aimes and I had left behind are still lingering. The men wear their unhappiness to be back as proudly as they wear their vests. I didn't expect them to hug and make-up, but if something doesn't break the walls soon, there might not be any of us left to hug.

Not that the local HOA is going to be making rounds anytime soon, but the porch is destroyed where the male problem solving took place. Amid the wooden debris and the glass from the ruined windows, sits Genny on one of the rockers. She is watching me with eyes so like my own that I have to look away. Need a warm body to run into certain death? I'm your girl. You want to sit and talk about feelings? Sorry, I'm already running to the whole certain death deal.

"Coward," Aimes whispers into my ear.

I roll my eyes, ignoring her and her comment with my boots crushing the glass underfoot. I can feel Genny's eyes on me with every step. The constant creaking of the rocker reminds me of a clock keeping time with my approach.

"Hey Gen-Gen," Aimes calls out, before we enter what is left of the house.

"Who's that?" Genny asks her, staring out at the arrival party.

"Leigh. She's Aim-Aim's new playmate," I answer, mocking the pet name Aimes tried to use to annoy me. I know I shouldn't have, but I did, and I smile when Aimes shoves me the rest of the way through the door.

"Is that her blood or someone else's?" Paula asks me, as I wait for my eyes to adjust to the dark front den of the house.

"Something else's, I think," I answer her, and the meaning is understood.

"What's in all the crates?" Peyton asks me from where he, too, had been watching our arrival.

"Not sure."

My answer brings his eyes to me as if I'm a kid trying to sneak away with a lie. His normally soft eyes turn a shade of something more while he stares at me. The man who once advised on how we all needed to trust each other seems to be a little more on the other shade of the argument.

"Honestly," I tell him, "I don't know. I wasn't there when they were loading it up. It could be stashed porn magazines to a holiday feast for all I know."

"If Rhett helped pick items," Aimes mutters, "it's most likely the first."

"Looks like he's brought back something more useful for that purpose than just magazines," my father says.

The look the room gives him is shared. He stumbles over his facial emotions as he realizes what he has said and what it implied.

"No, no what I meant was in the crates. For the feast comment!" Collin says, trying to save what grace is left for him to recover. "Looks like a lot of dry food. That will easily keep no matter where we end up."

Peyton looks back at the gathering of plastic milk crates and sighs. He knows the men out there are not going to wave any flags of peace or offer any branches of hope by just handing the items over. It's once again up to Peyton to make the first step to find a remedy to the divide so his group doesn't go without.

I can't help but miss Chapel even more at times like this. He would have already stepped up, divided the supplies evenly and dared the men to question him. He was our compass. He was our due north when the world always seemed to be heading straight south. We are drowning without him.

"I miss him, too," Paula whispers, to what is left of the window.

She doesn't acknowledge me when she pushes past. She has already slipped into her role of the nurse as Leigh stands mutely in the yard, lost as to what to do now. She will sink into the numbness, her white noise of her making. Her sense of duty always allows her to find it, because just like me, we aren't ready to accept the loss of the one man we both can't stop thinking about.

With the tension thick of unsaid things, Peyton and my father follow her out. My father's head is so low one would think he was obsessed with his shoes. Good to know I came by my fear of feelings honestly.

Aimes does her normal flop into the nearest chair. Her body might be limp, but her mind isn't. I can almost see the thoughts her mind is trying to work through. I'm honestly worried she might hurt herself.

"What?" I finally ask, taking what was once a matching chair. Now it's torn and stained from either stray animal abuse or something worse. I squirm a little thinking of what might be under me.

Her blue eyes lock onto mine with such a force I tilt my head back without meaning to do it. Something tells me I'm not so lucky as to have her thoughts focused just on Rhett's new toy. No, this is going to be something painful for me.

"You didn't tell them," Aimes whispers like a dirty secret.

I shrug, unwilling to help a conversation I'm still uncertain about. "Tell them what?" I ask.

"Are we taking them?" she whispers again, completely refusing to accept my denials.

"There is as much risk with numbers as there is safety. If we have to quickly leave a place, it's double the people we have to see out. It's twice the supplies. It's twice the-"

"Death," she says, cutting off my rambling. "It's twice the risk of losing someone you care about." Her whole face is calling me on my pathetic excuses, as she says, "It was easier when you thought he was dead. Now, he's not and he could be. You might think you don't care about him, but you do. Maybe not so much about him as a person, but no matter what your past holds, he is your dad and he is the only one who is left knowing the truth about your mom."

I shrug again, sinking into the chair despite the many stains around me. "There's Gen-Gen," I offer as a rebuttal to her logic.

"Chances are Gen-Gen only knows the PG-13 version of what happened. One doesn't normally add all their yearly details of their holiday affair to Christmas cards."

I say nothing, letting her simmer in her thoughts.

"If we take them, you're going to have to finally admit to what happened," Aimes says. "If we just skip out, you can keep right on running from your past like you have been."

"I told you. I've told you all that happened," I say, with a voice as cold as ice, unbelieving that she's wiggling her finger, again.

"No," Aimes replies, "you've told us the abridged version. Now, you're going to have to go all full biography."

She's right. It's not the fact of what secrets my past is obviously holding that keeps me from Genny. It's not the many years of unreturned love that's keeping me from Collin. It's *my* secrets that won't let my eyes look at either of them for too long.

"You want to try a practice run with me?" she asks me.

My arched eyebrow is enough of an answer.

"Just trying to do that supportive thing I hear so much about," she replies, with her hands held out in a surrender-like position.

The men's stomping in saves me. Both of us watch as the crates are lined by the front door just as the weapons once lined the windowsills. Those habits, so hard to break, I suppose.

"No nudie mags," Rhett tells Aimes and me, letting us know Peyton's attempt to bond was spent over our speculation of how helpful Rhett might have been in our survival selection.

"Nope, you have found a whole doll," Aimes says, without missing a space of a beat.

Rhett flashes her one of his trademark warning smiles. To others, it might be charming, perhaps even panty-dropping, but to us, we know the truth. Unfortunately for Rhett, Aimes isn't fazed by it anymore. She returns her own version with just as much energy behind it. They both might have met their match.

"Okay, love birds," I whisper, "that's enough."

"Take your pants off," Rhett commands of me.

Aimes and I both look at him as if he is either the boldest man alive or the dumbest.

He smiles slowly, like the man we have come to know. "Flattered, but it's Paula who wants you," he tells me. "We have bets on how many stitches you'll need this time."

I shudder, remembering the pain of the improvised needle and thread.

Rhett smiles again when seeing my discomfort. "Daddy could hold your hand if you want him to."

"Funny, but I don't ever remember calling you, or any other man, Daddy," I tell him, with my version of his dare.

"You haven't given me a chance, yet," Rhett shouts to my back as I leave the house to find Paula.

"I have, and I still don't call you Daddy," I can hear Aimes tell him.

The rest is muffled laughter as the two exchange jokes with their attempt to repair their little world. Whatever they are saying, it's enough to cause Genny to blush and rush from the porch.

Even demons have their desires and needs. A personal demon demands such a heavier price to soothe its damaging ways. My hope is theirs have finally found peace now that they have found each other. With their laughter growing bolder by the second, maybe there is hope for us all, after all.

Chapter 15

Four stitches later, in a better pattern than those of my stomach, half a bottle of discovered whiskey down, and a few too many smirking men, we find ourselves sitting around a slow churning fire in the fireplace of our new hideaway of a house we have claimed as our own. With the destruction from Rhett and Marxx, the other house was voted not safe, or worth defending, should we be ambushed. Now, we sit in the den of a home no one here could ever afford while the ones who could afford sit dead and propped as door stops on the exterior doors. Their hanging jaws seem to gasp at the irony of it all. Luckily, their eyes have long since glazed over to keep their glares subdued and muted.

"It's not funny," Aimes says, looking around the room for what must be the hundredth time.

"It's kind of funny," Rhett defends.

Lawless shrugs, wincing from his last chug from the bottle. He says, "It's not like we killed them. They were already dead."

"We just found a use for them," Rhett adds. "Consider us the new neighborhood recycling program."

He and Lawless smirk at each other, amused by their sense of wit, as they pass the bottle back and forth.

"Finding a use for that, too?" Peyton asks, as he leans on the doorway.

Once again, the two groups have naturally separated. Leigh, still not sure what to think about any of us, has taken the small office room on the bottom floor for herself. She has made her bed under the space of the desk as if still not comfortable being exposed after being secluded for so long. Her grey eyes watch us without any emotion from the curtains of her dark, black hair. The same empty-styled eyes that April uses to watch us.

The mood of the men around me shifts when Peyton appears, but the answer they give him is a shrug while they continue to pass the bottle around. They have been judged by better men and worse. I can almost hear the ghost of J.D. sucking his teeth from a far corner.

"You said we needed to talk?" Peyton tries again when he goes ignored.

Lawless does his normal quick sniff of agitation.

"About something you found at the school?" Peyton tries again.

Aimes and I both stare at each other. The men are staring at Lawless. Lawless stretches his neck side-to-side, trying to ease some of the tension from the room. His stiff movements only add to it.

"Maybe," Law says. "What if I told you we might have a lead on someplace that is supposed to be safe?"

"What if you did?" Peyton asks in return.

"Interested?" Lawless asks.

"I thought the high school was supposed to be safe?" Peyton asks. He isn't looking to the men, but to Paula.

Paula stares at him with a blank face and haunted eyes. "Nothing is safe forever," she says.

She makes her point, and possible vote should it come down to that, with one sentence. Paula has lost faith. The realization shakes the room with a tremor of fear.

"Then why would we risk it?" Peyton asks, riding that tremor. "We have a good thing going here. If we don't stay in one place long enough, those things can't find us." As if showing some presentation, he stretches his arms wide before adding, "Does anyone here really think we can add any more to this group at the rate we are going?"

I look across to Aimes and she meets my eyes with an eye roll before dramatically falling backward onto her sleeping bag. We both know it's about to grow dank with the scent of ego.

"Leigh over there seems to be blending well," Aimes says, rolling her head to look in the direction of the room across the hall.

"By blending you mean avoiding?" Peyton asks.

We are now staring across the hall to the woman whose eyes dart from face-to-face. Her face is still the empty mask, but the way her eyes keep increasing in speed, the panic is presented at being the sudden focal point of a conversation.

"Avoiding. Blending. Verbs of survival, my friend." Aimes smiles at Peyton.

"I would prefer if we could eventually become one…" Peyton's word trails off, but he has the courage to look to me with the suggestion.

"Me, too," Paula almost whispers into the room.

Our heads turn to the woman who has become the very meaning of separate. Paula has gone from the woman in charge of feeding and nurturing a whole community to simply being a supporting figure in the background. She once used a wooden spoon like a warning when we were brave enough to step out of line around her, but now she simply watches with disinterest and unmovable eyes.

Her appearance, which she once took pride in with her slicked hairstyles and almost pressed clothes, has become rumpled and limp. I have concluded that she, like so many others, has come to the point of being ready to meet their creators. With how many they have lost, and this in-between, is just a waiting room for them. Until now, I thought I was just being bitter, but maybe I was right.

"Me, too," Paula says, this time with a breath of more conviction.

As if her body is dust-covered and stiff, she slowly stands and looks around the room. Her eyes take each of us in, measuring us against some inner ruler of morality. Only I have the decency to look away. Unfortunately for me, it's me she keeps staring at the longest.

"Me, too," Paula whispers to herself one last time, before walking out of our area to climb the stairs where the other group has claimed the rooms as their own.

"What was that?" Aimes whispers. "Did the home team just lose a batter?"

We all shrug. All of us, but Peyton. Peyton is watching her mount each step with a mixture of amusement and curiosity. Is each step taking her from us and closer to them? Or, has she finally just overfilled her 'I'm over it' meter for the night with how the men keep poking each other?

I watch her until she slips from view. I know who is up there. A teen who just gained the same scars I wear like a crown. A man who is so lost in his past it provides slim hopes for his future. A man who mentally replays the death of his son a thousand times searching for a different outcome. A woman who has lost her very sense of self, but she keeps attempting to reinvent it each time we move. A group of people with nothing more in common than a common theme – loss. Maybe, that's what keeps them close. There are no chapters of a back-story to cloud their feelings for one another. Everything is shiny and new; blood-covered and open-mouthed screaming, but new. Maybe that is exactly what Paula is looking for right now. A new suffering to escape from the one we won't name – Chapel.

Marxx's deep voice pulls us all back to the room, "What would be the benefit of blending? We still share everything. We still watch your backs." He pauses from the remarkably interesting grime he seems to have discovered under his nails to look up at Peyton. "Seems to me, perhaps it's your group which needs to work on this so-called blending you want. We find the supplies. We fight those things. We seem to be doing just fine."

There it is. There's the ego Aimes and I knew would creep into the room to suffocate us all. To suffocate not only us, but any hope of ever stepping over the lines that have been drawn to declare the war zones, keeping us forever stuck in the trenches with verbal gunfire constantly coming from all around us, pinning us and defining us.

"When have you asked for help?" Peyton counters, not hiding the annoyance in his voice. "Helena storms off. You follow. Danger ensues and then you want to be petty about 'where were we'? We're here. Holding things down when everyone left us."

Aimes snorts. She literally snorts with her laugh. Aimes' loyalty lines zigzag. Everything is a war zone with her, and she likes to be the one with the grenade launcher.

When she feels their stares, she answers, "What? He has a point. You can't sit here and do the martyr dance when you don't let anyone else carry the cross."

"Chapel carried our crosses. Look where that got him," Rhett mumbles.

"Oh, so you won't let them help because you're what? Protecting them?" Aimes asks. "Thought you saved that for religious hookers and orphaned children?"

"We know how to get things done," Marxx states, quickly changing the argument Aimes is attempting to fuel. "They would slow us down."

"Yeah, but what would it be like to get things done without a body count?" Aimes ponders.

"Ask Hells. Her count is higher than any of ours," Rhett says.

Rhett meant it as a joke. He wasn't far from the truth, though.

"Boring," I reply quickly. "What exactly do we even know about this 'safe place'?" I ask, attempting to change the topic.

The silent until now, Lawless, pulls the ramblings of a demented teen from under his sleeping bag. He tosses it into the middle of the space between us all. It serves as some style of invitation to Peyton and he finally steps over the line. Luckily, this time, it wasn't rigged.

"It's some island up the coast," Dolph offers, as Peyton leans into the space to look at what has been presented. "It claims there is some kind of settlement there. The logic seems to be that the water keeps the things away, allowing the people there to live life without anyone having to live in constant fear or always moving."

"And you think that works?" Peyton isn't asking anyone specific. He's mostly musing out loud the revelations being presented.

"Those things only come when motivated. If the water keeps the distance from them and people, they wouldn't have a reason to cross it," Lawless says. "Out of sight. Out of mind."

"So, we should try for it?" Peyton muses out loud again.

"We should, but there is one problem," Lawless says, twisting his neck to peer up at Peyton. "How are we going to get there?"

"You signal for the boat."

The soft voice is like a scream amid all the chatter. Leigh is no longer under her version of a sanctuary. She's sitting with her back supporting the arch of the open doorway. Unlike Peyton, she's still kept to her lines.

"You signal," she says again, still peeking from behind that thick curtain of hair.

"…and you know this how?" Aimes, our ever-skeptical pixie, asks.

Leigh doesn't answer at first. Her eyes are doing that dance again, bouncing to some tempo only she can hear as she flutters from person-to-person. Pulling her knees to her chest, she finally speaks. "It's my home."

She says this as if we should have known. She says this as if had we just asked, she could have told us all about it and answered any riddles the discovery held. She says this with no eagerness to return or fear to, either. It's just a fact. A fact that not even Aimes' grenade launcher could top, despite her efforts to try.

"Good thing you didn't kill her for your body count," Aimes says towards me with a smile.

I don't smile. There should be some feelings of hope when rescued and discover your rescuers are going to take you home. There should be more details forthcoming, some excitement over being reunited with your family, whoever that may be. There's not.

I watch as she just sits there. She holds no interest if we vote to go or to stay. She's not trying to influence the vote either way with further explanations of the location or the logic of why we should go there.

Her eyes sway to mine when she feels me staring at her. We watch one another for a shared moment. I can feel her gaze settling deeper in my consciousness than a casual glance should.

"Yeah. Good thing," I whisper to the room.

Trepidation tiptoes into the room. She stalks the dark shadows around me. She's hiding the hand I want her to show me. Her movements are gliding, and she dances all around me now, taunting me with what she knows and with what I do not. She mocks me with what she is holding behind her dangerous back. She taunts me with what she knows is hiding behind those grey eyes and blank stares and as those eyes slowly close, her dance swallows my soul.

Chapter 16

"So, we are taking them?" Marxx asks. His voice trembles somewhere between a whisper and rage. Whispers are good. Rage is becoming more comfortable, though.

"What would you have us do?" Lawless asks. His voice is steady. He's refusing to give over to the angst Marxx now wears like a warning label, bold and highlighted with a lot of fine print.

We are standing in what was once a very expensive kitchen. Everything matches from the tiles on the backsplash to the granite counters with their swirls of shades. Now it's covered in fine dust, which clings to the corners and the once pristine, white grout work.

They have been doing this tit-for-tat debate since the sun finally peeked over the trees. Her bright rays may have chased away the shadows, but they are doing nothing to shake the gloom from the men around me.

For once, Rhett just watches. Whatever verbal volley he is having, he is having it mentally. The only hints to his opinions are the random facial expressions that leak through his detachment. Dolph has nothing to add, either. He's either picked a side already and is refusing to admit it or is simply waiting to be asked who's side he is on. I lean against the kitchen counter watching them. The male volley is quickly becoming boring.

"Why are you so against it?" I ask Marxx, throwing the first flint to his sparks.

"We have no ties to them," he begins, but quickly stops, hearing what he's said about the giant elephant in the house. "You know what I mean." He tries to recover ground, but all he's done is left a bigger hole. "You've hated that man for as long as I can remember. Now you want to convince me to save him?"

"It's not about him," I begin, adopting the elephant we've all been avoiding. "It's about the fact he, and the rest of them, are living people and deserve a chance just as much as we do. Besides, it's not our place. We can't keep it to ourselves. Who knows, maybe it's big enough we can all go our separate ways once we are there."

He's right, though; I have railed against the man I know as my father. I have wished for his death a thousand times, and in contrast, a thousand times I have wished for his love. Why should I defend him now? Why should I campaign for his safety? He's never cared for my life. That hope wilted a long time ago in a white kitchen and I've been searching for my white knight to rescue me from him ever since. Maybe it's because of all that I've lost, or because of the very little I have left, but either way, a part of me still lives in that dream, giggling with a man who once smiled back.

I look to April who sits happily munching away on whatever dry food Rhett has found for her at a large, wooden table. Her little feet sway back-and-forth with her limited height. She almost bounces as she eats having not a care, or concern, for the conversation flowing around her. Her blonde hair is pulled back in a high ponytail that swishes with her movements. I wonder when she grows older if she will have the same ghosts of parents haunting her with her 'what ifs' as I do.

Rhett chooses now to end his silent role in the room. "Where are they?" he asks.

Having watched my steady gaze on April, he asks the same question I have been asked by many people – where are the Hawthorn Angels? He's going to get the same answer.

"Dead," I respond.

"Obviously," Rhett says.

"Obviously," I copy, tone included. "Where they are isn't important. I'm just saying I'm not leaving any more behind to die."

I hadn't meant my words to provide so many clues. I was just attempting to end the debate. I can feel the heavy gaze of their eyes. They are waiting for me to explain, giving me the space to explain. I won't. April glances up at me amid the sudden silence, and for a moment, those brown eyes are awfully blue. They bring me right back to a hall with purple doors and a music box of horrors.

"Dead," I whisper again, stuck in my own mental revolving slideshow of hell.

"Where did you leave them, Hells?" Rhett asks. He's the only one brave enough to ask it, but even his bravery affords him nothing more than a slight whisper.

Time has stopped. It's just me, and my memories, revolving around their constant merry-go-round of tormented images. The battered and demented horses grow more antagonistic each time we do this.

They blare their images like a war flag of failures, waving it in the air with the bold colors of murder and destruction. Despite the many months, which have sunk me into deeper horrors, the original horrors hold their texture like no other. The scents of the gore seem to still cling to me. The lambs' bodies clash with the bright red colors sprayed across their black and white backgrounds. The blood still feels hot on my hands, which cramped from holding the knife so tight, but those eyes peering through the curtains of blonde hair, the eyes that never looked away, holding on to mine to guide her through the unspeakable things which were about to happen to her, they still tear my heart from my throat.

I feel the moan. I feel it from my soul. I feel it shred the strength in my legs. My whole body begins to shake with the truths I've locked away in the many dark rooms of my mind. Just as my last dam begins to crumble, forcing me to not only accept which I have hidden so deep but also admit it, it's refortified when I hear his voice from behind me.

"Where, Helen? Where are they?" he whispers.

Collin's voice is like a hiss. The whisper slides up my back and inch-by-inch I feel it straighten. Others in the room may have been stirred by the hint of remorse, a hint of mourning behind his hushed syllables. I'm stirred. Let me assure you, I'm very stirred.

Turning to him, much in the same way Ashley turned to me, peering through a dark curtain instead of blonde, I ask him, "I'm sorry?"

Maybe it was my tone that confused him. Maybe, it was some soft shade of green still lingering in my eyes he mistook as some invitation to touch me. When he placed that palm on my shoulder, peering at me with their eye color, the lost cherubs' eye color, it was my fist that cleared everything up for him. It sends him to the ground, shocked and angry with my conclusion to his question.

It wasn't planned. It wasn't even instinct. It was because I wanted to and when I connected with his perfectly shaped jaw, all doors and dams sealed tight.

"What the fuck?" he shouts his question through his hand holding his face.

I drop to my knees so I may place my lips near to his ear. I see the fear in those eyes as I lean close. The flinch which used to bruise my ego so deeply, now fills it with a fire. The same fire that I have been fighting to keep ablaze as it threatened to become embers.

Now, it's engulfed and the warmth of those fanning flames dances with my self-destruction like well-timed lovers, a phoenix of agony and torment. I place my lips so close to his ear I know he can feel the heat, as well.

"What the fuck is exactly what I have been asking myself every day since this started. What the fuck is exactly what I mutter to myself when I dare to ponder where our perfect father was that morning. What the fuck is everything I feel when I think of you letting your children die when you ran off to find your past fuck buddy and what the fuck is what I'm going to think every time from now on when I wonder why I ever let you matter so much to me."

We hold each other's eyes for a moment as I lean away from him. I watch his eyes swirl from anger to sadness with the thoughts trampling through his memories. I wonder if they wear the same flags. I wonder if he can smell the deaths of those he left behind. I wonder if Karma and Fate provide for him the same lessons those twisted sisters ingrained in me, but mostly, I wonder what he sees in my eyes. As I now stand over him in a kitchen just as grand as the one that was lemon-scented and gleaming white, at this moment, what does he see in my very green eyes?

I wish I could play him the chorus of his children's deaths. I wish I could explain where they are with so much more than just empty words retelling a tale resembling one so many have told. Instead, I walk away letting him wonder with nothing more than past events gluing together possible collages of explanations. Meanwhile, I know nothing he pictures, from even the deepest of his fears, could really prepare him for the truth.

Even in my moment of self-obtained glory, there's always the double-edged knife. Genny stands a mere few steps away from the whole show. She no doubt has heard the references I made towards the woman whose death has carved a hole in her own soul. As suddenly as the fire was flamed inside me, I'm completely cold now. I let that chill climb to my eyes, meeting hers with a glance of a warning. When the first tear glides down her cheek, I buckle and storm from the room like the defeated villain I have become.

Walking on to the back porch, I let what's left of the morning sun warm my face as the door slams behind me. No one follows me out. No one is either brave enough or interested enough in another one of my moments. Truthfully, I don't blame them. Even I'm growing tired of my constant bullshit.

Try as it might, the sun does nothing to remove the chill from my soul. That ice is too thick for such a simple warmth to melt it. The ice is like scar tissue, holding the many cracks and fissures of my wounded heart together. Not even the fire fanned from my self-destruction could touch that ice. Like a plague of its own making, it is spreading more every day. It eats slowly away at the flame which spurs me towards each new day, giving me the courage to constantly keep fighting beyond my own measure of exhaustion.

I had told Aimes I would never give up or give in, but we both know my seat in the waiting room is inevitable. No one can hold on forever. Closing my eyes with a sigh, I know I would welcome the chance to cave under it all.

I was asked if I was going to leave anyone else behind to die. A few moments ago, when I was among the rusted horses of my personal apocalypse, I had said no. The growls now coming from my left, they hint at a different answer, but that ice, that spreading numbness, it does more than just hint that I just might.

Chapter 17

Near me, I hear the footsteps on the wooden porch. I hear the boards creaking, singing like a slow song of a chorus holding a warning. It doesn't stir me. I don't respond to the waltz which once fluttered my mind with panic. I don't even uncross my arms or open my closed eyes. I don't brace for the dance. I have no plan of defense against the attack. This should worry me, but I'm not worried. I'm exhausted. I can almost hear the intercom in that imagined waiting room.

The smell is the classic roll of death and rot. A smell only layers of gruesome acts can accumulate with such a depth. I welcome it around me like the familiar must of an old room.

It walks with the Shadow of Death and all the Deities of Destruction following closely in its trail. It has become the end-all, the last sight so many have seen, but it has yet to meet me. I'm not sure if Deities still walk with me but I'm certain Destruction does and she's stronger than any prayer I could offer up for protection.

It's halted near me. What's left of its voice is making soft growling sounds, yet there is no move to attack. Instead, it licks a slow line of sludge from the concave crevices of my neck to my temple. A cold slime is left behind from its sandpaper-like tongue. The sludge chills where it's left, causing an almost hardening effect like a candy coating now that it has finished its tasting tour of my flesh.

My mind starts to weigh the pros and cons of what should happen next. I should never have let it get this close. I can hear the imagined doors of the waiting room swishing open, challenging me to change my fate. My repeated attempts to constantly prove I don't care may just be the fatal flaw that escorts me past those doors, deeper than its lobby and somewhere even Paula can't save me. Finally, my heart skips its first beat. The ice feels its first thaw.

I hadn't heard the other set of footsteps. I was so lost in my own attempt of suicide; I hadn't heard Irony throw her dice into the lot. The chambering of the gun, that I heard.

The impact was instant. The force of the explosion of vile fluids flew across the left side of my body in a shower of frigid shards. It didn't drip the way fresh blood does after it smears you; something, as of late, I never thought I would know. This is sliding down my face and arms with a heavy gravity, clinging to me in thick patches making me thankful my eyes are still closed.

Turning my head with the feeling of the slime-like juices slithering deeper into my shirt, I slowly open my eyes to see whom I will thank or curse. I hadn't expected to see Leigh, nor the barrel of her gun still pointed directly at my head. I don't waste words to ask her what she's doing, or of what her plans hold. I wait with calmer eyes than my heart portrays.

We stare at one another in a locked gaze of eye contact. She's wearing her perfect bored mask of a face with her pink lips almost curving over the power she thinks she's holding over me. Her eyes aren't doing their panic dance. They are flat and level with mine with no hints of the shy creature we rescued.

"You're welcome," Leigh says, slowly lowering the gun a moment after her eyes dart behind me.

The screen door does a slow creak. Lawless and Marxx are slipping their way onto the shared porch. Their posture portrays their confusion over which role to slide into, having obviously walked into female drama. More so since one of those potential land mines is holding a gun.

"Who gave her a fucking gun?" Marxx asks.

Having reapplied her veneer of delicate and distraught, Leigh's eyes are back to their dancing, but the gun is steady in her hand.

"She did," I reply, keeping my gaze on the woman who keeps presenting more questions than answers about herself. "You're welcome to try to take it from her."

Marxx, sliding down the same suicidal slope as I am, actually takes a step towards her to my amusement. To my disappointment, the burst of screams from overhead stops us all in mid-drama.

"There are more upstairs," Leigh says, using her facts as grenades, again.

Lawless and Marxx are already running back into the house. Leigh and I, we are still standing on the porch, and I watch as her façade melts back to boredom with it just being us, again. The screams don't unnerve her. She doesn't flinch as the many tones of voices join into one shriek of panic. She doesn't head into the house to help or run into the yard to escape. She turns, wearing the same bored face, and strolls along the edge of the wrap around porch to the side of the house. Sharing one last glance, she keeps walking in her slow pace around the corner, blocking my view of her.

Rhett is running across the side lawn from the opposite side. His jeans are stained with more patterns than I remember them owning. In his arms, April is almost impossible to see as they make their way to the line of vehicles. Risen may not stop my heart, but the sight of Rhett running from danger, that does. The only reason our dark monster would run, leaving so many behind to the real monsters, is if there weren't that many left to save.

I wait a spare second to see who else from our family will soon follow his path. When none do, I do what I do best. I run the opposite direction from those who are fleeing.

I don't follow Rhett to safety. I follow the screams. The same screams which follow us time-after-time. Screams which have become a bird song to our soundtrack, constant, and always flowing in the background. When I reach the side door Rhett must have exited from, I welcome the numbness I was moments ago worried over. I revel in the white noise, blocking my thoughts and worries. I welcome it like an embrace from a lost friend. I let it settle over my mind and racing heart, in a way I can use instead of being used, because sitting just past the door is a slumped blonde pixie. She's draped over the bottom stairs with something more than just biting exchanges flowing from her.

J.D. murmurs from the back of my mind. I can smell his whiskey-laced breath as if he's standing beside me, taunting me.

"Do you know what day it is?" he asks me, without shame or remorse. Pulling me mentally back to a death-filled hallway, he smiles at me.

"Helena, move!"

This time it's Peyton's voice pulling me along. He is closely followed by Genny and Ginjer. Their wide eyes express what they are running from better than any verbal exclamation.

I push past them to reach Aimes, Peyton grabs my arm.

"Don't," he simply states. "Come with us." His eyes aren't wide, but they are just as expressive.

"Is this your idea of coming together?" I hiss, jerking my arm free from his grasp. "I'm not leaving anyone behind."

I ignore the repeated shouts of my name as his group exits the house. My eyes are only for my friend who Peyton so easily just stepped over. Her body has collapsed, alone and broken, draped across the steps in front of me. In denial, I call her name over the shouting surrounding us, but it's not my arms that reach her first.

Rhett reaches around me, scooping her lifeless body from the ground. He doesn't look at me. He doesn't look at her. He doesn't utter a single sound, as he too dwells in his denial about who he holds. Securing my arm in his other hand, he drags both of us from what was a moment of respite. These walls provided a small lull to the endless cycle we are in now, allowing us to secure our mishandled treasure.

I stall, straining to catch a sight of who is still left upstairs, but Rhett doesn't allow any disobedience to his plan of action. His fingers become almost talons, driving the strength of the man into the flesh of my arm.

"Don't," he says, repeating the same word command Peyton had used before.

Rhett should know better than to expect me to simply walk away. He should know I always look. Even when everything inside me pleads to just once listen to the advice I gave, I don't. I'm not about to start now, either.

Risking the loss of my arm, I pull from him using all my strength and the downward pull of gravity to free myself. He doesn't fight twice. His fingers waver for a moment, but we have both made our choices. Like a cherished goodbye, he lets me slip from his grasp. With one more look to the other, we go our separate paths, our eyes saying to the other what our voices cannot.

He doesn't look back. He doesn't waver to see if I will change my mind. Rhett knows better than that. He knows I have to look. The grinning skull upon his back fades through the sunlight. For a moment, I can't help but wonder if that grin is of a warning or mockery of the decision I have made.

Chapter 18

I climb the stairs one slow step at a time. There are no tell-tale signs of what is ahead. No proverbial writing on the wall, unless you count the many running streaks of red clashing with the crisp white paint. The screaming has long stopped, and the silence before me has a different taste of dread.

It's easy to mentally put together the moments I've missed. The stairwell is littered with claw marks and various signs of abuse from a goal-centered mob. I can almost piece together the puzzle, interlocking the many jagged edges to become a whole picture of how the Risen were able to sneak past us. When I see the open window on the first ledge, the pieces become glued together, framed like an outline of bad decisions. The creatures heard the laughter and sounds of food from the yard below. The soft sounds were too tempting to not accept the unsent invitation. Where are those sounds, now?

The first corpse stares at me as I come around the winding ledge. I freeze from taught lessons of the past, waiting for it to move or acknowledge me. Even my breath is held in irregular patterns to hide my discovery from him, but he doesn't see me. His glazed eyes finally see nothing. He is in such a state of decay, I can't tell how he found his final death, providing no further clues as to where I may find the others.

I step over the next three bodies. My small feet suddenly feel large as I strategically find spots on the gore encrusted carpet to place them between the broken, discarded dead. The vile scent of rot seeps along the path I take. Every step releases it further into the air around me. It used to gag me, coil my stomach into knots. It's almost a comfort, now. The Risen can't lose this much fluid if they are still alive.

The further I creep into the area, the more evidence I see of Lawless and Marxx. What began as simple disposal has now dissolved into pure slaughter from the many gashes placed upon the bodies. In typical G.R.I.T. fashion, they don't just do the job, they enjoy it. Yet, still no sign of those who did this.

A noise from behind the door of the room ahead paralyzes me. Every muscle in my body comes to an abrupt halt. Except for my brain. This muscle is suddenly in full tilt, flooding my mind with images of possibilities watching me through the thin slit of the doorway. My ears strain to hear any clues as to what it came from, or who, but it's just a soft sound; a sound which could be many things and nothing at all.

She's daring me again. Truth is pushing to see if I'm still the same reckless girl I was when she first started teaching me the ways of this new reality. She's just a few inches away, waiting for me to peek at what she holds for me. She attempted to take Lawless from me once before. Has she finally fulfilled that threat?

She spared Marxx once already when he put his life on the line. Will she do it, again?

Paula has invited her, almost begged her, to take her. Has her wish been granted?

Do I look? I could just head back down, chase after the ones who begged me to come with them, but where would be the fun in that? Removing my knife from the holster in my very well-worn brown boots, I answer Truth's dare.

My fingers tremble as I extend my hand to push the door wider. The white wood is cold, lifeless as those laying around me. Yet, it isn't silent. It whines with its reluctant weight. As it shatters the silence around me, it might as well have been screaming in duress with the slow swing it provides.

It's a teasing look into the room. My heart beats in time with the slow pace. Sliding my back against the door molding, I prevent any more mute footsteps from slipping up behind me.

The handle of the knife in my hand is causing it to cramp with how I'm clenching it, raised and ready to defend myself. My eyes stare into a room that should be bright with sunlight. It's shrouded in shadows from the backyard's tall trees, keepings its secrets well hidden. This does nothing to settle my heart into some form of a normal pattern. It's beating against my ribs. The walls of my chest feel battered by its abuse. Yet, I keep going. I have to look.

Unwilling to put my hand into the dark room, I use my foot to nudge the door open wider, but it swings back, removing any progress made. I nudge it again, harder this time. Mockingly it swings back but with the same slow rhythm as before.

"Fuck," I whisper to myself.

I use the word to steel my resolve. It's not eloquent, but it eloquently describes my thoughts of the door in front of me. Taking a deep breath, I kick the door to remove all doubts of my sincere efforts to open it.

I should have listened to the door's hints. I should have given up with its protests. I should have walked away. I should have done a great many things since this all started. This, right here, this will just be another one to add to the list. Sitting in the corner of the room, half-hidden in the secret abiding shadows, is something covered in its latest victory and it's looking right at me like I'm about to be the next conquest.

It's what it is kneeling over which has my eyes locked and throat closed. I've interrupted enough of their meals to be shaken, but not damaged by the sight. I've been their meals enough times to not be devastated by it, either. Despite all of this, the one thing I will never grow used to seeing is their hands, wrists deep, in the body cavity of someone I know.

With his face turned away from me. His caramel-brown hair is loose, free from the small ponytail these last months have resulted in. The shade is slightly off from what I know it to be, but there are a thousand reasons for that to happen. The subtle shading from his facial hair has caught chunks of the gore the demon-possessed creature sprayed with the attack. It shades his face like a death shroud, dark and heavy with its meaning.

Marxx lies before me, spread wide like a Thanksgiving dinner for the damned, but I'm the one sliding into Hell. The descent rips my sanity. It suffocates my breath, catching it in loud, locked patterns burning my lungs only to repeat the torture over and over again.

I can't look away from the carnage in front of me. I cannot see anything else in the room. My mind fights against the whispers Truth hisses in my ear. She's gleeful in her vindication. She rolls my mind with memories of a crowded back room, stacked deep with death. It rolls back to the day Marxx risked everything just to reach me and how he kept reaching for me every day after that. It rolls to a house haunted with the ghosts of a birthday party and the man who followed me into those walls of purgatory. Even as our leader fell to his knees, Marxx was reaching for me. Again and again, he was reaching for me and I wasn't here to reach back.

I don't know how much time has passed as Truth and I danced down memory lane. I was living only in those lost moments. Time belonged to a dead man's watch and the ticking was the sound of my heart breaking.

I don't know when I lost the ability to stand or how I ended up sitting, propped up on the same molding I had thought to use as a barrier of protection. Now, as I sit here, watching handfuls of flesh being torn, I know what the sound was I heard. It was the soft sounds of still wet meat being lifted from the bones they held together. It was the soft sucking of rotting fingers. It was organs being scooped out as if they were fruit at the bottom of a blood-bathed ice cream sundae. It was my friend.

"Helena," Marxx calls to me.

His is another voice now added to my soundtrack of regrets.

"Helena," he calls again, and I turn my eyes from his body to the sound of his memory.

I'm staring into those same steel-resolved eyes. As if even he can't handle the sight of his death, he is squatting down just on the other side of the doorway looking only at me. He isn't covered in his final moments the way my ghosts are normally. He isn't watching me with the judging eyes of my Angels or the mocking horror of Margaret and her friends. Marxx is simply there, holding his hand out for me to take. He's sitting there to guide me out from this mental prison of which I have locked myself. He's there to be sure I don't scream, to be sure I don't break.

As I reach for those fingertips, I completely expect them to dissolve under my touch. My hand hovers, knowing this will be the last moment I can hold onto before denial is inescapable, but when they slide against mine, the warmth is startling.

"Will you please get the fuck up?" he whispers, between clenched teeth.

When Marxx asks you to get the fuck up, ghost Marxx or not, you get the fuck up. So, I do but it's not graceful, at all.

My legs are limp from how I crumpled. As I attempt to crawl through the doorway with his request, I might as well as trample through my exit like a toddler throwing a reluctant fit. Every noise I can possibly make, I do. Every wooden surface which could tattle on my retreat, it does. Boots may be great for winter and protection, gentle escapes, not so much.

"Damn it," Marxx sighs. He pulls me towards him with a jerk. Spinning me behind him he asks with a heavy voice, "What's one more?"

In my confused mind, I'm not sure if he's asking about his death-- or mine. Watching him lift the muzzle of his gun to what is heading towards us from the room, apparently, it's neither.

It's a single shot. He doesn't even wait for his murderer to fall. With all the confidence he has always conveyed, he turns to walk down the stairs. He doesn't step over the scattered limbs strewn around the room or their attached torsos. He doesn't have the same fragile mindset as I did when I had entered the second floor. The brittle bones break under his thick boots. His prints leave stains upon the spots of unmarked carpet darker than the ones which have already soaked the thick fibers around us.

My confused mind fights to put this new puzzle together. The edges don't line up. The pieces don't mesh. Nothing is locking into place with any solid answers or even half-clues.

I follow him just the same. I've followed worse people to much more confusing places. After all, it's Marxx with his warning labels of rage now no longer highlighted, but just as bold. He glances one more time over his shoulder to be sure I am following him. I am, but I can't help but worry where his fine print is taking me.

Chapter 19

"About damn time," Aimes states, as I step back out onto the porch where this whole thing started.

I look to Rhett with confusion coloring every corner of my face. Like some dark gargoyle, he is leaning on the frame of my truck where he can watch over April with her legs dangling out the open door. His eyes glance towards me before adjusting back to the little girl. As always, they give no answer to his mental state, just a brief recognition of something shared over what must have happened only a few moments ago.

Without his help, my mind is stuck, looping through what I saw in there and what I am seeing out here. They were dead and now one stands mocking me and the other just lead me through their tomb. I can't help but wonder if this is how Alice felt when she first fell down the hole.

"What did you do to her?" Aimes is waving her hand in front of my stunned face. She turns to Marxx asking, "How did you make her shut up?"

Marxx does his normal half-smile before saying, "Found her that way."

I can feel Lawless analyzing me from behind his dark sunglasses where he sits on his bike. He says nothing though and I wonder if I've finally gone insane.

"You were dead? I saw you both, dead," I force the words to form. "Rhett…" I look to him for help. This time not physically, but for help just the same.

If he heard me, he doesn't answer. His eyes are all for the little girl he's been using as a shield and as an excuse wrapped in one big ball of avoidance. His fingers fidget. They shake, tapping out a pattern along the metal of the big beast I stole. Rhett doesn't have many tells, and when he does, it's normally not a smart idea to push him. Unfortunately for me, I've never been very smart.

I close the gap between me and Rhett in a few quick steps. I sense Lawless moving behind me, unsure of what mood swing I'm riding now. Rhett doesn't turn to face me, not entirely. He lowers his head so that it swings towards me with his eyes blank and lips half curled. If his tell was a warning, the blank eyes should have been a screaming signal of caution. His half-smile is a declaration of danger. Yet, I stand here, face-to-face demanding answers.

We don't exchange words. We just stare at the other, each waiting for someone else to say the first word. Who it is, is not what I was expecting.

"It's my fault," Genny's voice shouts from where Peyton has gathered their group.

Ginjer stands, letting her long hair announce her movements before her body does in a way I have only seen her capable of accomplishing. "It really is," she says, having no guilt for throwing the teen under the blame bus. "I told her it was a dumb idea, but she takes after her mom. A bleeding heart, that one." She whispers the last part as if the woman might overhear her opinion of her.

Genny makes a noise as close to teen angst as I have ever heard. "What was I supposed to do?" she shrieks at the woman. Turning to Peyton, she asks again, "What was I supposed to do?"

"What's the plan?" Ginjer's words crush Genny.

I have no idea what hidden wounds those words hold, or why they do, but I've been around 'family' long enough to know a manipulation move when I see one. Ignoring the brute in front of me, I look to Lawless, and by his posture, I can see it didn't slip past him, either.

I cradle my head in my hands, asking in the self-made dark shelter, "Can someone just tell me what I'm missing?"

"Boobs. Personality. A butt?" Aimes offers.

I meant to glare at her. I was fully prepared to level her with our silent eye games. I wasn't prepared to have my eyes land on the dumped body of her doppelganger resting on the edge of the driveway.

Rhett's watching me with a different interest, now. When our eyes meet again, that damn puzzle allows another piece to fasten into place.

"Wait," I can hear Aimes behind me also matching the picture forming to the box it belongs to, "you thought that was me?"

Rhett and I say nothing. It's a different type of look we share, now. Before we were waiting for the other to speak first. Now, we want to be sure neither of us speaks at all.

Aimes comes to stand beside us close enough to make herself be seen. "You *both* thought that was me?" she asks, letting the words unite Rhett and I, and hitting an annoyingly high pitch.

We watch her walk to where the body has been discarded. She squats with not an ounce of shame to her investigation. She leans over to peer at the woman below her, tilting her head various angles. All she is missing is a stick to poke the deceased to complete the picture.

Sighing, she stands and turns to us both. "I don't see it."

"Blonde," is all I can offer her, with my own explanation being bleak.

Aimes turns to the body again. "Really, Hells?" she asks. "Like my roots aren't a mile long?"

"I wasn't looking at her roots," I shrug, shutting off the words which want to spill out.

I want to tell her all I saw was that morning in a crimson-caked hallway. I want to explain to her how every clinging moment of fear of having lost her that day was all that I could feel again, but I don't, and neither does Rhett.

"Obviously," she mutters.

Rhett mock whispers, "Carpet doesn't match the drapes."

"Self-esteem doesn't match the shaft," she counters without a pause.

Paula clears her throat. "Children."

"Them or Genny?" Marxx asks, already over the scene and settling into the seat of his bike.

Sliding onto the bench of the truck, Aimes blows Marxx a kiss wrapped around her middle finger.

"Children!" Paula glares at Aimes when she takes the seat beside her.

"Definitely them," Lawless echoes, but I can feel him still watching me. He's waiting to see if the bomb has been diffused or if the explosion is still counting down.

Aimes leans over to shout out the open door, "Why are we still standing around after we've just escaped attempted number two-hundred billionth on our lives?"

"Where to?" I ask the two men who have become the rulers of our civil club.

"Home," Leigh glides past both groups, from who knows where, to throw a leg over Marxx's bike. Wrapping her arms around him, she settles in behind him as if there was an invitation granted to her.

"Home." Lawless echoes, when Marxx doesn't baulk over his new rider.

"Sure thing, Polly," replies Aimes, with a shout.

I slide into my seat to start the truck's engine. Black horses weave between my truck and the red Jeep parked near me. April watches them with a smile I used to wear when first hearing their engines come to life.

"Start 'em young." Aimes pats April's head and playfully tugs on her ponytail.

She's rewarded with a gentle laugh and it sets the whole cab of the truck into a smile.

I nod to Peyton, letting him know to take the lead. Following him out, I brave the question to finally put the puzzle to rest, "What did Genny do?"

"She opened the back door for two people running from the monsters," April offers. "Then the monsters followed."

"She thought she was helping. She couldn't stand by and listen to them die." Paula tries to add more clarity. "We didn't know how close the infected were or we would never have allowed it."

"And the plan?" Aimes asks.

Paula leans a little deeper into the back of the bench seat. "It was the rules her mother used to have her repeat. Part of it is referenced to only help others if it were safe to do so."

"You've picked up a lot with the short time you've spent upstairs," Aimes delivers the compliment with a backhanded meaning.

If Paula was offended, she doesn't admit it. She continues to run her fingers through April's long hair blocking Aimes' attempts to annoy her. Not many can ignore Aimes, but Paula has always been able to completely throw ice water on Aimes' antics.

Now I understand why Genny was instantly defeated by such a short phrase. We believe the dead hold higher expectations of us than they ever did when living. It makes failing them so much more painful.

"So, the two I saw…?" I trail my question into the shared space, not caring which one of them answers.

"Not yours truly." Aimes smirks. "Touching, though. Did Rhett actually cry? Or, just pout?" she asks, making my mental breakdown all about her.

"They were the two Genny tried to help." Paula crosses her arms over her chest, still ignoring Aimes. "The girl never made it upstairs. We thought we were trapped until Lawless and Marxx arrived. They cleared a path and we went out in two separate directions for safety. Peyton took the two down the stairs. Jacob, so he said his name was, separated and went into a far bedroom. The rest of us climbed out a fire escape someone had installed on their child's window. We met at the front, but when you weren't there, Marxx rushed back in to find you. Lawless and Peyton stayed back to keep a path cleared just in case they missed any roaming in the house."

"And my father? Did he offer to look?" I don't know why I asked. Some wounds just crave the salt.

"He had his hands full with Genny." Paula attempts to smooth over what she knows she is avoiding saying. The lemony zest hurts just the same.

Aimes leans over April sitting between us to whisper, "That's a no."

"Yeah. I got that," I tell her, still tasting the salt of their answers.

Aimes covers April's ears and in the same attempted whisper asks, "Can we kill him, now?"

"I can hear you," April says, with an amused voice.

Aimes shrugs, settling back in her section. "So home, huh?" she asks to no one and anyone.

Home. It's such a word filled with longing. We've heard it so many times here recently. Each time the 'home' proves to be anything but something for which to belong. Each time it's been said we earn more scars, figuratively and literally. We lose someone we love. We are torn apart. Home isn't a word I long for, anymore. It isn't something I even crave as I once did with child-like hopes for safety.

Home is just another word Truth and her sisters taunt us with. It's a carrot on a stick, and to their amusement, we jump after it each time. We jump right off the ledge, never stopping to gauge the distance of the coming descent. Home isn't where the heart lies. It's just lies, and our hearts are the prize.

Chapter 20

I'm not sure how long we drove. My mind was weaving in and out of thoughts like the forgotten traffic patterns left along the cluttered roads of abandoned cars I steered us through. I traveled through thoughts of Chapel and how we seem to be lost without his gentle guidance. I thought of J.D.-- wondering where his leadership would have led us with the many twists and turns we have encountered to reach this point. With so many winding roads, and morale mishaps, how would the two of them be guiding us if they were among us? They each held their shades of grey, but J.D.'s was always so much darker than the rest.

Marxx had taken the lead once we arrived on the main roads. With gentle nudges from Leigh, he had navigated our troupe through forest laden scenery. The long tree limbs reach for us like the nightmares from which we keep running. As if the limbs reminded Paula of the same thoughts, she has kept her eyes roaming the area, searching for any movement. When Aimes and April were on their billionth round of a random hand game, and just to the point of pushing me to pull over to trade them with another set of passengers, Leigh finally signaled for us to pull over and park.

Around us, various other vehicles are tucked away in this almost hidden spot. Some look as if they had traveled their last mile years ago. The vines of the forest have overtaken them, stretching their way across their hoods and roofs to secure them as part of this new landscape.

A few look as if they have just arrived, windows open, and awaiting their passengers to return. Only the streaks of various weather patterns left upon their paint tell of their discontinued use.

As the truck slows, Aimes begins to mimic Paula, peering around the many thick trunks of trees surrounding the makeshift parking lot. "Seems kinda sketchy."

I shrug and exit the moaning door of my truck. I'm just happy to escape their chatter.

"So, you're not even going to wait and let them look around?" Aimes shouts.

The slamming of my door is her answer.

"April, don't grow up like your Aunty Hells," I can hear Aimes saying to the little girl beside her. "She's moody, rude, and totally bi-polar."

They are sliding out of the truck now behind me. I don't acknowledge that I heard them. I simply keep walking to where the group has congregated.

"What's bi-polar?" April asks.

I figured I would hear some quip from Aimes, but it's Paula who shuts down the conversation.

"It's what men make women," Paula says.

I smirk as she walks past me.

"Well it's true," she adds, looking as if she needed to defend her point of view.

"Chapel, too?" I don't know why I ask that. The words tumble out with him having been so present in my mind during the trip.

I regret asking instantly and my face shows it. She lifts a hand to stop my pathetic attempt to apologize.

"That man could drive a nun to sin," she begins, "but he had a heart which would make a nun want to sin."

It's the only explanation she shares as we come to join the others. Ginjer is doing full body rotations, keeping every inch of the wooded area in her sight. Terrence is resting on the body of the Jeep where most of the men have spread out the notebooks. His mind and cares are far away from our current situation. Genny and my father have somehow managed to end up right across from me. Like a battle line in the sand, our stance copies those emotions. Genny has a right to have that anger in her eyes for me. It's not my nature to look away first. This time, I do.

"The plan?" I ask the men gathered around the hood of the Jeep. I hadn't meant to repeat the words Ginjer had used as a weapon earlier. I hadn't meant to, but I can see their impact on Genny from the corner of my vision. If anyone else caught my mistake, they didn't show it.

"How about we just follow Crazy?" Aimes is pointing to the shoreline where Leigh is walking, having once again slipped away from the group without anyone noticing her.

Rhett is the first to break. He walks to where Leigh is headed, saying, "Works for me."

"You running to follow a crazy brunette? Shocked!" Aimes follows him, to accompany or berate, not sure.

I watch Leigh walk along the shoreline. She has no real motivation to her steps; no joy at the thought of rejoining her family. It's the same slow, bored walk she has always displayed. Warnings tickle the back of my senses, whispering hints as to something I should be seeing, but since when have I ever listened to such sensations.

I follow the slow progression everyone else has already started upon. Even in our descent to the sand, our group is segregated, divided into smaller sections. Except for April. She dances and skips through the divisions as if they were left to make room for her adventures, finding childhood innocence all around her.

If Leigh notices us following her, she doesn't turn to acknowledge it. Her slow pace takes her to a clump of downed trees. She stands there staring into the space of an empty trunk. Reaching her hand in, she pulls forth a long orange tube.

"What's that?" April's small voice penetrates the silence.

Rhett turns his head, hearing her angelic sound, to smile at her. "Flare."

"Is it loud?" she quizzically asks Rhett. Her brown eyes shine with her questions.

Leigh doesn't give time for him to explain. Twisting the white cap from the tube, she uses one end of it to strike against the tube's top. In an instant, orange smoke begins to pour forth in a dense, thick cloud. She tosses it onto the sand and then leans against the trunks of the trees which hid her summoning device, waiting and still bored.

Peyton seems confused. He is looking to Leigh and back at the giant cloud before glancing around us. "That's it? We drove a whole day for a flare?"

Lawless shrugs, "Makes sense, actually. I mean, you could try shouting to some island out there and see if they hear you but most likely you'll just gather every Risen from that day ride to here before they do."

I'm watching Leigh listen to the men further debate the logic of it. Her eyes aren't the panic-filled tennis match they once were. In fact, there is no panic. There's nothing in them at all; not in her eyes and not on her face. She doesn't even bother to move the dark hair the winds are churning around her face. With arms crossed, she's simply here, and when our eyes meet, the same taunting creeps up my spine. The broken, hostage front has faded from her and no one seems to notice.

"So, we just are supposed to sit here until someone shows up?" Peyton's shouting drags me back to this moment.

"You can always leave. Maybe go for a nice swim? See how well you fare alone," Marxx answers.

"You'd like that wouldn't you?" Collin, my father, joins the verbal attempts of battle.

I'm not used to hearing him raise his voice. He always tip-toed around Carol, inserting himself between our passive-aggressive antics only when he was desperate to keep her calm. Unless putting on a show for her, not even to me did he raise his voice. Mostly, he just didn't speak to me, at all.

Marxx smiled. He didn't have to say anything. That smile, and the matching smirk from Rhett, was enough of a sentence without having to string a single word together. Whatever act of bravery Collin was attempting is instantly extinguished.

"Is this bi-polar?" Ashley's little voice whispers to me, amidst their veiled threats. But like all children, it wasn't really a whisper, at all.

"No," I tell her, "this is moody. That's why *I'm* bi-polar."

April scrunches her face with confusion. She confesses, "You're *all* making me bi-polar."

"That's fair." Aimes nods with the accusation.

Genny steps from the shadows of the trees. She's hugging herself as the early evening temperature begins to drop. "How much longer?"

Leigh points to something in the water. While the men were measuring their bravado, among other things, we had missed the boats heading our way. It's still a black shape floating along the waves, but it's heading towards us with certainty, using what is left of the orange smoke trail to lead it. Behind the nearest shape, is another close behind it. Two bobbing shapes headed towards us, but are they sanctuary or destruction? Like the sheep J.D. always preached about, have we just walked into a trap?

Leigh's face tells me nothing. She wears her mask better than anyone I have ever known. Just the same, I can feel her trying to measure me, and for an instant, just a flicker, there's a different shade to those bored eyes. For a moment, something flickers between her and me, and as I tilt my head to try to encourage more of her silent conversation, that flicker dies. It's drowned in waves of black hair and porcelain pale emptiness.

Ginjer is already primping. She runs her fingers through her high, perfectly shaded ponytail removing any knots from its length. Fluffing it, she smiles. "Won't be much longer, now!"

Aimes look towards me, making a fake motion of sticking her finger down her throat as she rolls her eyes. I would have joined her in the eye roll. I would have smirked, sharing in her assessment of the woman, but I didn't have time. Just as the boats had, something else has slipped upon us. This time, I didn't have to wonder if it was sanctuary or destruction. Destruction is all they have ever had on their minds.

I feel April's tiny hand take mine. I look down, distracted from Aimes, to see wide brown eyes watching me.

"Monsters."

It was a little word she said. A word too small to encompass the things she is talking about. A word too small to explain the damage about to be done. Such a small word. Such a small, small word.

Chapter 21

"Monsters," April says.

Her eyes are locked with mine. She is refusing to move or look behind her at what she is certain is waiting just behind us. I look. I always look and there, amidst the many trees and overgrown roots are looming statues. Even from this distance, I can see their glazed eyes watching us.

"Go," I tell her, handing her small hand off to Aimes.

Aimes doesn't argue. She doesn't pout anymore when we shove her off to the distance. After all we've seen, I think she's grateful.

Lawless and Marxx come to stand beside me. Rhett takes the space between us and those fleeing for the boats. An enforcer till the end, Rhett knows he is the last defense. Whatever makes it past us, is his job to finish.

Dolph is trying his best to keep the fleeing groups in some form of formation, herding them to keep their natural responses from spreading everyone too far apart. Ginjer's panic has caused her to leave a gap between her and the rest of them. Despite Dolph's attempts to bring her back, she keeps running wide and he must finally choose to let her go to keep up with the rest. Even with how far I am standing from him, I can see his distress.

"You should head with them," Marxx suggests. "You could help Dolph."

He offers this with a hint of yearning, tossing in an ounce of guilt for leaving Dolph on his own to keep so many safe. Marxx hopes I'll take the bait and avoid what may happen if I don't. He's never been hesitant before, but it's easy to see he is now. He hasn't pulled a weapon, yet. He's waiting to see which one he'll need first before committing to the act, as his doubts carry him along with their drowning current.

Lawless laughs. It's a short laugh, one born more from frustration than humor. "And leave the main action? You know her better than that."

"The fact you two can carry on a conversation while we are being watched, makes me wonder about our sanity," I tell them both.

My words are met with smirks and raised eyebrows. I guess I'm not the only one with doubts. Not having quite as many doubts as Marxx though, I do commit to a weapon. Some girls have teddy bears to comfort them, or journals filled with pretty scrawl to record every moment. I have a double-edged hand knife which would make a croc hunter envious and we both remember everything I've shoved her into.

"They aren't moving," Peyton stands a little to our right. He's set himself up in the gap Rhett provides, adding another layer of back-up should we fall.

He's right. These aren't moving. That wasn't their role to play. They did their part of the murder masquerade. Their dance card was simply to not dance, at all, but to distract. We may have never known if it wasn't for the different degrees of screams now surging from behind us. As we pivot to face those sounds, I almost swear I saw one smile.

Behind us, the beach is being closed off by the sheer number of shambling forms rushing towards the boats and our scattered family. I've done this run enough times to do the math in my head. We won't make it. There is no equation that will allow us to reach those we sent ahead thinking only of their escape. Even knowing this, I still run.

Half of my life is ahead of me, fighting the waves to make it to outstretched hands waiting on the bobbing vessels. Half of my life is beside me, running as we always do to protect who we can, despite the odds against us. I don't want to have to choose which half I lose today. I won't have to. Fate will do that for me.

Dolph is fighting to get through the Risen to reach Ginjer. Her wide pattern of retreat has left too wide of a stretch. He knows it's hopeless, but he tries. The constant screaming of his name is spurring him on, but the sheer number of Death's army isn't making it easy. I watch him stumble a few times, struggling to not be overtaken himself. I'm certain every time he fades from my view, he won't be seen again, but he is, despite the sheer impossibility of his task.

My boots are in a constant battle with the sand below them. The sand pulls them down, holding onto one, before freeing it to grasp the other. Fighting against these invisible hands, my progress is slowed even more, eating precious seconds from minutes I don't have to spare.

The men around me are separating, picking their targets to either save or attack. Peyton is heading towards Ginjer and Dolph. Lawless and Marxx are heading towards the center with Rhett close on their trail. I'm running towards the boat with Aimes. I know I cannot take on such a sheer number, but I can keep a path cleared. I can do that, at least. I can provide a space for them to run to once we know everyone has made it clear of the beach.

We collide with the confusion of sounds and panic. It threatens to engulf us, ripping our plans of action from our minds. The sheer volume robs us of bravery, and we slither into hopes for survival.

I can hear the high pitch of Ginjer's voice begging for help. I can hear Aimes shouting for Paula. The sounds of hand-to-hand combat merge with the fear floating around me. Everywhere I turn there is an outreached claw, grasping for me, with its skin missing from the tips of the fingers from the deaths it has served. Jaws are snapping, surrounding me with hopes of just one little taste. Spinning in circles, I can't focus on one. I don't dare turn, losing sight of the others. I keep taking steps backward, shifting sideways and all it does is close the gap around me. Their choir of lethality hits octaves which trigger every last sense of panic I was holding at bay. It floods my brain. I'm paralyzed with it, and despite every effort not to, I feel, rather than see, my double-edged blade of comfort slide from my hand and to the sand at my feet.

The first body lands against my back. The attack sends me to my knees, unhinging them from under me. Bracing myself with my hands, the compacted sand connects with my palms. The vibration travels through me, knocking the air from my lungs and the panic from my brain. Rolling to face whatever is going to be above me, I bring those same jarred arms up to protect myself, but I didn't need to. It's who is above me I now need to save.

Genny stands there, swinging a small knife she must have stolen from the kitchen of the house we just left. The small blade will be of no use to defend her from what is encroaching upon her. If she knows it, it's not apparent with how she stands, just as defiantly as I once did, facing down what could be her last moment.

"Get up," she shouts. "I don't know how to do this but even I figured out you don't drop your weapon!"

Her pose is completely wrong. She's exposing every inch of herself for the attack. She's solid, knees locked, and the first shove will topple her just as she did me.

Rearming myself, I stand. Placing my back to hers renews my resolve. I'm reminded it's not just me in this battle. Nor is it just me I'm fighting to keep alive, and I hate how Aimes' words from before are washing me with scorn.

"Come on, you ugly piece of shit," she mutters, jeering the nearest one, and from such a diminutive person, it is somewhat impressive.

"Start 'em young," I mutter to myself, recalling what Aimes had said just hours ago. "Be ready," I tell her.

Until now, they haven't forced their fight. They jockey back and forth, making sure we can't escape, but they haven't launched into their normal disorganized frenzy. This feels familiar. I've done this before, but it wasn't a sand-covered serenity. It was a scream-filled courtyard with snow keeping it echoing among the silent, retreated trails of my past.

"They aren't going to rush us," I tell Genny.

She turns her head to see me better. "What?"

"They are hunters. A pack. They separated us making us easier to take down."

"I didn't think they were supposed to be this smart?" Genny looks at the ghouls around us with a new caliber of fear.

"They weren't," I tell her, already mentally mapping an escape route. Once the attack does begin, we won't outlast this many. "Keep your back to mine and follow my lead."

"Why?" Her voice is anything but trusting.

"Because we are still smarter."

She makes some style of an annoyed sound. "Says the one who dropped her knife."

I don't reply. Instead, I just start a slow slide towards the floating promises of sanctuary. If their plan is to wait until we are weak before rushing us, I plan to get us as far from the center of the confrontation as possible.

The Risen begin to settle. Their minds are aware there has been a change. I keep a mental track of every one of them standing before me. I watch their eyes watching me as they try to formulate a new plan. Their voices are a low growl, a warning, but not on the offense. At least, not yet.

I pick the two weakest links of the mob as I plot my path. A man who was of thin build in life is now a composite of meat and joints. His white shirt is no longer the once bleach-beaming pride. It's yellow and brown, and so much more than I want to identify. The smell from his oozing frame is acidic. He leaves blobs of black mud-like fluid to clot in the moist sand. The one next to him isn't much better and my stomach is arguing with my brain.

My other pick is almost the complete opposite of his counterpart. His gelatinous shape seems to hold no real true style. As he rocks in place, his whole-body sways with the movement, rolling and sliding with gravity placed upon him. His clothing is fighting to contain him. It's stretched and threadbare in shades of what was once grey sweats. His eyes are focused on me. As if he may figure out my plans, his eyes slide over me, pausing at my feet and their path before coming to rest on my face again. If I didn't know better, I would have sworn that I saw him smirk.

Fear and the pure smell of bile has my stomach rolling faster than the waves around me. I am almost in arm's reach of the two, and whereas one is still glazed and waiting, the other has figured out where I am headed. His fingers begin to twitch.

Keeping my voice low and hushed, I whisper to Genny. "Ready?" She has kept tight to my pace, only now upon hearing my voice, do I feel her slow. "Stay with me," I hiss. "If we become separated in the midst of all of this, we won't make it."

I don't have time to elaborate on my words. It seems to happen all at once. I raise my blade to attack the mentally slower one only to be countered by the large force of the other. With nothing to hold onto, it feels like fighting a heavy, wet fog. Any solid plan is now forfeit. Using my elbow to connect with his face, keeping his mouth away from me, I use the small window of his recoil to slash at anything I can reach. Landing a long slice upon his torso, it erupts like the overflowing sack he has become in this life. I'm soaked in cold, thick fluids of which makes my stomach shudder. But like a deflated balloon, he sinks to the sand. His weight is shifted from so much sagging flesh. It pins him, rendering him unable to stand again.

Genny doesn't need instructing. With the flexibility of youth, she kneels mid-step and finishes the glaring face watching her before standing back up to keep her presence felt behind mine. With the fears of youth, she kicks his head so that it no longer faces her. Monsters are less scary if you don't have to look them in the eyes and I'm starting to rethink kitchen knives.

I waste no time putting down the oozing one. Just as I had expected, his body has already passed its limited expiration date. His face conveyed the message of attack, he was just unable to do it. The same method of defense with my elbow to the side of his jaw rotated his head just enough to expose the tender temple where I slid the blade. Gravity freed my knife. Genny's foot freed his jaw from his face.

One-by-one we tunnel a path through them. Only the ones I confront become some form of alive with their nature triggered. The evil which stimulates them becomes rampant, rushing through their system with thoughts of hot blood and warm meat to feast upon. Each is disappointed as Genny and I dispatch their expired lives.

Genny lets me lead the way. I take the brunt of the fight and she, the ever-confident shadow, finishes those I leave scattered around us. She never breaks more than a whisper of space between us. For a moment, I hold hope we're going to make it. For a moment, in that same whisper of space, I hold faith. Faith is damning like that. She shows you a promise and then drowns you in her denial.

The well-dug tunnel we have created isn't holding anymore. Too many have sensed our possible escape. The same one-by-one logic we are using, now they use against us. It starts in front of Genny, the one of us seen as less of a threat. It was a slow flowing of tones. Tones of aggravations, and hunger that starts with the ones in the furthest back to slowly spread to the ones near us. I know this sound. My soul knows this sound. Every hair on my body knows this sound. Each one is now reacting in warning and fear of us escaping them.

I can see the boats. The path is technically cleared in front of us. It's now or possibly never with their desperation overriding their nature.

Grabbing onto Genny's shirt, I spin her, propelling her ahead of me. "Run!" I shout, with every ounce of air my lungs hold.

She doesn't pause. Whatever life she endured with this new horror has taught her to take direction well. She runs and only when I see the flowing of her hair from the action, do I turn to keep her from being followed.

I run backward, letting the shouts of my name in the wind guide me towards those who are waiting. The now running things ahead of me propel me from those who aren't. I glance around through the air-tossed knots of my hair and see no one left upon the beach. There's just one cluster of the damned hovering over something on the sand, but I won't allow my mind to dwell on that, nor acknowledge what it may mean.

We were the last ones to be free from our fight. Everyone is either on a boat, running to a boat, or wading in the water to help those near them into the boat. I am the last one on the shore.

Turning to fully run, I see Rhett fighting through the cold water to head my way. Marxx is shoving, half carrying Dolph towards the boats. Paula is holding onto Lawless. I shake my head, signaling for him to stay. The closest boat is already starting their engine as Genny is hoisted into it. She, too, has turned to watch me. Collin has his hands resting on her shoulders to discourage what seems to be a family trait of self-destruction.

I feel the rake of a hand in my hair before it clamps down upon it. Sharp nails dig into my scalp to anchor itself in those same knots I saw my family through. Instinctively, I pull forward, not connecting the reason why I'm feeling what I am feeling. My eyes and focus are on the targets ahead, blurring out all other thoughts.

My body is rocked backward. My spine extends and it pulls my feet from underneath me. My fall is graceless, denial fueled, and gravity hindered. Despite the hand securely holding my hair tighter than any rubber band I've ever used, I crawl forward, seeing only the boats ahead of me, hearing only the sound of my name on someone's lips and not the sound of my death in something's throat.

The claw is paired with another and now there are needle-like sensations in my shoulders. My mind refuses to admit they are teeth. My sanity refuses to grasp or accept that logic. Instead, I dig my fingers into the wet sand and use that as stability to force me forward. Something is running hot and fast down my arms. I don't want to look. Once I do, there will be no doors to hide my mind behind. Once I see what I'm refusing to give into, my mind will break, taking any lingering resolve with it.

Hands have secured my legs. I stretch onto my stomach making the still tender flesh scream, or perhaps that's me screaming and my flesh is agreeing with me. I can feel the thread in my thigh popping through the meat it attempts to secure. I'm no longer crawling forward, but I make the motions, just the same, clawing at the sand in refusal to admit defeat. Just hours ago, I had stood under the same sun, with a different type of defiance. A defiance colored with exhaustion and remorse. A defiance born of pure ice. This defiance is heat, a fire and a determination to live. I was defying life, and now, with every last ounce of strength I have, I am defying death.

When the pain rips through my calf, a scream rips from my throat. It breaks my concentrated efforts to contradict the part of my mind living in the denial over what is happening. I look at my arms, finally seeing the bright red blood that has been streaked like some style of war paint. Turning my head further, I meet the eyes of what was once a brunette. She stares at me while her jaw works the bones of my clavicle, trying to separate the tendons and muscles from their protective bones.

It was her hand which found my hair, securing my body for her fiendish friends to feast. My brain fights the dam that is fracturing with the truth. It tries to re-plug the facts leaking through its thick walls. Despite the efforts, the dam is fractured, splintering, and compromised. Truth rushes through and washes away the last slip of denial to which I was clinging.

Like Ginjer, my screaming stops. I stop. Everything stops. My head is suddenly too heavy to hold up. I let it rest upon the oddly soft sand, sand softened by the blood I am spilling, while keeping my eyes locked with the one who finally grants me escape. I watch her until she blurs, becoming a picture of haze blending into the many shades around us. Then, I close my eyes, letting it all go. The waiting room doors open, and I'm almost grateful to see who is waiting for me.

Chapter 22

I know where I am. I know these pastel walls which surround me and the colorful tiles I am walking upon. I know the path I am unconsciously taking. I know the purple doors, now looming in front of me, taunting me yet again to open them, to just take a small peek.

"Is that wise?"

His voice comes from behind me. Turning, I stare at the one man I didn't know I leaned on so heavily for life support. There's a different type of tears escaping my normally hate-filled eyes. I rush to him. I rush to Chapel.

His arms consume me, and they are the soul-soothing perfection I remember. The smell of his leather vest is more calming than any blend of lavender I have ever encountered. He holds me as long as I need him to, to hide me from the world he left me in. He doesn't grow impatient as time extends. He lets me drink from a well I thought dried. It sates a thirst I didn't know I was craving. Only when he starts to stroke my suddenly groomed hair do I pull away to really see him.

Like the father he is, he wipes away the tears as he inspects my face.

"Are we dead?" I ask him, allowing him to treat me like the kid he has always seen me as.

"One of us is." He pushes back the hair from my face, smiling into my green eyes.

"Am I?" It's a whisper, faint and barely audible, but asked all the same.

He doesn't answer. He simply smiles again. A smile blended with sympathy and secrets.

"Comforting," I tell him.

"What are you doing, Hells?"

"Standing shit-deep in my own created nightmare."

Chapel smirks. "You always were gifted with your words. That's not what I'm asking you. What are you doing, Hells?"

I'm confused. Honestly, when these little dreamscapes take place it's normally J.D. lurking to rip off the scabs and marinate them with lemon juice. I don't know what he's asking. So, I don't answer with anything, but the look upon my face.

It doesn't deter him.

"Why, Hells?" He's looking past me now to the dreaded purple doors.

Turning to view them myself, I battle with the many different retorts my 'gift' wants to use to reply. Instead, I answer him the way only he can get me to. "I have to look."

"Why?" he whispers.

I can feel the words clawing my throat. I want to keep them stuck, trapped deep behind locked doors and closed curtains. There, in the darkness I have created for them, they can fester, eating away at me internally while being ignored externally.

"I just do."

It's what I tell him. It's not the truth. It's not why I always have to look, but he already knows that.

His hand cups my shoulder, splitting my mind from here and seconds ago when a different type of hand steered me to the truth. "Then look."

He doesn't stop me. He lets me walk towards the moment I ruined everything. He doesn't follow me to my damnation. He waits. As all good guardian angels do, he waits.

The metal doors are the same heavy metal weight they were then. They emit the same groan. They, too, want this locked forever, but I keep showing up to refuse their slumber.

I wasn't aware that I had closed my eyes until I was forced to open them to look around me. The smell of rot and bile doesn't greet me. I can smell the copper scent of blood, but it hasn't turned yet to something darker, deeper in scents. The sounds are of panic and screaming, but a different octave hangs in the air around me.

This is a tone of terror for what is happening to someone, not the screaming of what is being done to them. The rushing around the room isn't one of escape. These people are rushing to small children stacked high on the bleachers who convulse, shattering their own bodies beyond their normal strength. Their screams are over the damage their small charges are doing to themselves, slamming their bodies against the metal until bones break and fluids escape.

I've heard enough stories of when it started to know what I am watching. This is when it started here. The walls hold onto this memory like a body part clings to trauma. Wearing it. Sharing it. Exposing it for others to notice since there is nothing these walls can do to change it.

When I arrived, the ones who are now fighting to stop the inevitable became the inevitable. I recognize those raven curls, the security guard still standing by the door, even the principal shouting orders. I recognize them. I want to shout, to scream to get away, to come with me now, as if it will save them. As I watch them, my hands itch with the facts resulting in me clenching and releasing my fists. They are already dead. There is nothing I can do.

"You didn't cause it, Helena." Chapel has come to watch their confusion. "You didn't cause it and you couldn't have stopped it that day."

With the ending of his words, the room shifts, becoming something utterly different. Now, it's how I witnessed it that long-ago day. Those who were just running around the room to be heroes are now victims. They lay spread out through the room, exposed, destroyed almost to the point of not being recognized if it wasn't for the small slips of identity Ashley had pointed out.

The children are gone. At least, they appear to be, until I hear the echo of my own scream deeper in the hallway. Each shriek I hear pulls a tear from my eyes. I know where the children are. They have found my pink-clad Angel. This is the moment they took her from me and all I did was watch.

"You didn't cause it, Helena," Chapel repeats himself.

He is here being a witness to all of my dark sins. He's viewing the very failures which walk with me every day, motivating me to never again turn my back. The failures which dance around my mind, spreading their dark effigies into every moment.

"It was just a simple shot," Margaret says.

I turn to view what I am sure will be a death-cloaked minion. She isn't. She's perfect. Her white bows bounce as she skips around me before heading back towards those purple doors. She is something a mother would sigh over with pride, not the nightmare of which I was introduced. She pauses, right at the doors, and smiles at me before finishing her innocent exit.

"You didn't cause it, Helena."

Chapel smiles at me and standing on either side of him are two small children. They take his hands into theirs, smiling a smile like their father's. A woman appears behind him. Smiling the same warm knowing smile they are all sharing.

Chapel's smile widens with their arrival and I know this must be the family who he was so ready to return to. The small children must be Kay and Ken. The woman, Trina, his wife. Chapel is finally home.

I start to smile at him, but it freezes on my lips. Trina is no longer the image she was when she first appeared. Her hair is now sweat-matted. The complexion of warm tones is grey and pallor. Her smile isn't one of warmth. It's to expose teeth she uses to latch onto Chapel's neck. She tears apart the flesh, stretching what she pulls from him in her mouth. Blood gushes, spraying the wall beside us before sliding down the grooves of the cement blocks.

"It was just a simple shot," Margaret sings from down the hallway, "and wherever Helena goes the lambs are sure to die."

I scream. It isn't an imprint this time of an engraved memory held by unrelenting ghosts. It's my voice. My fear. My torment. My pain as I watch Chapel's family devour him while he smiles at me.

I'm no longer seeing the gym. The room is dark and illuminated by lamps smelling of burning oil. I'm still screaming, though.

"Hold her down!" I hear Paula scream from somewhere near me.

A sharp sting is felt in my arm. The frenzy in my heart slows, slipping away just as the room is doing around me. I can't scream anymore. My voice is too weak to obey.

"What was that?" A voice my mind doesn't recall asks.

I know it's Rhett's fingers tracing my face. It's the same style of caress of which Chapel had used before our tour. If Rhett is showing a room filled with people such an open example of concern, I understand why Chapel couldn't answer if I was dead.

"Purgatory," Rhett says. "That was purgatory."

The sounds of the room fade away. The sensation of his touch lingers along the lines of my face. It's the last thing I cling to before everything becomes muted and void. It's the last thing I cling to before hearing a red-haired little girl sing my name from the darkest pitch of the blackness I am tumbling down into. When the chorus of condemned cherubs begins to sing, it's the one thing I wish I could feel again.

Chapter 23

I don't know how many times I've bounced from Margaret's little games to the dark room that I'm lying in. There were times their voices mingled with the gym. I would try to call out, begging for someone to hear me, but the visions slide, meshing and flowing the two worlds to one, or colliding them together into a tragic blend. This is one of those tragic times.

I can feel Lawless holding my hand and the soft vibrations of his voice near my ear but all I can see is the piles of dead children as I'm sitting on a long-ago-abandoned kitchen floor. Their heads aren't turned away from me as they were that day. Now, each one stares at me with their eyes peering into what's left of my soul.

"Haven't you had enough yet, Girl?"

I cringe, sinking even deeper to the floor when I hear his voice. I let the congealing blood soak into my jeans. I even trail my fingers through it reminding me of Jell-O before it's fully set. Anything to distract me from J.D.

Letting out a slow whistle of appreciation at the scene around us, he tours the kitchen with his normal slow walk. He squats down beside

Margaret, turning her limp head back-and-forth upon her neck. "This is the bitch that keeps tormenting you, ain't she?"

I submit a quick arch of my eyebrows for my answer.

"Why don't you just burn her? Isn't that what you do to the dead you wanna keep dead?" he asks.

I know what game J.D. is playing. I didn't miss the dig he just inserted. I'm just not interested in going round-for-round with one of my imaginary friends.

"Why don't you just wake up, Barbie?" he asks me. There's a tone to his voice that pulls my eyes his way. His face holds a look I've only seen a few times in the span of our lives together. That soft sound comes again, saying "Barbie, wake up."

I sit up, hearing him speak so softly to me. I'm used to his verbal banter, the way his words can strip you of ego or fill you with rage, but not this pleading pitch. I watch him walk over to me, kneeling so close I can feel his breath on my face. His hands are on my shoulders. It's comforting at first, until he starts to slam my body against the metallic door.

"Wake up!" He begins to shout over-and-over, each time it becomes louder and more urgent. With a sudden breath, I do.

The shaking stops. My body is moaning from the damage it has caused and my voice shares its opinion.

"There," I hear Aimes say, when the hands are removed and whatever bed I am laying on shifts its weight. "You just had to shake her. She's stubborn like that."

"Bitch," I slowly whisper to wherever she is standing, with an almost hiss characteristic

The sound of my voice results in such a commotion around me. I instinctively flinch with it. It sounds as if a thousand voices are speaking at once. They bounce off the walls of my skull resulting in a different type of pain. There are hands checking random points on my body, spreading my lips, shining a light in my eyes, and various other tests only they understand. The light did nothing to help my eyes focus or the throbbing their voices were creating in my head.

"Leave her alone!"

This voice I know. This is our resident shield maiden of medicine. The bass of her voice sounds as if she's about to start a war.

"I said, leave her alone," Paula repeats it again, this time slower, shockingly putting a punch to each word hiding a threat among the vowels.

"Ohhhhh, you're in trouble," Aimes is taunting someone. Which isn't shocking at all.

The hands disappear, leaving me feeling somehow more invaded with their absence.

"Go tell them." The way Paula's voice softens, I know she is talking to Aimes without having to witness it.

"Okay," Aimes declares in her normal, sing-song pattern, "but if she starts to slip under again, you know where to find me."

I listen to the sound of her retreating feet. I hear a door open before she shouts into the room, "Love ya', Hells."

"Sure, you do."

I hadn't intended to say it. My voice found some will to live and expressed it, though.

I feel the bed sag under added weight. "I can't see." I don't know who I'm talking to, or who is sitting near me.

"Shhhhh," Paula whispers. "It's going to take a moment for your eyes to adjust."

"Adjust to what?" My confusion carries to my words.

Paula chuckles. "To being open."

It makes so much sense when she says it like that.

"How long?" I'm scared to ask, but my voice is doing that trick where it just vomits words before I can stop it.

"Not too long," Paula croons. I can feel the moisture from a damp rag on my arms. "Long enough," she finally concedes.

"Chapel wouldn't tell me if I was dead or not." Part of me knew better than to mention his name to her. Part of me also is still tripping along a cloud of destroyed sanity.

I can feel her tensing, picking the right words to say without revealing too much. It makes me wonder if we are alone in the room or not.

"Well, for a while there we didn't know either."

The cloud tripping part asks, "Am I dead?"

She chuckles again. "Not yet, but you sure do keep trying, don't you?"

"Better me than Genny," I reply, letting the words become more of a sigh than punctuation.

"Why?" Marxx barks.

Anger is good. Anger means they are safe to let me know what they really think without having to worry about how I will handle it. Anger is real, not candy-coated with a mockery of sweetness Death seems to convince us to use with someone.

"She's just a child, Marxx," I reply to the angry man somewhere in the room. I believe I'm looking at his outline, anyway.

"So was I," I hear Margaret murmuring from the darkness.

Paula touches something near my shoulder and the pain becomes almost adrenaline. I'm wide awake. Margaret slithers away.

"Stay with me or I'll let Aimes bounce you a few more times." Paula threatens.

I watch the outlines become a little more in focus, like someone is adjusting the knobs of my grandfather's old television.

"I'm just tired," I reply to her concern.

"Each time you take a nap you stay out a little longer," Rhett's voice comes from the darkness behind me, somewhere near the head of my bed.

"Tell me about it," I reply to his massive shadow. Rhett doesn't need to remind me of the many intervals which seemed to never end. "So then talk to me."

"What were you thinking?" Lawless is close to me. His voice is velvet and it hovers right near my ear.

"Don't want to talk about that."

"Outvoted," Marxx's voice is still further away, holding somewhere near the door.

I sigh. There is no way to explain to a group of men who believe that if it is not our own then they don't matter. They do understand debt, though.

"Genny came back on the beach because of a mistake I made. She risked her life for me. Seemed like a shit thing to not do the same." My voice is weak and I know they find my explanation the same.

"Why do you always have to be the hero?" Rhett is chastising me. Yet, there's a hint of amusement mixed in there, as well.

"Hero's don't need as much saving as I do. I'm more of the cliché sidekick who always lands in trouble despite her efforts to avoid it." I point out.

"You didn't put in a lot of effort this time." Marxx is bitter. He answers each response with an angry retort. I know it's going to take me some time to climb out of the hole I am in with him.

"To avoid trouble or land in trouble?" I ask, mostly to irk him. "How bad is it?" I ask, to fill the void of muted awkwardness due to Marxx's behavior.

"Well, you didn't turn," Aimes says, and we fall into our normal verbal volley that only the best of friends can do.

"Turn?"

"Into one of those things."

"Was I supposed to?"

"They think so."

"They who?"

"They who be in the room, your eyes can't see."

"Oh…" I try to focus my sight, but it's still just shapes and shades. I look to the shape of Paula still sitting near me. "I thought you didn't turn into racoons?"

Paula doesn't answer right away. She's doing that thing where she busies herself with something in hopes of looking important enough to explain the stalling. This allows her time to pick and choose her words amid the awkward silence. "There's been some discussion about that topic."

"They aren't holding a bible, are they?" I ask, as my eyes fight to stay open.

"Not that I've seen," Paula says.

"Should I shake her?" By the sounds of it, Aimes is already walking over before she finishes her question.

"No," Paula replies. "This time it's just sleep."

As my eyes lose the battle to stay open, I hope she's right. I hope I'm not about to descend to the sin-displaying darkness. I know what awaits me there when the fog clears. When I don't hear the singing of a red-haired devil, I believe Paula.

With a silent prayer of my own, I hold onto that belief just as tightly as Travis held on to his bible. It's not Margaret's song I hear from the far corners of my mind. It's 'Amazing Grace' that welcomes me into this exhaustion-driven slumber. The gentle notes of the song remind me there is nothing sweet about my soul left to save. The little blonde child running through the fog in front of me assures me of it.

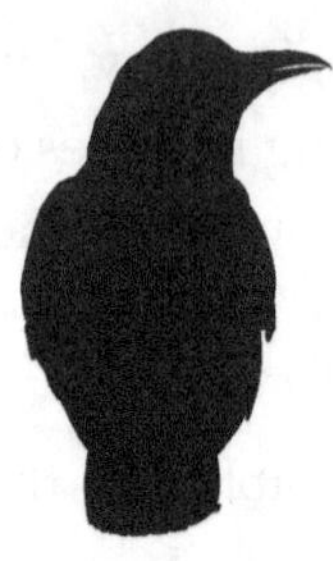

Chapter 24

It was several days before Paula released me from her tender care. I never spoke of Chapel, again. She never asked. She explained to me I had managed to tear open the wound on my stomach and completely rip every stitch in my thigh. I also earned new stitches for my bravery.

The brunette was kind enough to only gnaw on my flesh, leaving a nice gap for Paula to perfect her craft. My legs will heal on their own, as long as I don't try to relive my goals of being a human serving tray. I assured her I would try my best. The only questions she wouldn't answer were about what else happened on that beach. She finds something else to do each time and the haunted look in her eyes make me drop it, each time.

I know Paula is watching me even now. She has a way of watching without ever having to actually look at you. Which is why I wasn't surprised to hear her told-you-so tone after I winced upon standing.

"Your stitches would heal much faster if you would stop trying to constantly rip them out."

The glance I give her explains every thought in my head before turning to stare out the window of the red brick interior building. I haven't been able to venture far, but it's amazing to see how these people have turned an old civil war fort into a new, thriving community. It's almost like peering back in time, before that fate-filled morning as life moves around the courtyard. Families go about their normal days, no fear of sounds, or lurking shadows. I'm almost envious of how untouched they seem to be by what is going on in the world around them.

Children play openly in the grass-covered yard. Their laughter is not the sounds of those who have been warned of what their shrieks of childhood excitement may lure. They are pure adornments of innocence and trust, something I thought was lost to us.

I watch the leisure strolling style of those in the marketplace. Stands of various construction rest along the far walls. Each stand displays different items from food to clothing, even household comforts of books to linens. Things we never thought we'd miss until it was too late.

"How do they shop?" I ask to the only person in the little house with me.

Paula looks up from what she is doing to see what I am looking at. "They barter."

"Barter what?"

"Whatever they confiscated on a trip to the mainland or whatever they no longer have a use for." She's watching the same display of attempted normalcy.

"They don't just pool it all together for everyone to use?" I wrinkle my face with the thought. "What about the elderly who can't go to shore?"

"There aren't any."

There's something about how Paula says that, that makes me turn towards her. "What?"

"You'll see." Is all she shares.

She hasn't shared much of this new place in the time I've kept her captive. At least, that's what I thought I was doing to her. Now, with how completely disinterested she is in those who surround us, I may have been just the excuse to avoid them.

"What are you knitting over there?" Crossing my arms, I watch her, waiting to see if she gives any more hints.

"The basket we are all going to Hell in."

Paula holds up what looks to me to be nothing more than a few rows of cotton knots, but her smile is either pride or sarcasm. I can't really tell.

"You're going to need a lot more rows to fit us all." I slide my feet into my boots which look as if they are ready to wave a white flag at any moment. "Going to go find the crew and let them know we need to all start losing weight for your basket."

Paula shrugs. Returning to her knitting, she doesn't offer to join me. I was definitely the excuse.

Various conversations envelop me when I leave Paula's self-made prison. It almost feels as if somehow nothing has ever happened; nothing has occurred to disrupt life to a whisper-guided routine for safety and survival. I watch for a moment as April sits with a group of girls around her own age. They are playing a game I remember from what feels like decades ago with another little girl and her friends. Each girl holds in her hand a plastic replica of how adult life is supposed to look, complete with the plastic cars and house. Like a lost album, the sound of their laughter is something that should be recorded and preserved. It's so rare to hear it anymore.

"Hey! Helena!"

I turn to the direction in which Genny is shouting. Part of me wants to keep walking. The other part of me, which I haven't been able to label yet, almost becomes giddy to hear my name. That part and I are going to have a conversation later.

She's standing a bit away on what resembles an attempt at a football field, mid-pose with one foot resting on a soccer ball to secure it from the other teens around. They are annoyed and are waiting for her to mentally return to the game. As if me looking right at her wasn't enough to convince her she has my attention, she's waving frantically in my direction. I mentally whisper to the giddy part of me to shut up.

"Yeah?" I don't wave back, but thankfully, it's enough to make her stop hers.

She kicks the ball to a nearby teen, letting the game continue without her as she heads my way. "Can we talk a moment? Now that you're able to?" she's shouting as she heads towards me. Little does she realize this totally negates my ability to answer 'no' without looking like more of an ass than I really want to upon my first day of release.

"Sure." I shrug standing firmly planted just in case I need to make up some medical excuse to escape. I've learned to always leave an out when someone asks if they can talk. It's just safer for everyone if I have a clear exit plan with my mood swings.

The overhead sun plays across her young features. It toys with the many thoughts she is having, and wearing, across her face. She is almost practicing the words, running them through various filters before she says them. Obviously, that's a skill I've never learned.

"What all have they told you?" She's beside me now, but looking beyond me at something she's pretending has her attention. She's hiding her gaze in some further object with the hope of disguising any emotions attached to the question. That is a skill I've learned well.

"Nothing." I shrug, again. "I remember something about proving I hadn't turned, but that's really it."

She makes a soft noise of agreement before continuing. "You don't know about Ginjer?" Her eyes are on me now. "Or, Terrance?"

I hesitate. I can hear the carousel music faintly start. Somehow, I know I'm about to add a few more horses.

"No." I don't look away from her eyes. For once I'd like to see the truth and not just feel it rip my heart into smaller fragments of what is already left of it.

Hugging herself, Genny doesn't look away, either. "Dolph couldn't make it to her in time. He tried, but he couldn't."

She doesn't need to fill in the blanks for me. We both know we've seen enough to understand what she isn't saying, or maybe not willing to say, yet.

"Terrence?"

I can hear the music playing a little louder. Part of me already knows the answer to what I have asked. Part of me has blocked it for my own protection, but like always, I'm about to ruin it.

"When we saw you being overtaken, a few rushed the beach, but it was Terrence who made it to you." She looks away now. It makes it easier to hide whatever may be in her eyes. "He shot the ones he could and dragged you back to where the others were waiting." She pauses. I know by the gaze she is not in this place right now. She is back on the beach reliving that moment. "He could have made it, but he just stood there. Collin kept telling me not to look, but I couldn't look away. It wasn't slow like yours. They didn't attack one-by-one. They overtook him as a force, breaking him apart before he fell. Sometimes, I can still hear his screams."

Her voice trails off, hitting the highs and lows a survivor will fall into when retelling the horrors.

"They blend with your mom's?" It's a bold question I ask.

"No," she says, turning to look at me. "But they do with yours."

I can feel the air rush from my lungs. It's as if she has physically hit me, but I can't understand why I'm reacting. Until just recently, I didn't even know a mother other than Carol. There's no reason for her words to hit some hidden part of me, but they do, they really do.

Something must have shown on my face. Genny looks away again, but she doesn't apologize.

"Do yours blend?" she asks me.

"If I'm lucky." My answer confuses her, and she turns back towards me. "Otherwise, I get a personal reminder of the things which have happened. When it blends, it's just one giant blur of torment. When it's a personal tour…"

"…it's torture." Genny finishes for me.

I nod. I don't have to fill in the blanks for this, either. All this time I've allowed myself to think I'm alone in the depth of suffering I drown in. Somehow, I almost felt better for it, more prepared to handle the things others can't or won't do. I'm not. Everyone is just handling it differently, and defiantly, in their own ways. Aimes had said as much in the truck one afternoon but seeing it raw before me on such a young face, I know I can't fool myself anymore. I'm not special. My nightmares aren't rare. They are just pages to the many tomes around me we have all privately written upon our souls.

"It doesn't get any easier, does it?" Her face is almost hopeful. There's also a shadow of fear with what my answer may tell her.

I don't want to spread that shadow. I don't want to lie to her, either. Mentally, I toss a coin. Unfortunately, it lands on truth and I ponder for a second how soon is too soon for someone to lose everything and still remain unchanged.

"No, it doesn't," I tell her, aggravated it must be me to chip away at her innocence. "It doesn't because it can't. It can't get easier when we grow close to new people. It means we take new risks. We will push harder each time, and each time, life pushes harder, too."

"The only winner is whoever is more determined to live and to live with what they have to do to keep pushing. So no, it doesn't get any easier, Genny, until there is no one left, or nothing left for someone to give."

"By then it's too late," Genny whispers, and I know she's speaking about the many scars life would have left before reaching such a point.

"Then it's too late," I echo.

"Is that why you dropped your knife?" She isn't accusatory when she asks, but she's still whispering.

Genny is good at finding every weak link in my armor. She doesn't quite go for the soft spots. She pokes at them, testing them and me. Aimes has taught her well.

"Maybe," I answer as honestly as I can. There weren't any real thoughts or plans on the beach. The porch, that's different.

"And now?" Genny is watching my eyes, my face, even how I am standing for some hint at my next answer.

"I have new risks to take," I answer her and she almost glows.

"Because you're growing close to new people?" Her voice is hopeful, almost giddy and I squash the resounding mimic inside of me.

I smile at her, letting that be my answer and she returns it.

"Oh, one more thing?" she asks, as I begin to walk away. "Can you talk to the scary one for me?"

"That doesn't really narrow it down."

"Right," she pauses trying to think of a better way to describe someone. "Not the really tall dark-haired one, but the other one that's kind of like him, but worse."

I chew on my bottom lip to hide a different kind of smile. "Marxx?"

"Maybe?" Genny shrugs, looking lost in a broken, sad way.

"What's he doing?" I don't have to ask. I already caught a touch of it.

"He thinks it's all my fault." She sounds like a child who has been chastised by her favorite person. "Like I somehow almost killed you myself."

"What was Aimes' advice?" I notice her blush. I'm not the first person she's cornered about Marxx. I didn't think I was.

"She says they are all just acting like a bunch of babies because they had to leave their bikes behind. Something about a limb of theirs not feeling adequate without them and I should just ignore him." Genny answers innocently, making the innuendo sound that much more risqué.

I smirk, tilting my head with the thought. "She's probably not wrong but I'll see what I can do."

"What do I do till he's in a better mood?"

"What Aimes and I used to do." I do smile now, recalling our days at the bar. "Avoid him if you want to live or tease him if you want to break him. He can't stay mad if you can tease him. It has to be something to which he can't answer with a quick reply. It's how Aimes got over her fear."

"I don't think I want to tease him," she says, as if Marxx is the very essence of some boogeyman. "What did you do?"

"I left him alone. I wasn't always suicidal."

I leave her with her thoughts to find the rest of our group. I never would have thought to describe Marxx as scarier than Rhett, but is Rhett the man we once knew? Has all of this broken the very embodiment of the nightmare we once pictured him? Has the once silent, resilient Marxx now taken that mantle, striving to become more of a demon than those who stalk us? Or, are the men so used to being one they simply fill where the other slips, a give and take of responsibilities? If that's it, who now becomes the monster we once feared? Who now becomes the saint we are missing? Or are we all just discovering how much more we have to give before it's too late, once again?

Chapter 25

"Why are you sitting on a giant cannon?"

Aimes is sprawled across what was once thought of as an untouchable landmark of civil war history, right where a young man said she would be found. The sun stealing through the rounded brick archway warms her face, and with her swaying foot, she looks like the perfect example of leisure. She turns at the sound of my voice. Smiling one of her trademarked smiles. I'm almost afraid I asked.

"Why aren't *you* sitting on a giant cannon?" Aimes' smile grows wider.

"She's not used to having that much power between her legs," Rhett says behind me, before patting my head as he walks past me to collapse on a cot.

Aimes makes a tsking sound and I know her reply is most likely going to be targeted at me and not Rhett, this time.

"Whatever is between her legs is powerful enough to make her think she's indestructible." She smirks now, letting the smile become more of a taunt. "Love the new stitches," she purrs.

"Want them?" I mockingly smirk back.

She's made such comments in her frequent visits, annoying Paula more then keeping me company in my seclusion, and it still isn't any more amusing than the last.

"Nah, I'm smart enough to run." Aimes sits up, stretching her arms high into the air above her. "I'll leave the undead snack tray to you, but I am glad to see you've finally been released from your latest round of idiocy."

"Want me to find a window to dangle her out of? I don't remember her being so cocky after her round of idiocy." Rhett asks from his cot. He's pretending to be asleep, listening to every word, and very aware of what's going on, but asleep.

"When were any of you going to tell me about Ginjer and Terrence?" I ignore his joke.

Aimes spins, looking at the area around us. "I only see Rhett and me. Not sure who was supposed to tell you, but I don't make those calls. You know, due to what's between *my* legs."

"He picked his fate. It's more than most of us will get to do." Rhett doesn't answer in any way which shows he is moved or phased by Terrence's passing.

"Ginjer?" I let the name hang between us.

"We don't talk about that," Aimes whispers. "Trust me. Don't talk about it."

Her eyes hold a haunted look. A look earned from things which should never have been seen. I take her advice, for now. I won't talk about it.

"Well since you love to gossip so much," I sit down on the cot by Rhett, who automatically moves before I reach him only proving he's very aware, "tell me what's going on with this place. I seemed to have missed our grand arrival."

Upon hearing the magic word 'gossip', Aimes spins around to face me and fully begins to unload.

"Well," she begins with an almost twinkle to her eyes, "it's some kind of fort. They seem to be run by a woman named Marigold. Her daughter, Torri, is their second. Then follow the family tree down. Marigold used to work here doing tours and stuff so of course, she knew all about it when everything hit the fan. She loaded up a few of her favorites, kicked everyone out of here, and then peed on the walls to claim it as her own." She pauses to make eye contact. "I don't mean that figuratively. Real hippie-like family." She settles back on her new throne to begin anew. "So yeah, they have a few rules; most of which Rhett and Lawless have already broken out of boredom. They play so well with others, after all."

"Marxx?" I ask the newly self-appointed queen.

"He plays even less well with others." Aimes pauses, trying to think of how to fully explain it. "Remember Mr. Shepperd? Always walking around his yard, bitching to himself while throwing threats around about staying off his lawn or he'd kill you to everyone in the neighborhood? Which you were never really sure if he would do it or if he was just crazy, but you weren't willing to risk it?"

I nod, slowly and with caution.

"That's Marxx!" she exclaims, almost ready to clap over her comparison.

"What's Marxx?"

Much to Rhett's amusement, we both jump when we hear the very man we were just speaking about.

"Went by to see you," Marxx says, glaring at me as if I've already done something horribly wrong. "She said you walked out."

"Did you want her to crawl?" Making herself small, but vocal, Aimes settles back along the long line of the cannon.

Marxx shares his glare now. "I want her to stay where she is safe."

Aimes extends an arm towards my direction. "She's sitting with Rhett. What's safer than that?"

Rhett opens one eye to peer at his brother-by-choice to see if he will let his anger seep towards him. Marxx caves to Rhett's bluff-calling with folded arms and his face close to a grimace.

"Anything else about this place?" I ask Aimes.

She's more than happy to skip over the male drama and dives right into our new neighbors. "Well, they seem to think once you're bitten, gnawed on, raked, or any other of the many things you keep allowing to happen to you, you turn into one of those things. They totally didn't want to let you in."

I twist my face with the confusion of what she is saying.

"Yeah. When Marigold ordered those on our boat to dump your body into the water, Lawless grabbed her and put his gun to her head. Luckily, she backs down easily."

"Why would they think that?" I ask those around me.

No one has an answer. If they did it's the various forms of shrugs in shoulders or facial twitches.

"Whatever their reason, they firmly believe it." Marxx offers. "Marigold demanded you stay in that hut with only Paula. She even kept the door locked."

"Law camped outside the door. Pretty much daring anyone other than us to come near it." Aimes smirks. "He hasn't made a whole lot of new friends."

"Is this our new little hideout?" I look around the little enclave they have claimed.

Cots are spread along the walls, keeping their distance but still enclosed enough for protection. Various flannel blankets are spread across them with thin, filled pillows for cushions. Even being in such a state of depletion, I'm sure if I walked over to each one there would be some style of weapon under those headrests.

The walls are a time faded brick red with what appears to be a mixture of oyster shells for a floor. There are tall, thin slits of windows, or spots, where cannons once stood. Their absence leaves gaping holes in the walls. Something one wouldn't normally want in a place where walls are sometimes the only protection one can count on.

I point to the obvious flaw. "How is that smart?"

"The several miles and feet of water all around us," Marxx says, as if I should already know this. "Seems they don't swim, or at least don't care to, once the boats escape them. There's a few spots where the walls are completely missing."

"Doesn't seem smart, does it?" Aimes asks, thinking of the same inevitable doom's day.

"Not really," I agree.

"Wanna know what else isn't smart?" Aimes is pure joy waiting to answer her question.

I roll my eyes and shrug, not willing to fall too easily into her verbal trap.

"Look further down the hall and count." Aimes almost giggles and the two men beside us make a groaning sound knowing where she is heading.

Looking down the hall, I spot more cots. Nothing of any real hint as to what she's giddy over.

"Count," she encourages. "Use your stitches if you have to."

Exchanging my own version of a middle-finger-greeting, I do as she suggests, minus the stitches part.

There are ten cots spread along the hallway. There seems to be some form of grouping or at the very least a type of division. Three of the cots are spaced closer together than the rest, but at the same time, spaced further from the rest. Seems Peyton and Paula have gotten their wish. The dwindled number of cots holds my attention more than their spacing. What should have been a simple venture turned into a life-changing event, and despite what Chapel kept saying, I know this time I'm to blame.

"Don't worry," Rhett's voice mutters, heavy with sleep. "We put yours far from Daddy."

"…and Daddy far from Lawless," Aimes counters. "Hell, we put Marxx far from everyone."

"So, it's going well, I take it?" My head already hurts thinking of how this has been playing out.

No one answers. Just Aimes, and her signature Cheshire cat smile, fills the silence around us. It's answer, enough. It's the very answer which drains me of patience and hope for any type of resolution between our groups.

Leaning further on the long legs of Rhett, I sigh with my frustration and Aimes doesn't miss a beat.

"Live. Laugh. Lucifer." She smiles, mocking the once-popular slogan people hung along walls of homes before she dismounts the metal weapon. "It's almost dinner time. Let's go meet the crazies."

Rhett nudges me off him. "You really don't want to miss the show."

"Show?" I stand, but I'm not sure it's what I really want to be doing. The last group I woke up to holding a show was more than a high school, thought to be impenetrable, could hold.

"Oh yeah," Rhett smirks.

Now I know I don't want to be standing.

"It's audience participation." Aimes is already walking away, leaving me to either follow or stay.

I'm pretty positive I'd rather stay, but I always have to see for myself. I'm never satisfied until I've walked up to the monster and stared at it in its eyes, always ignoring the blaring warnings and living for only the self-sabotage I create.

Following her, I'm sure I've made the wrong choice with how Rhett's laughter trails behind us. Glancing one last time over my shoulder to where the three separate cots have attempted to hide in plain sight, I wonder where the two who are missing now sleep. Are they too hiding in plain sight, waiting to join my many other tragic mistakes? When they reveal themselves, will it be torment or torture?

Chapter 26

It's not exactly a cafeteria. What once greeted and held visiting tourists as a lobby, has been overtaken to become a central gathering place. People sit among glass cases, which once held artifacts that have long since been looted. The velvet ropes which guided tours now guides lines towards self-serve food stations, which have yet to have been entered. I can feel Aimes watching me, waiting for me to catch on to something I'm missing, but I'm completely missing it. There's something about her smile which makes me nervous. It's the same smile she wears right before the fan gets turned on high and the shit flies everywhere.

"What?" I finally relent.

Her smile grows just a little larger. "What, what?"

"What am I missing?"

"Oh, *that* what." Shrugging she leans against a glass-encased poster telling of the battle that took place here centuries ago. "You'll see."

I don't roll my eyes a lot out of habit. I roll them out of situations. Situations I seem to be habitually put in. Like this situation, right now, where I'm rolling them.

Once again, I glance among the crowded room in front of us. It's simple enough in its appearance. Nothing screams of warnings or any danger. There are no obvious signs of an impending disaster. The cultivated paranoia in me starts to wonder if that is the warning; the fact that there seems to be nothing amiss. Can things be too perfect?

Looking to Aimes again for guidance, which in itself should be a warning, she whispers, "Notice anything missing?"

Something Paula said earlier sparks my memory. Scanning the room again, I do notice a blaring oddity. Everyone here is maybe touching mid-fifties or lower. There are also no children under the age of five running among those gathered. The normal sounds of babies, or even toddlers, are non-existent, and with a random gathering of this size, those sounds should be bouncing off the walls.

Aimes watches my face as the clues begin to present themselves. I'm just not sure where they are going and to what end they will form. The last puzzle I had tried to put together on my own wasn't my finest moment.

"If you say they are cannibals, I will just give up right now and take my chances back on that beach," I whisper to her.

She tilts her head with her thoughts. "Don't get me wrong, the food here tastes a little off, but I don't think that's it. It would be refreshing though to deal with a type of crazy I could understand and maybe agree with."

"You could understand, and agree, with cannibalism?" I let the judgment spread across my voice as I'm looking at her.

"Supplies are running low. Numbers are growing larger. People die," she says this, as if it all makes perfect sense.

"By the way, how close is your cot to mine?" I ask her.

She responds to my question with a genuine smile of mirth.

We watch in silence as the crowd finishes gathering. I spot my father and Peyton in the same shared restlessness. Genny stands between them, as they, too, seem to be waiting for something to start. I don't see any of our men, and like the perfect best friend she is, she already has read my mind.

"They don't attend this. They barter and their food is brought to them," Aimes answers in such a way, that results in more questions than explanations. Upon seeing my confusion, she tries again. "Around here, you're only as good as what you can provide. Provide them different things, you get different rewards."

"What do you provide?" I hadn't intended for it to be an insult or jab, but her sudden pout suggests it was.

"Nothing. Which is why you and I will be entering that far line." She points to the section where Peyton and his are waiting.

"What line is that?"

"The 'thanks for not messing up so bad today it got someone killed' line."

Aimes says this with such an attitude I can taste the bitterness of her words. I almost feel sorry for her. She's always been protected, never really given a chance to prove herself. I can't help but consider if we may have done more harm than good to our little pixie.

"Is there a line lower than that? Considering my wide range of talents?" I ask, attempting to change her pouting to taunting.

"Yeah. It's the lake." Aimes once again leaves more questions than answers, but she did at least permit me a small smirk.

She doesn't take my well-placed bait. Her soured mood leaks to all her features, staining her normally playful face with her darker thoughts. She chews her bottom lip, keeping whatever those thoughts are locked tightly behind her sealed lips.

Having already burned my conversational bridge with Aimes, I weave my way towards the grinning Genny. She's the only one of her group smiling upon seeing me. Peyton's eyes don't glow the way they used to upon my arrival. I don't take it personally. I have that effect on people once they have been around me for a while.

"We don't talk about it," Aimes hisses behind me, reminding me of her earlier rules.

She knows eventually I'm going to talk about it, but for now, I nod and silently vow that it won't be today.

"Hi, Helena." Genny is genuine in her welcome when we first arrive, but her smile soon wilts under Collin's stare.

Ignoring my father, as I've spent a lifetime doing, I return her smile. For a brief second her lips curl before she catches herself. I rest my back against the same wall as Peyton. He doesn't turn to acknowledge or greet me. Aimes is watching the interaction like a bored house cat. She's mentally taking note, but not showing any signs of recording it.

I don't take well to being ignored. Peyton should know this by now.

"What landed you two in the non-useful line?" If I could sharpen my nails while asking, I would be doing just that. Instead, I just smile with my question.

"Nice to see you, too." Peyton returns my volley before Collin gets a chance. "Paula said you were healing well. I thought she was just in denial, but here you are."

"Here I am." My smile doesn't shrink.

"How many close calls is it now?" Peyton finally turns to look at me.

"From my own cause or from not rushing to my safety while others are in danger?" My smile is still holding.

Peyton doesn't return any form of a smile. His eyes are a cold winter. His face seems to age with a weight he never thought his shoulders would have to carry. I won't accept the award for the damage he is wearing. I won't deny my part in it, though.

"I hope we are as lucky as you seem to be," Peyton's voice is harsh, half-filled with his raw emotions that his nature just won't let him explore.

"Me, too," is the only response I can form under his gaze.

We both become distracted when seeing Genny waving to someone across the room. I watch as Paula returns a brief 'hello' before entering a different section. She meets my eyes before turning away in an almost shameful way.

Looking to Aimes to once again guide me through this labyrinth of confusion, I arch one eyebrow. It's enough to convey my questions.

"She's medical. Way more important than us," Aimes explains. "So, she gets promoted to the line over there."

I shrug. "Makes sense. So why is she hiding?"

"She doesn't like the status. She doesn't agree with subdividing based on some imagined social status." Peyton's lost some of his wrath, but he's still frosty with his words.

"To be fair, isn't it all imagined?" I shrug with my question.

No one offers anything in return. Whatever this place is, it's broken every one of them in some way. This, too, should be a clue to what Aimes had prompted me to see. Even she, normally full of spite, and the vocabulary to share it, is demure with her responses. For the first time, I'm starting to hear the silent screams of a warning.

I watch this seemingly lackluster group before me. They don't have the shades of battle-hardened along their features. Their eyes don't dart around the room from one too many nights of lost sleep and imagined sounds. They mingle freely, not restricted by fear or isolated for protection. Laughter and conversations flow casually around the room. They seem so helpless, powerless in their compliance. Yet, somehow, this place, and their people, have chipped away the hard-earned exterior of my family.

"Her name is Marigold and that's Torri beside her," Aimes cuts through my thoughts.

I had missed their grand entrance. The crowd parts for them as a hush smothers the room. Some kneel. Some reach their hands out to grasp or touch the two women as they pass through. Lips are pressed to the hems of their clothing. Hands are held out with a desperate need to be grasped. This isn't the same adoration Travis and Selma had managed to stir. Travis was seen as just the voice of a god. These two are seen as Gods. This adoration is something much more dangerous.

Marigold wears a long white cotton robe. The robe's wide arms and full length seem to swallow the older woman. She looks deceptively frail underneath the weight of such a garment with her bare small feet occasionally exposed as she walks. The way she carries herself speaks to the complete opposite. Her head swivels to meet each person she passes with a keen awareness. Her frame, where slight, is fully erect with no curvature of her age. Her silvering hair is thick and heavy with well-cultivated dreads. Her serene appearance isn't from something invented in the recent events but from a lifelong goal of discipline. She seems to soothe the souls of those she touches, but she's touching something completely different in mine.

Torri trails behind her wake with a different energy. Her smile is infectious in those who reach for her, returning the wide smiles she offers. Her blonde waves flow around her, moving in perfect harmony with her motions. Unlike most hair, it doesn't cover her face as much as it frames her pale, pink-toned skin. She wears a simple gown of green. It, just like her hair, seems to float with her almost waltz-like procession to their seats.

Once the two are seated at their designated tables, the room becomes a funneled effect of sections finding their route. Groups who once clumped for amusement spread apart with merriment and waves of farewell. Paula seems to be alone in her discomfort of the predetermined social benefits. No one else seems to look at their parting friends with any harbored feelings of the shame, as she is still exhibiting.

"What if you don't stay in your line?" I ask Aimes.

Her sullen mood brightens when hearing the vibration of annoyance in my question. She knows me so well.

"Are we going to find out?" Aimes asks and I'm certain she's not asking just to ask but to encourage me.

Accepting the encouragement, I arch my eyebrows with my shrug. "Why not?"

Not needing an invitation, Aimes follows right beside me adding, "Oh, how I've missed you."

I don't just switch into a different line. Slipping under the velvet ropes, I don't merge into a different section with some small act of rebellion. I ignore all the imposed rules, the guidelines, and the many sounds of shock to bring me to Paula's side. She doesn't glance at me with shock, though. She smiles at me with the same smile she would wear at the high school when she was amused by my mischief. Her smile secretly repeats the same statement Aimes had said when I started my social uprising.

"I see you still have your talent for making 'friends'." Paula is still wearing her smirk as she stares at the head table watching us. I didn't miss her sarcasm.

With her arm fully extending into the air, Aimes waves without shame to those who are not hiding their stares.

I don't wave. Instead, I'm staring into a pair of very observant brown eyes. As the rest of Marigold's table melts into hand-covered whispers, she is composed and calm. She collects the table with a swift movement of her hand, but her eyes never break from mine. We watch each other as predators, acknowledging the other as something above the scattered forest of prey around us.

With a face void of the serenity Marigold has been displaying for all to see, she briefly nods in my direction. Mimicking her, I return the gesture. Before our eyes part, returning Marigold's attention to her table, I know Paula is correct. I just tested the links of chains used to keep social order and found them lacking. Unfortunately for Marigold, I'm not through, yet.

"Wave at Genny," I tell Aimes.

Aimes' smile is the widest I remember. "Really?"

I answer with the same eyebrow arch I used to answer her last time.

Paula sighs, but she doesn't stop Aimes.

Marigold doesn't miss Aimes' arm launch into the air again. She follows the direction of Aimes' gaze before returning hers to mine. I don't have to look to know Genny accepted the invitation. The chatter filling the room informs me of it. What it didn't tell me was it wasn't just Genny who came when summoned.

Peyton is standing close enough behind me to whisper, "I hope you know what you are doing."

"That would be a first," Collin responds.

Between giggles, Genny whispers to me, "This is awesome. They are losing their minds."

Torri isn't sharing an infectious smile, anymore. She's gesturing wildly to those sitting around her. Her fingers punctuate words I cannot hear, but those around her are listening with full agreement. She begins to stand, but the same swift hand motion from Marigold shrinks her back into her seat. Torri is almost pouting, as she watches us.

Marigold isn't exactly watching us. Her eyes are only for me. I see through her peaceful veil. It's flimsy, well-worn, and easily discarded in a swift change of winds.

Aimes hands Genny a tray and they both happily make their way down the newly selected path ahead of them. "Wonder what the important people eat?" Aimes asks, and all Genny can do is giggle.

Paula sighs once again. It's mixed with exhaustion and amusement as she follows behind them with Collin on her trail.

Only Peyton holds back long enough to share a glance at Marigold. "Do you know what you're doing?" he asks me.

"It would be a first," I answer, repeating the words used earlier to describe me.

I hold no malice or sarcasm in my tone. It's a simple fact. I don't have a plan. I've never really had a plan in any of my random outbursts.

Upon hearing my answer, Peyton chuckles with bewilderment before following the rest of them.

Keeping my gaze with the table, I defiantly hold back a moment longer before taking my tray. A group that was completely animated now sits in silent judgment of what I have done. Scanning those who sit among Torri and Marigold, I smirk when I spot a familiar face wedged among them. Leigh, with her naturally bored pale face shares my amusement. It evaporates when Torri turns to look at her, but as Torri turns back towards me, Leigh's smile returns, as if it never left.

Marigold watches me with a cautious stare. She hadn't wanted me on her island when we first arrived. She thought of me as a threat to her little colony. After seeing what she has done to my family, she wasn't wrong.

I turn to follow those ahead of me. Predators don't turn their backs to those who they are unsure of or fear. I had acknowledged her as something on the same level as myself, something daring and dangerous, but I saw past those brown eyes. She's a different type of dangerous. With so much to lose, she's watchful and cautious of me. Like a gossamer glove, her hold is paper-thin and easily torn. I've displayed that to everyone around her.

I've displayed my colors, my war paint of trauma. They are bold in their shades of black and blue like the bruises of which life has covered me. Like a rare Picasso painting, the closer Marigold looks at my painted lines, the more dangerous I become to her. Perhaps she will show her teeth. Perhaps, her colors are just buried deeper and have yet to have surfaced. Time will tell, and maybe by then, I'll finally have a plan.

Chapter 27

The chorus of laughter dances around our new makeshift group as we head back to our selected haven. The dark shadows which covered their faces, aging them in such a rapid time, slip their hold just a little. The heavy burdens they've encased themselves in shed a pound or two. Conversations which started strained are a little easier once again. Like a river, we flow over topics we know to avoid. Our minds always swirl around the questions we want to ask, but we don't. In this moment, we let the river bubble with our shared jokes and smiles, knowing soon enough those unasked questions will reach from the depths to possibly drown us all.

Aimes explodes into our new gathering spot with her arms wide. "Hells is home!"

"What did you do?" Rhett asks, with less than thrilled feelings.

Aimes answers for me. "She pretty much told Marigold no one puts Baby in the corner."

With more theatrics than were actually present, Aimes and Genny re-enact what the men have missed. I'm only focusing on Lawless. Sitting on his cot, he's only half-listening to those around him. His head is down, making random nodding motions when the conversation is directed towards him. He's shutting down, keeping an emotional distance from what is being said, until he can't.

Lifting his head, Lawless looks directly at me. "We've worked hard to try to blend this time. We talked about it. It's what we decided. Why is it just after a few hours of being released you risk it all without talking to us?"

"Why is it just a few hours after being released, I've seen nothing but broken-down people?" I counter. "Why is it just a few hours after being released, I've had to hunt down our group instead of us all being together," I pause to let the verbal blade sharpen before continuing, "like J.D. taught us? Last I checked, you were supposed to be leading us. Since when do you let outsiders divide us?"

"You think you can do better?" Lawless stands, meeting me eye-to-eye.

He's holding himself one inch from a fight. The energy around him is like a storm waiting to unleash its furry. It's not me, or the emotions my words stir. It's so many other things hiding under a blanket fort of anger.

Removing the heat from my voice, I say to him and his many fears, "I think you can do better." I turn to face each of the people near me. "We can't blend. We don't blend. We don't know them well enough yet to blend. We've always taken care of our own, no matter where we have gone. Why is this so different? Besides, Aimes said you've already broken most of their rules. When did this blending come into play?"

No one speaks up. No answers or explanations are given vocally. Their faces say plenty. Plenty of hidden accusations reside behind the masks before me. I'm sure most of the accusations are for me, but no one is willing to show their hands just yet.

"Why is Aimes left to fend for herself?" I ask.

Aimes shuffles uncomfortably. She's not used to being the center of this type of attention.

"It wasn't exactly like that." Her voice is strained, almost unwelcomed.

I look towards her, waiting for her to clarify. "What was it exactly like?"

Aimes hugs her body only proving it was exactly like what I've suggested.

I continue, turning to face Marxx. "Since when do we pick on teenagers?"

Now that I've singled him out, Marxx isn't hiding his emotions. His face appears to twitch as they flow from one extreme to another. I should brace for what is about to flow from his mouth, but I never bragged about being smart. Why start now?

"Since when do we give up and put a teenager at risk?" Marxx steps from the brick wall he was resting his shoulder on to begin what I recognize as a verbal assault. "Since when do we give up, putting *everyone* at risk?"

I'm mute in my confusion.

"We had to choose Helena," I hear Dolph's subdued voice float from somewhere down the bricked hall. His voice echoes with something thicker than the vibration of the cement around us. "When you dropped, we had to choose."

"Stop it," Genny pleads, knowing where this is headed. She seems to crumple, folding her body down instead of sliding to the floor.

Despite her plea, Marxx pushes on. "When *you* gave up, when *you* fell, *you* put a teenager at risk. We couldn't make it to both of you." He hits each word with added heat letting me know who he truly feels is to blame.

I'm confused. I had made sure Genny made it safely to the boats. There was no need for them to have to choose between her or I.

"When you dropped, and they didn't see, Genny did. She didn't even hesitate. She slipped right past Collin to run to you." Peyton doesn't hold any anger. Like a disappointed father, he's just trying to explain my mistakes. "Ginjer was lost, but maybe if they didn't have to run to save Genny, or you, Helena, they might have had time to fight for her. They had to make a choice." Peyton pauses, letting his words sink in.

"I thought you were safe," Dolph's words stumble, fighting past the memory I have gifted him. "You were beside us when we started running but then everything just went to shit." He pauses, fighting past the images. "Ginjer was too far out. She let her panic break her. I headed for her. I didn't even really think about it. She was screaming and I just went to her. There were so many of them when they saw she was alone, and I just couldn't get through to her. I had her hand once or twice, but she kept getting pulled back. It's like they were toying with her instead of just…" He doesn't finish his thought; our minds do, though. "I heard Petyon screaming for Genny over all of it. Then I saw you, what I could see of you." His pain is painted in the hues of his eyes as he looks directly at me. "I couldn't get to Ginjer, but maybe I could get to you. I chose you."

His words have become such a soft whisper. Soft and fragile like crushed petals, his words litter the floors of my mind. They perfume the guilt-carved rooms as I realize, I killed Ginjer.

The hallway is a vacuum of silence. Everyone is watching me, waiting for me to see the taboo; the very thing I was warned about asking, I have not only asked, but demanded – and now my requests are being answered.

"We didn't make it before they circled you," Marxx shatters the silence first. "Genny did."

Peyton nods, adding, "Terrence and I grabbed Collin to keep him from following her when we saw the circle close. Terrence told me to take him to the boat. So, I did."

"We were halfway to you when Genny came running out," Dolph's bruise-filled voice pulls my attention to him. "We turned and headed to the boats, thinking you would be right behind her."

"Terrence was the first to see it. When Aimes screamed, he was already headed to you." Peyton shuffles as he explains, but he's unsure of how to continue.

Genny saves him the effort. "I already told her. She knows."

"So, you know you killed two more people?" Collin's voice creeps from the shadows where he has been sitting. "And it wasn't your men who saved you. It was one of ours. Yet, you have the nerve to ask us what caused us to be so broken and divided?"

The men shuffle around me. Some adjust to starting a fight. Others adjust to stop a fight. I don't adjust at all. As my father continues, I'm just going to stand here and let it happen.

"Want to know what else they aren't telling you?" Collin asks. "The reason for their blending, as he put it, is because if we didn't all bow down and do what they wanted, they were going to refuse to let Paula keep treating you. Paula wouldn't let them send you to some other place called 'the lake' without her. We either had to all step-in line or lose both of you to who knows where."

"I guess I know which way you voted?" My arms cross in my self-conscious way of deflecting when I ask him.

"Thanks to you, Genny is the only family I have left now. I wouldn't do anything to upset her. That's how I voted." Collin is standing now with an attempt of intimidation.

I hadn't intended for my sharp tongue to melt the space around me into a civil war. It just did that on its own.

"Funny. I don't remember being there when my real mom died." I felt myself smile as I heard myself say it.

Paula has become a professional at saving me from myself. She grabs me from the erupting discord, placing a hand over my lethal mouth and a threatening glare on her face. I will willingly fight hordes of rotting people, but an angry nurse is where I draw my line of bravery. I say nothing to argue with her while she pulls me from the fighting males behind me. Her glare even has the power to make Aimes cough to cover her giggles over what I had said. Genny is saying nothing. She follows in our wake with complete uncertainty over which side of the war she belongs – her fake uncle or her fake cousin.

"I should go back." I slow my steps as the commotion behind me gathers decibels.

"Why?" Aimes asks, her voice matching the confusion on her face.

"I caused that. I should go settle it," I explain.

"You didn't cause it and you're not going back there." Paula latches her hand onto my arm again. "If they are fighting, they are at least working stuff out. It's better than the invisible act they have been doing to each other. Let them punch each other for a while. Thanks to you, I'm really good at stitches now."

Paula pauses, reflecting on how she phrased it.

Waving my hand, I smooth her internal debate on how to retract her words. "It's fine. I'm not going to deny my many contributions to your continued education, but the lake thing, is that true?"

Paula looks almost guilty with my question. Her claw-like hand relaxes, adjusting invisible creases on the sleeve of my shirt. "Marigold found their weak spots quickly. Lawless embarrassed her, made her look weak by having her break her own rules. When they continued to taunt her leadership…"

I cut her off to say, "…as they do."

"…as they do," Paula copies my words, confirming them as correct, too, "she had to find a way to stop them."

"She used me?" I ask.

"She used us both," Paula corrects me. "I wouldn't let them take you there without me and the guys wouldn't let you out of their sight."

"And because the sight of the guys caused too much gossip, the way Rhett always does, Marigold did one better and said if they did the heavier of the jobs, the guys could have their stuff brought to them verses eating, or such, with everyone else." Aimes is staring down the darkened corridor as she explains. "Marigold found things for them to do. Basically, things they do alone, to separate them. They've become glorified housewife meat. She even pointed out how our guys do more useful things than Peyton and Collin, nailing the coffin shut by putting the rest of us in the useless line. It's just caused even more tension."

Aimes turns towards us exposing the worried look upon her pixie face. "We thought Selma was good. Hells, she was amateur night. This bitch is pro leagues."

"Why don't we just leave?" I shrug with something I think should be simple.

"We thought of that once you were stable," Paula begins. "Lawless and Marxx went all over this place looking for a boat while Rhett caused his idea of a distraction."

"Do I even want to know what that was?" I cautiously ask.

"Nope." Aimes quickly answers, but she smiles such a wicked smirk with her declaration.

Genny shakes her head but she, too, is at least grinning with the memory.

"No. You really don't," Paula rings in with their assessment. "Despite Rhett's little act, they couldn't find any boats. Leigh said they are kept on the lake. This way it prevents people from coming and going as they want to from the fort."

My face contorts with my confusion. "Then how were we picked up with boats?"

"Remember when I said pro leagues? This lady keeps the big boats at the lake and only small row boats by the fort," Aimes explains, filling in the holes for me.

"Okay, how do we get to this lake?" I ask the three sets of eyes watching me, but they don't answer, all for different reasons. One, they don't know. Two, they are afraid I may go alone. Three, they are afraid the men may go alone.

"Through the tunnel."

We each jump when we hear the new voice, with Aimes and Genny adding an extra sound effect from being startled. I don't know how long Leigh had been standing there, but there she was, standing just on the crest of a shadow watching our little debate. It concealed her perfectly with its irregular shape and her dark hair helping her blend into its embrace.

"Has someone not told you that's how you get shot?" Aimes is holding her chest, staring at Leigh with exasperation. "There are people walking around freaking eating people and you're all over here creeping around? That's exactly how you get shot!"

"I've heard about your aim," Leigh counters. "I'm not that worried."

"Oh, pasty over there has jokes," Aimes mutters. "Real funny, pasty."

Leigh doesn't show any concern over Aimes. She's watching me with the same grey eyes that seem to somehow always tiptoe along the vertebrae of my spine.

"There's a tunnel which opens at a dock behind the fort. There's a boat there. What you do with the boat," Leigh stalls, letting the silence fill in the gaps of her words, "that's up to you." She turns to slide back into the shadows.

"What's that mean, pasty?" Aimes shouts to Leigh's disappearing back.

From further ahead of us, Leigh answers. "You could leave, and never wonder about what really goes on here, or you could go to the lake, take a look around, and find your answers. It's up to you."

Leigh tosses her dare in the air behind her. It floats in her trail with the most beckoning of ways. Her voice has no weight to it, lending neither outcome any personal preference. Yet, somehow, that causes the dare to be so much heavier and almost personal, for a different reason.

"Oh, she's good." Aimes is overcome with her amusement. She crosses her arms over her chest with delight and admiration. "Like a fat kid and cake, Pasty knows you won't be able to help yourself."

"We don't even know where this tunnel is." I dismiss Aimes' observation.

Genny slides past Aimes and I. There's a pattern to her walk I recognize. It's the same self-destructive gait I have when exploring a path of provocations, despite the slim grasp of common sense I hold.

"I do," she tells us, without glancing to see if we are following her.

Aimes gestures to Genny's back. "This whole related thing," she says, "it's possible."

I feel my spine tighten with the thought of this teen being family. "It's going to get her killed."

"You're still alive." Paula smirks. As she follows the three of us, I can see she's mentally praising herself for that little dig.

"At what cost?" I ask the keeper of my health.

Paula answers by pointing to the teen we are following. "At whatever cost keeps the light in those eyes from fully distinguishing. It's not just you that she sees, Helena. She sees her aunt, your mother, and she can't fully lose the connection."

I don't respond to Paula. I turn my head, shielding whatever she may see in my eyes and focus them on Genny. Throwing myself at monsters has always been so much easier than facing my truths. It's why J.D. held such a grasp on my soul. He was my monster when monsters were only things we invented in the pitch of night, but the monsters broke him, and now I have nothing but truths to face. Throwing myself at monsters doesn't scare me anymore.

"We are really going to this lake thing tonight?" Aimes asks.

"You have something better to do?" Genny calls to her.

"Yeah, totally possible," Aimes hisses to me, upon hearing Genny's retort.

Genny sweeps her hair up into a high ponytail. She pulls it tight as if she is preparing to enter a battle. Maybe she is. Maybe, like me not too long ago, she's warring with herself over what she knows she is about to walk into. Maybe she's already pushing past the sounds and screams of those she's lost with fear of them tormenting her. Maybe she has her own carousel of beaten horses who circle her, as her doubts taunt her.

I watch her grow bolder with each step she takes. She settles into her gait, eyes locked forward, leading us to a place only she knows, without a care or thought about if we are following her down this bricked path of good intentions. She's already made her mind up to what she knows she has to do, and she'll do it, at whatever the cost, to keep some flicker of hope circling her soul. Maybe, just maybe, the whole related thing is possible.

Chapter 28

"If you fall off this dock, I will never forgive you," I threaten Aimes, but the laughter in my hushed whisper ruins it.

I'm holding her hand as she teeters into the metal rowboat with her normal theatrics. It rocks violently in the water from her indecision, and lack of commitment, to either the boat or the dock. Genny and Paula cling to the railings of the boat's hull. Neither are amused with the rapid bouncing nor the threat of being overturned as Aimes and I settle into our rows amid jeers and playful banter.

Freeing us from a wooden post, Paula exchanges a look warning of her constant exasperation with the two of us. Aimes, upon seeing the glare, the constant badge of maturity she is, sticks her tongue out at the other woman. Genny watches the exchange and I worry for a moment about her source of role models.

Finding the tunnel was uneventful. The door being unlocked and unguarded added another layer to Leigh's dare. The fact we accepted it added another layer to Genny's.

"How do we find this place?" Genny asks me, as if she wasn't the one leading us through this whole crusade.

"They came to the beach with two boats after Leigh sent the flare." Paula and I are already rowing away from the fort as I verbally muse. "They have to have the time to make it to the lake, get the motorboats, and head to the beach after seeing the flare."

"Don't stop now, Sherlock," Aimes goads, when my words stall.

Ignoring her, I let my mind roam. "It has to be somewhere close, but not too close so she can protect the main community from whatever is on it. Close enough to where it wouldn't be taxing to travel back and forth often to also tend to whoever is there."

"We don't have a motor. It can't be too far away," Paula joins in my musing. "And there would have to be some kind of beacon to guide people to it if there was a need to go there in the dark."

"Like that?" Without a pause, Genny points at something to the side of our boat.

"Like that," Aimes agrees.

To our left shines a faint, red light. It almost twinkles like a grounded star ahead of us, encouraging us to drift towards it. Paula glances over her shoulder to the back of the boat where I am sitting, steering to her pull. We share the same doubt over that flickering light. It's etched in the furrows of her concerned face.

This all seems too easy. Leigh just showing up at the same time we mentioned the place. Doors unlocked when the whole purpose is to keep people away. Now, like a welcome sign, here sits a convenient light to guide us to the shore.

The dares keep mounting, luring us to them with little restraints, and we follow their crumbs with little hesitations. The question being, how long until these crumbs turn into self-ingested poison. Like moths, we glide right to the light where it hangs in the trees above us until our little metal boat wedges herself into the mud of the shore.

"It's one of those solar-powered things people used to use around their driveways," Genny announces her discovery with a hushed whisper and astonishment.

She's right. It's been tied to a thick branch of an ancient tree. The flickering was from the way the wind nudges it, casting its one-dimensional ray to shine in random directions. The ease of the solar-powered battery pack keeps the concern of tending to it at bay. It's amazing in its simplicity.

Genny and Aimes, lost in their amusement of Marigold's cleverness, continue to debate in whispers. Paula and I are looking for the next clue, the next mark of ingenuousness, to be displayed. We visually search for another marker, a new star to follow from this rocky shore. A blaring banner of hints of what's located around us would even be more beneficial, but I'm not the type of girl to count her blessings.

Paula motions with her head towards a barely-there clearing among the tall trees and their surrounding brush. Under the sun, the trail may have been something spotted upon landing. Under the moon, it's near invisible; just a part in an overgrown hairline of the forest. The thick, evergreen branches whisper neither encouragements, nor warnings with their slight sway. These trees have stood witness to things which make our short moments around them meaningless, but just the same, they watch with half-invested interest.

"Ready for this?" My eyes are for the surrounding area, but my question is for Paula.

She sighs. "We're here. Might as well."

It's not the resounding vote of confidence Genny or Aimes needs right now. I let my facial expression share my thoughts with the woman these two have deemed the most logical among us.

Smiling, she corrects her statement. "It's supposed to be a place where their old and useless reside. I think you can handle this, Helena."

She motions for me to lead the way with a look that declares 'tag you're it'. Paula is over her responsibility to keep others safe. She's passing that chore to me, the one who has let so many fall for her poor choices and pride. She may have just signed all our death certificates. For fear of being correct, I don't point this out.

Aimes and Genny are stuck in our wordless volley. They watch us as two kids watch their parents' passive-aggressive fights. I paint my face with my false confidence and take the lead. It's just another day in our neighborhood and we are off to discover our new neighbors.

Once the shore is behind us, the trail becomes well-worn and gutted. Water still stands in the depths of the ruts. The collection of water and muck is as dark as oil, reflecting our lost faces back at us when we pass. The trees have stopped swaying. Their whispers are hushed, watching us trudge along the winding path. There are no markers to share secrets with us.

Genny jumps with every noise. Her eyes are wide, showing mostly white. Her thoughts project her fears. It isn't hard to understand with her behavior, she's mentally convinced herself that at any moment some unnamed horror will emerge from the nearest tree trunk. If it wasn't for Aimes' constant taunting, she would be completely undone.

Aimes tugs at every low hanging branch, letting it swing back to find Genny's face. Aimes isn't as rattled as our younger counterpart. With the things we have seen, a dark trail is a commercial break in the insanity, or perhaps, we've grown a touch insane. A leisurely stroll through a forest the Brothers Grimm would be envious to explore doesn't even ring our warning bells.

The minutes keep rolling, turning into curve after curve of the trail. I'm preparing my speech for reasons to turn around, completely settled in my defeat.

"That's cool." Genny points ahead of me, pulling my attention.

Tucked to the left of us sits a once proud, southern mansion. The hidden years haven't been kind to its crumbling porch and white, fading exterior. The many rows of broken windows seem to be missing teeth in a once-perfect smile. Pillars, which once stood as support and a welcome, have become smothered in the same vines climbing along the walls of the once grand home. With nature stretching her green fingers to reclaim it, the whole structure appears to be a footnote of memories long rotted and decayed.

Despite all of this, there are subtle hints of life among the ruins. Well-frayed lawn chairs nestle among the lawn in patterns implying small gatherings had been recently held. Curtains float from random windows, shielding neither the weather nor the space behind them. There seems to even be a glow cast behind random broken shards of glass. Someone, or something, is nestled inside.

Paula and I exchange a thousand unspoken words with our mutual glance to the other.

"Do we knock…" Aimes trails off with her question.

Genny tilts her head. Her ponytail bounces with mock cheer. "I don't think you're supposed to announce when snooping."

"Not everyone is a threat," Paula interjects.

"Better to think everyone is." Genny doesn't stand to listen to any rebuttals. She's already heading through the trees, skipping the wide loop the trail would have us use to arrive at the house.

Aimes crosses her arms as we watch Genny slip silently away. "Definitely related," she tells me with words and a glance. "There's a whole family trait of distrust and destruction."

"It's like you've never met my father?" I ask her back, as we follow Genny's lead.

"You're right. The idiot genes must run on the mother's side," Aimes agrees. "Your father doesn't have the balls to do even half the stupid things you two do."

"You're just jealous," I tease her.

"About not having balls? Maybe," Aimes shrugs as we continue on the path. "Apocalypses would be much easier if one didn't have to worry about tampons and toilet paper each month."

Paula nods silently, agreeing to the other woman's logic. For once, she's smiling a genuine expression of mirth, not just one of tolerance.

Genny is already climbing the porch's steps. My stomach rolls with her boldness. My mind has already gone to a thousand dark places with as many different scenarios as to what's beyond those wide, wooden doors.

Aimes and I wait behind the pillars to hear from Genny. She's already crouching down to peer into the nearest broken panel. Paula is roaming to the side, examining the side of the building. She shows no care or concern about being seen. Aimes points to her, her eyes widen to express her shock over Paula's actions.

"Leave the house," Paula says, still staring at something we cannot see.

"Why?" Genny whispers, unaware that whatever cover we had Paula has already discarded.

Paula doesn't answer. She slips from view, following whatever has her attention.

"At least if she gets us hurt, she can fix us." Aimes jumps down from the porch to follow the older woman.

I wait for Genny to fall in behind Aimes before I leave our discovery to explore a new one. I want to be sure none of the things my mind painted for me will slide through the white doors when our backs are turned, as they so often seem to do. The house sits, keeping her secrets. If we had disturbed her, or anything inside of her, she shows no signs of it. She sits as she has sat for the many past unfolding years - cold, disinterested, and lonely.

Paula walks with trance-like motions. Whatever she is seeing in the large, matching white barn behind the house, the rest of us don't, but we follow her with our own brands of curiosity. It's just as weather abused as the house. It projects a look of yearning to be demolished, like bones begging to be reburied. There are parts of the roof missing. Timbers can be seen peeking through, further hinting at what shambles await inside. Paula walks on, pulled by an invisible thread connected to some deep part of her. A thread no one else feels.

Aimes and Genny look back at me. Their faces wear unspoken questions, wondering if they are alone in their thoughts and confusion. They aren't. They just want me to be the one who asks.

"Paula…" I let my voice trail with the shared unasked question.

"There's a little girl in there," Paula responds. Her voice is soft with a mixture of wonder and concern.

Aimes twirls her finger near her temple hearing Paula's answer.

I cast a look of displeasure at Aimes. After all, who am I to judge people for seeing invisible little girls? Aimes rolls her eyes and continues to follow Paula's lead.

Paula doesn't wait for me to enter first, as she did on the trail. She pushes to test the weight of the doors, letting them bounce back with only a slight sound of protest. Pushing harder, she listens beyond the door's answer to see if there is a different sound of an answer deeper in the building. Just like the house, whatever these structures are keeping in them makes no sounds of introduction. For some, that may be a welcome change. For us, we have learned silence is sometimes more deadly than a scream.

With how they swing, there is no lock on the doors. Nothing to keep anything in or out. Paula finally commits to opening them, letting her eyes adjust to the darkness swallowing everything in our sight. My hand instinctively reaches for my knife, resting on its long handle to settle something fluttering in my stomach. I'm waiting for any hints, any murmurs of what may be watching us from the shadows, but the barn keeps her mysteries wrapped tightly in her shadow-covered arms.

When nothing lunges to hurt us, or worse, Paula nudges her way into the shadows. She's keeping to the center of the building. Gaping sections of the roof allow for the moon to pierce the looming darkness around us. The faint light turns the barn into shades of greys with the outer edges being the pitch of the night.

"You know there are flashlights along the wall here?" Aimes asks.

She's toying with the hanging objects. Pivoting back and forth from her torment, they almost mock our fears.

"Obviously, we didn't." Paula reaches around her to release one from Aimes' games.

The circular ray dispels any hidden opportunities of the space. Like a monk with his censer, Paula swings the light, chasing away the darkness encircling us. It reveals what one would normally discover in an old, abandoned barn. Stalls are framed with thick timber used to separate the animals they once contained. Various rusted instruments of farm life are strung up along the opposing wall. There are no eyes reflected in the shine of her light. Nothing is crouched, staring at us from the depths of the building. It's peaceful and still.

"Where is the girl?" Genny, encased in youth's bravery, has begun to walk the length of the stalls with her own flashlight showcasing each interior and still nothing moves.

Paula, refusing to admit to defeat or insanity, is casting her light towards the rafters. In her mind, or her pride, a floating child makes more sense than an invisible one. Finding nothing, she avoids our gaze.

Refusing to admit defeat, Paula mirrors Genny. She doesn't just walk to the horse stalls, she enters them. She is still holding to the belief she will stumble upon a small frame nestled into a makeshift hiding spot. I follow mutely behind them. Aimes' face conveys she's convinced Paula won't find anyone. I'm worried she may. Little girls have a way of showing up with sharpened teeth and terror-filled lullabies.

Walking to the last stall, I skip ahead of their efforts. The lock on this swinging door is different from the other's rusted counterparts. It's almost glossy with the metal looking new. Having been replaced recently, it's a stark contrast to the rest of what is around us.

I slide the bolt a few times. There is no tug from age. It slips back into the locking sleeve with no effort. This dare is metallic, and gloss covered. It waits to see if I will cave to the doors' mockingly, hushed whispers. I do. We both knew I would.

I let the wooden rectangle of the stall door be pulled by gravity. I watch, waiting to see if the hinges will disagree with the lock, telling of a different age. They don't. They don't even voice a whine of complaint with the heavy door pulling fully on them.

The other stalls are thick with molted hay. Genny's investigating steps release their acidic perfume into the air. In this one, what appears to be hay, or other light brown lawn clippings, have settled in a far corner, leaving the rest of the floor clear. Such a simple thing shouldn't trigger anxiety. It shouldn't roll my stomach with worry. It's the simple things, though, which seem to always do the most damage.

In my mind, Fate seems to giggle. She's calling her sisters, gathering them to see what I will do with what is before me. Truthfully, they already know.

"Hey," I whisper.

My hushed voice might as well have been a battle cry with how it startles them. Whispers are warnings. Things to be heeded. It's a simple thing.

Aimes is the first by my side. Genny isn't far behind her. Paula, just as torn over the hopes of finding who she saw and the fear of it, stands along the furthest timber of the stall.

Aimes is searching for some comical retort to my discovery. She discovers none. Her blue eyes stare into mine with apprehension and fear.

Genny kicks at the ground covering. It's clumsy. She's not willing to invest her whole leg into the action just in case the action bites her – literally.

When nothing moves, Genny kicks harder. She's pushing the hay further along the back wall. It scatters with each effort finally revealing a perfect square of newly colored wood. A thick length of rope has been strung through an opening resulting in an exposed loop. Once uncovered, it's obvious and yet somehow still holds an unanswered mystery as to what it is.

"Go ahead. Lift it. What could go wrong?" Aimes has recovered her wit.

Her comment motivates no one. It doesn't have to. The wooden door begins to lift itself. Light escapes from the framed hole. As its rays reach out towards us, we step back to escape them. The knife is in my hand before I realize I had grasped it.

A little girl's brown eyes with matching brown hair stares out at us. She is shocked for a moment before her child-like voice says, "Oh. Hi."

Paula exhales the breath she was keeping hostage. "Hi," she says, to who must be what started this whole adventure.

The little girl lifts the door the rest of the way, flopping it to the ground. "Come on," she says, slipping back down into the hole.

Aimes and I share an exasperated look to the other. My heart is still pounding from what I had expected to crawl from the space below us. It was just a little girl, as Paula had said. Once again, such a simple thing. All these simple things. The welcoming red beacon, the soft hay, the subtle hints with their whispers and warnings – simple things. Like the small shards of a long-ago broken picture frame, it's the little things, the simple things, which always cause the most damage.

Chapter 29

It's a sharp contrast under the ground to what is above. Someone, long ago, built the barn over a stone basement, but it's not the simple, outdated thing it once was. It's been renovated to appear almost hospital, or lab-like. Rooms have been built with doors of thick wood and thicker brass locks. Unlike the unguarded barn, something is definitely meant to be kept inside these doors.

The little girl skips ahead of us. She treats us as if we are long-time friends, but I can't remember ever seeing her. Her long hair is unkempt. The dirty watercolor of the brown sways in clumps instead of curls. The shine is not from health or youth but neglect. Otherwise, she looks to be cherished. There is no gauntness to her frame. Her eyes sparkle with life. She wears an old smock style dress with scuffed black boots, but not even the weight of such footwear slows her joyful passage in front of us.

"Where are we going?" Paula asks.

Her eyes have rested upon every point of the child's body. I thought it was of a mother's concern, but with her eyes cold and shoulders rounded, she's flipped her mind to medical. In the same way I grasp my knife when situations become unclear, Paula grasps onto her

215

rational mind. She lets it encase her thoughts like a protective shield, a barrier between herself and who she needs to be to be safe.

The girl stops skipping to turn back to us. Her forehead wrinkles with confusion before asking, "Aren't you here to check on them?"

"Yes," I quickly reply before anyone else. "She's new," I say, motioning to Paula. "We wanted her opinion on how they are doing."

The little girl looks from me to Paula. Paula smiles, nodding to assure the girl of what I said. I don't turn to see what the other two are doing behind me. With Aimes, one never can be sure.

"She's the new doctor, right?" the girl asks. She's looking to me, but side glancing at Paula.

"Nurse," Aimes corrects her.

The girl's forehead wrinkles again. "What's the difference?" she asks.

Aimes squats down to be on the same level as the little girl before answering. "Doctors just tell people what to do. Nurses are the ones who actually do it. Nurses equal action. Doctors equal lectures."

The girl looks horrified saying, "I don't like lectures!"

"Me either!" Aimes agrees, standing to her full height.

With the innocence of a child, the girl reaches her hand out to Paula. "I'm glad you're a nurse. I'm Wren."

Paula, figuring now is not a good time to do any corrections to Aimes' logic, extends her own hand to take Wren's. "I'm Paula," she says, shaking the offered hand.

"Cool," Wren smiles with sincere pleasure over meeting a nurse. "I just fed them all so they should be pretty well-behaved" Turning to me she asks, "You know which ones to watch out for, right?"

I don't. I don't even know what she is talking about. I lie. "Sure do."

"…and that's how we all died," Aimes whispers behind me.

I don't turn to acknowledge her comment. She's most likely correct. I smile at Wren and she smiles back before leading us to the next door.

Still wearing her smile of complete confidence in me, she slides the lock open. The smell hits me first. It rolls out with a familiar greeting.

A greeting we've all encountered too many times in the past. Wren is watching me, waiting to see what I do now. I keep my fear corked, sealed tight in the bottle of panic. I can't let it leak onto my face with her watching.

Genny takes a step back, pulling Wren's attention to her. Our bluff may not be as strong as I hoped.

"Don't worry," Wren says, watching Genny try to recover. "Their meal wasn't fresh. I had to pull some old stuff from the lake. It's not that bad."

Her words were meant to bring some inch of comfort. They resulted in a mile of the opposite direction.

"The lake?" Genny, even as she doesn't really want to know, asks anyway.

Wren has a moment of confusion again. "Yeah. The lake. Where we store the dead? They have to eat somehow and sometimes it's just less of a mess to get the old stuff."

"Small blessings," Paula says with a smile, recovering for us. It's thick with sarcasm but Wren being a child misses her true tone.

"Well, have fun," Wren says, as if all of this is just a normal day for her. She leaves us with the open door standing wide with an invitation. Before she makes it back to the ladder leading above us, she turns, saying, "Be sure to make sure they are all locked up before you leave. Okay?"

She doesn't wait for our answer. She is already up the ladder and gone. We listen to her feet overhead retreating towards the door that started this rabbit hole. Once the barn doors shut, it's just us, the door waiting to welcome us, and things we must remember to lock up before we leave.

"Do I still have to go first?" I ask, stalling.

"Wuss." Genny pushes past me, taking the lead I was dreading.

I look toward Aimes waiting for her to invent another joke about family traits. She just shrugs, holding her hands in the air. She already knows we are both sharing the same thoughts.

"There was a time we wouldn't have been able to keep you from that room," Paula says. She's watching me with concern, and something tinted with disappointment for letting Genny go first.

"What's the matter? Worried you won't have anyone to stitch back up?" Aimes asks, as she, too, pushes past to follow Genny. "Zombie Barbie is only activated when someone is in trouble. Don't worry Pauls, if one of us starts to get eaten you'll have plenty of work to do."

"How much to stitch her mouth shut?" I ask Paula, as I too follow them in.

"You're not the first to ask," Paula responds, with a smile and a song.

The smell doesn't become any better when we cross the threshold. The lights are low, lending to the smell feeling thicker, suffocating. Genny and Aimes may have entered first, but they haven't gone far into the room. Both are still hanging in the safety the hallway lights provide.

As the lights overhead brighten to reveal the room better, I wish Paula hadn't found the dimmer. What is hiding in these shadows is everything and more from what was missing in those above us. Cages, like those of a pound, are stacked on top of the other almost to the ceiling of the room. Inside the cages are mute dolls, gore-covered, and watching us with the blank faces Risen wear. They hold their bodies as if someone had pushed pause, freezing the room in a moment of time. Fingers are wedged inside mouths dripping with liquid my brain doesn't want to admit to seeing. Hands are pushed into what appears to be limbs, or various body parts, waiting to scoop the meat from the bones. Their eyes are the only things moving. They have been watching us way longer than we were even aware they were here.

"Shit." Aimes sums up our mutual feelings perfectly.

"Are they all kids?" Genny asks. She's lost in the waves of horror, fear, and revolt with what the cages hold.

I step closer to the first cage. The child inside doesn't move. She's still frozen, paused with her meal hanging from her cupid's bow of a mouth. Her eyes follow me. She doesn't react as prey or predator, just watching and completely passive.

"They aren't reacting," I comment. "Not a single one is even trying or making a single sound."

My comment brings a different mood to the room. With the beasts being passive, bravery is easier found. Genny roams the rows, looking into each cage. With her face pressed almost to the bars, not a single creature makes a motion to grab her.

The children range from tiny toddlers to maybe four-year-olds. Their clothes are hanging on with slim hopes for tomorrow. Their many frays confirming the tragedies. Their decomposition should be more noticeable, but other than obvious signs of death, their bodies appear to be intact.

Aimes and Paula are flipping through the charts attached to each cage. Their faces hold different measures to what they are reading. Aimes' face displays her shock. Paula displays her pure interest.

"They have charted everything," Aimes says. "Literally."

She lets the last word hang as a complete sentence in itself. It is.

Paula begins to mummer through her charts. "Date of death. Type of death. Eating habits. It's all here."

"Yeah, but what does this mean?" Aimes tilts her chart towards Paula's trained eyes.

"Not sure. It's on all of them," Paula replies.

"What is?" I ask, as I stare into the dead eyes of the little girl in front of me.

"A name. Just a single name." Paula comes to my cage and opens the chart to show me. "Some have the same name over and over."

I begin to flip through the chart. "Parent's names, too." I point the page to Paula. "Do you know these names?"

I know she does. I know because she's flipped her mask to cover her thoughts. She stands completely upright, turning to the cage near us. She's not looking for random facts, anymore. She's looking for a certain highlighted page. Going from cage-to-cage she turns only to the page I showed her. Her mask never slips, but her hands start to shake.

"These are all people from the fort," Paula tells us. "These are their kids."

She's staring at the little boy in front of her with a different type of horror. This horror surpasses the horror of what he is and rolls into the knowledge of who he was; a little boy collected and kept.

"And these are the people who are able to breed." Genny has found a different chart. She flips through the pages with the same frustration Paula had done upon finding her chart. "Our names are on here," she says, handing the pages to Aimes.

"Well that's a first," Aimes replies as Genny points to their names. "No one has ever said I'd make a good mother before. Good in bed, sure. Good for breeding, not so much."

"None of this makes sense." I'm pacing the row of cages near me as my thoughts pace in my mind. "Why keep them?"

"Better question," Aimes interrupts. "What's in the other rooms?"

Paula drops the chart she was studying. It rattles the cage wall and finally, the creature inside reacts. It's a deep growl, pulled from the bottom of a pit of pure hatred. A sound a three-year-old girl should never make pulls similar echoes from around the room.

There is a shift in the children. They no longer just watch, but crouch low, posed to spring into a form of either self-defense or attack. Their eyes don't shift from each of us but sway, keeping a note of where each of us stand. Something about their defensive nature is more unsettling than the mindless slaughter we are used to seeing from these half-dead nightmares. There are three who make no noise. They aren't crouched nor do they show any signs of apprehension. Their eyes glint with something familiar, something unnerving and calculated.

"Guess we've worn out our welcome," Genny says. She's stepping backward, afraid to turn her back to the room. Even in cages, she doesn't trust them. "Let's go see the other rooms."

I'm the last out of the room. Only when they have reached the safety of the hallway lights do they turn their backs to the children. I don't. I'm watching the three, who are still watching me, as well. The rest of the room has slowly settled back to the meal we interrupted, but those three, their bodies slide the length of their cages to keep me in sight. Their eyes aren't the glazed, empty orbs of the others. Their eyes almost shine with their thoughts. Something human is still in there. Something dark and twisted, but human.

"Helena," Aimes hisses, when I don't follow them right away. "If this is what's in this room, we may need Zombie Barbie for the others. Get out here."

"So nice to be needed," I mutter back to her.

Closing the door, I steal one more glimpse at the trinity of terror. They steal one more glimpse at me, too. Just before I close the door with hopes to seal these nightmares behind it, the oldest of the girls smiles at me. She waves those tiny, gnawed fingers in a goodbye she shouldn't be able to understand.

"What?" Aimes asks, seeing me leaning against the closed door.

My mind is trying it's best to dispute what I just saw. It's throwing all the facts and proof from my past against the walls of the memory, but the vision of her waving stands firm despite all the logic. Death's army has new tools and she's so very proud of her children.

"Nothing," I tell Aimes. "Everything. I don't know."

"Genny and Paula have found nothing but more charts and papers in the other rooms," Aimes states, looking relieved.

"Then we go back to the house." I'm nodding with my words, as if that will make them sound more of a good idea. "I want to know what else is out here before we head back."

"You think there's more?" Paula asks from the doorway of a room.

"You think there isn't?" I return.

The silence among us is the answer. We know there is. We just don't know if we want to know what it is.

"We still haven't found the lake," Genny offers. "Wren said that's where she got their food."

"She said it was the old stuff. I wonder what the new stuff would have been?" Aimes joins in our debate. She and Genny alike, have crossed their arms, hugging themselves for some comfort due to where their minds have traveled.

"Where does a child get such things?" Paula's shudder is visible.

Paula is traveling a motherly path. The rest of us are tripping along mental images of things only movies once held; things we thought were impossible have become warning tales for others.

I don't wait for my mind to travel too far into the darkness. My darkness has teeth, and songs of twisted comfort. My darkness isn't just a space to keep me awake at night. Mine is a whole dwelling of things waiting to remind me of what can go wrong should I stay too long. In the darkest of the rooms, is a little girl watching me through blonde hair with blue eyes that condemn better than any holy scripture translated by man. I don't stay in my darkness long. As I climb the ladder in silence, a part of me knows I'm always one step from landing there forever.

"To the house we go," Aimes calls from behind me. "What could possibly go wrong?"

"Nothing," I call back, helping Genny onto the barn floor.

"And everything," Aimes whispers.

"And everything," I agree.

Her pink-streaked hair isn't as vibrant as it was when we started that day in the bar. Her brown roots are seeping through, coloring her blonde with truth. As she stands now, hugging herself while waiting for us all to be regrouped, she too isn't as vibrant or playful. It's not just her hair which has become truth-covered, but her reality, too.

Truth can be a damning thing. She robs one of joy while providing glimpses of hope. She steals with one hand, while placating with the other. The trick to Truth is to understand her game. Unfortunately, she makes up the rules to her game as she wants. Right when you think she's going to be kind, and everything is going to be okay, she shows her other hand. As of late, her other hand is blood-covered, and sin-scented, reaching from dark corners and thick, hidden woods. It's this hand we've come to learn is always waiting for us. Everything could go wrong, and she'll smile with delight as we fall.

Chapter 30

"Where do you want to start?" Genny asks me.

We are standing in what is left of the kitchen. It has just enough appliances to understand what the room is intended for. The wallpaper hung long ago with pride is almost bleached to non- existent patterns. Scraps are drifting, hanging limply from where they were once glued in long rows. The sink is full of dirty pots and such items, lending proof this house isn't empty of inhabitants.

Aimes strolls over to the back door we entered through. Without any style of a word of warning, she bangs the screenless door a few times against the frame of the doorway. It's as loud as gunshots with the deep silence enveloping the dwelling.

"What the fuck?" Genny asks, forgetting to hide her teenage slips among the adults. I should disapprove, but it's perfectly phrased.

"What?" Aimes asks, appearing to be confused by our reactions. "Look, if something is going to barrel out from somewhere to eat me once it realizes I am here, I want to be by a door. A clearly marked exit. You two can play murder buffet if you want, but unless it's my eyebrows, I prefer to keep my body thread free. No offense, Paula."

"None taken," Paula half-heartedly responds.

She's listening for any sounds Aimes may have triggered, instead of listening to Aimes herself. Our eyes follow hers, traveling the length of the ceiling above us. The silence remains tight and heavy like a tomb.

"Well, that's a plus, right?" Genny asks. "If something bad was here, she would have woken it? We would know?"

Genny is asking the question as if she's a child wanting a mother to rationalize the fear away. She watches the three of us with hopes we will calm her with some truths, or even a well-told lie. It's times like these I remember how very young and fragile she really is despite the bravado she hides behind.

"Let's hope," Paula offers to calm her.

"Let's find out." Is what I offer. I've never been the one for comforting but confronting, that I do well.

I pull the knife to my side when I exit the kitchen. It fits into my hand like a lost lover, molding to my flesh with warnings of what may come. My boots click along the discolored wood, tapping with each cautious step. The small sounds seem impossibly large in the slim hallway.

Nothing looms around any of the corners we cross. There's no smell of death in any of its branded scents lingering in the air. The house feels empty, deserted, and forgotten with the perfume of neglect clinging to its surfaces.

"All's that left is up," Aimes says, as we stand at the bottom step.

"Any more doors you want to bang first?" I ask her.

"Any more opportunities to stall?" Aimes banters back.

"Asks the one who's always in the middle," I tell her, refusing to admit that I am stalling.

Stairs are slowly becoming my new style of purple doors. They hold the same stomach knotting fear when I see them; the same unanswered puzzles which are normally nothing like what their boxes promise.

"You'll just waste your time going up there," a voice calls from the front of the house. "Unless you risked everything just to say hello to our elderly? Did you risk it all for them?"

Marigold stands proudly in the rounded archway. She's traded her robes for jeans and a long grey sweater. In front of her is the little girl we had met in the barn, Wren. Wren waves to us, but Marigold wears a smile of warning. Like ethylene, she appears sweet, but too much trust in her would be deadly and she's been saving several doses for me.

"We were just bored," Genny speaks first. "The men were being stupid so we thought we would get out. You know, like a girls' night?"

Genny tries to look convincing. Her brown ponytail even seems to sway with the show. She tugs on her pink flannel shirt trying her best to look harmless, just one of the girls. She cocks one hip, as if resting on the banister while exploring old homes is our normal evening outing.

Marigold looks to each of us to see if we will contradict Genny's story. I shouldn't. I should for once just be silent and see where things go, but I won't.

"Why are there dead kids under the barn?" I ask without hesitation.

Genny turns to me. Her face explodes in an expression of disbelief. She looks at me like I just ratted her out to some authority figure. Maybe I have, but with Wren standing with Marigold, chances are we were ratted out some time ago.

Marigold's deadly smile widens. Her eyes almost light up with excitement when I asked. Running her hands through what she can of Wren's brown clumps of hair, she appears to be petting a cherished pet, not a small child.

Marigold says to me, "I was wondering how long we would play this charade. I knew that moment in the dining area when I first saw you, you would be bold, direct, truthful even. I wondered how long it would be until this day arrived. I must admit, it came much quicker than I had anticipated."

She takes Wren's hand in hers and begins to walk to one of the larger rooms of the home. We follow as she continues to talk.

"Where did you find Leigh?" Marigold asks.

She leaves the question to the room, but I know she's asking me.

"In a daycare. Locked in a room." I take the bait.

"Was anyone else there?" Marigold asks.

"Alive or dead or in-between?" Aimes flashes a warning look to me when she answers. She's once again picked up on something I have yet to.

Marigold stops. She spins slowly to look at us, wanting to see our faces with her next question. "Were there any children there?"

"Alive or dead or in-between?" Aimes asks, again.

Marigold is chewing on her words. Her jaw moves with either the self-control she is fighting for, or the correct phrase to get past Aimes' riddle.

"In general?" Paula asks. "Yes, there were children there."

"What happened to them?" Marigold is looking at me with her question. Once again, we were ratted out long ago.

"We killed them," I tell her what she already knows.

"The boy?" she asks.

"Oh, pick me!" Aimes excitedly says, raising her hand as if waiting for a teacher to call upon her in class. "I shot him. Well, he stabbed Hells. So, I did what besties do. Murder!" She widens her eyes with the last word, making it the exclamation point in more than just tone.

"Why? Did you know him?" Genny tilts her head with her question dripping every ounce of mock sincerity.

Marigold is staring at the two the way a cat does its prey. She says nothing but turns to continue whatever path she had started on. She drags Wren along with her, making the little girl stumble in attempts to keep her feet under her.

"Did you know him?" I ask, in a nicer tone than Genny had as we again follow her.

"Yes. You could say I knew him," Marigold answers me, leaving no eagerness to explain further.

"And those kids under the barn? Did you know them?" I push for some answer; something to settle the many currents of questions running through this whole night.

"I know them," Marigold tells me. "But it'd be so much easier to just show you."

"Show us what, crazy lady?" Aimes asks. It's not her best punchline, but at least she is still trying to hold on to her spark.

"Why there are kids under the barn," Marigold answers with the same cyanide style of a smile.

I look to Paula when I notice Marigold left out the word 'dead'. She arches her eyebrows quickly as her answer and as her plead to let it go. Pursing my lips, I nod, letting her know, for once, I'll play along. I'll even play nice, so to say.

When released from Marigold's hold, Wren runs to push back a corner of an old rug that serves as the only décor in the large room. It's threadbare, sun-bleached of most of its once red color, but it did the job of hiding yet another trap door.

"The most paranoid people in the world built this house," Aimes loudly whispers.

"Nonsense," Marigold says, still with her back to us. "Where do you think they kept their spare meat and such things?"

"Obviously, under the barn. Maybe in a lake?" Aimes answers boldly. I may have agreed to play nice with others, but she did not. She never does.

If Aimes struck a nerve, Marigold doesn't show it, at least not from where we are standing. Wren doesn't hesitate to scoot down another matching ladder upon hearing Aimes' answer. We may not see what is across Marigold's features, but whatever Wren saw was enough for her to hurry the show-and-tell along.

With a defiant glance towards those of us behind her, Marigold also descends into whatever is below us. Before she fully disappears, she stares at me with a mixture of a challenge and a warning. Whatever she is hiding under there, and as eager as she claimed to be to share it with me, there's a part of her warring with doing it. Glad to see my reputation still holds everywhere we go.

"We aren't really going to follow the female version of zombie Peter Pan down there are we?" Aimes hisses.

"Never heard you use the 'z word' before," I reply. My feet are already taking me to the ladder while my mind weighs out the pros and cons.

"Been reading a lot of books. Oddly enough, they seem to collect that kind here." Aimes takes my arm, stopping my slow progression. "We do a lot of stupid shit, I agree, but this seems the cherry of our adventures. Like the sprinkles of all sprinkles."

Her eyes are pleading with me and I'm lost as to why now she is filled with fear. She's right. We have done a lot of stupid things, but this is the first time she's showed this level of fear over doing them.

"Since when did you read?" I ask her, trying to flip her back to the banter she uses as her shield to hide the little girl inside of her.

Paula doesn't miss a thing, saying "Figured you were one more for the pictures type and not the articles."

"Fine. Make me into your verbal pinata," Aimes begins, dropping her grasp on my arm, but her eyes still hold the fear even if her voice is steady with false anger. "But don't come to me when she's stitching you up again because you became a pinata for whatever the nanny to the dead has waiting for us down there."

Aimes said the last part loudly. She doesn't do her battles with a knife in hand. She does them with snark in mouth. Her tongue can become sharper than any blade I've ever held and faster than any gun I've fired. Like a fighter prepping themselves for battle, Aimes just donned her armor. It's dented, unsecure, but it's hers and sometimes that's the only thing that matters when the battle finds you.

"It's fine," I tell her fragile nerves. "What could possibly be worse than the barn?"

"Oh, you just had to put that in the universe?" Aimes asks, with trademarked eyeroll.

She's right. I should know better than to put such dares into the air around us. I should know the evil sisters are always waiting, listening for their opportunity to remind us who is in charge. They wait in the shadows to teach us there is no escape; to make us always question – are we the hunters, or are we the prey? As I take the first step to descend into the lower, hidden level, I know the game of survival means we are always both. At any given time, we are always both.

Chapter 31

What's under the house has its own stains of immorality. It holds its own scent of acidic corrosion with their flesh festering under what Marigold has done to these people. It holds sounds of depravity and insanity and we have found ourselves standing right in the center of it all.

There are no cages this time. Thick chains around necks and waists hold adults in random places along the stone wall and dirt floor. They are in different stages of decomposition from their deaths. Each adds a different layer of stench around the small room, matching their fates.

The metal snake-like chains slither, testing their limits before striking. Their eyes watch us with fascination over the prospect of new toys to break and bend with their twisted urges for delight. Growls from the deepest hollows of their throats reverberate along the stones. It echoes inside our bones with a warning. A message understood at the very basic of primal level. We just became the prey.

Marigold stands tall. Her silver clumps of hair tightly round into dreads catch the low wattage of the bulbs. The strands twinkle with the same shine in her eyes. Like a mother proud of her children, she stares at each one of these things. Her eyes take in every aspect of them, making some mental note to jot down later while Wren sits with her back against the farthest wall. She, too, is watching them, but her small face doesn't hold the same pride or enjoyment as Marigold's.

"What is this?" Paula is the first to find her voice.

Mine is still caught in the back of my throat. It's clawing the tender flesh, screaming against everything I am doing as I stand here willingly in the middle of such depravity. The reality of what is around us has tied my feet with fear and pumped my heart with panic.

"Who," Marigold corrects. She is kneeling next to a young woman. "Who, Paula."

Marigold runs the tips of her fingers through the woman's red hair spilled along the dirt floor. It mimics the pools of blood I'm sure she's spilled with its ruby tint of deep red to almost black. Her skin is the pale grey of death, but her eyes hold the color of life. Those jade eyes watch us with boredom. If she's aware of how close her next meal is, she shows no reaction to Marigold's touch.

"This is Ranya," Marigold explains. She continues to pet the woman's hair and somehow, it's the most unsettling thing I have yet to see. "She's new. I have great hope for her."

"Hope?" Paula asks. There's something in her voice with hints she already has an understanding.

Marigold looks to the other woman with a smile, confirming what Paula's voice held.

"That's impossible." Paula has lost sense of herself. She's walking down the middle of the chained possibilities of death to stare at them, just as Marigold had done. "It wasn't supposed to happen like this."

"Oh, it didn't," Marigold says standing. "These are the ones who have survived the different blendings. I've lost so many trying to save these."

"Paula?" Genny's fragile voice holds so many questions.

Paula sighs, almost in tears she, explains what we aren't understanding. "To keep combating the sickness the shots were made to eradicate, the antidote's DNA has to keep evolving. It was supposed to take pieces of the illness each time it mutated and then mutate itself into the cure in the human body. Each time it would grow a stronger strain of itself, fixing what the host lacked to fight the illness.

"Do you remember the strain Travis and Selma had? That was a mutated version, something stronger to go to third world countries where their living situations aren't as regulated. It's the reason we were seeing a different type in the woods. They were smarter, using the weaker ones as pawns. The strain has already taken a different hold on those hosts, doing what it was programmed to do; take what the host was lacking and make it better, stronger.

"Marigold has figured out how to make it progress even further. By having the hosts infect each other, it blends the different types of strains the hosts have made making an even stronger version of the mutation."

"Whoa!" Aimes holds her hands up to stop Paula. "You said you don't become a racoon when a racoon bites you. So now we can become racoons? Because I really don't want to become a racoon, Paula!"

"I hadn't thought so." Paula's shoulders hang. As if she's at fault, she's becoming more defeated with each explanation. "But when I saw what was happening to Selma, I was afraid it had started. They introduced the stronger strain without ever really knowing what the real consequences would be."

"Okay, double whoa," Aimes stops her again. "What do you mean hosts infecting hosts?"

It isn't Paula who clarifies the choice of words. Marigold holds the arm of Ranya up for us to see. All along the greying limb are small bites. Some of the bites are clean with clear prints of tiny teeth. Others are raw, weeping something thicker than blood from the shredded flesh. Reality hits like bricks, pulling my brain into the undertow of blood-filled water. The nightmare all starts with the children.

"Patrick, the young man you murdered, had the right idea. He was just going about it the wrong way. He thought he could keep her by using the children. Those children were not the carriers he hoped they would be, though. So, naturally, she didn't come back to him, as he thought she would. Plus, she was already sick when he let the children bite her. You can't cure the old sickness with the old sickness. It has to be from the improved cure."

"It's not a sickness," I correct her. "And they don't come back from it."

"You're wrong," Marigold stands, rushing towards me to clasp my shoulders firmly. "I lost so many when it first hit. When this became our normal life, losing people left and right to what our friends and family had become, I knew there had to be a way to save them. I was right! I couldn't save the first of them, but now, when they become sick, we don't lose them! Not completely. I have discovered how to keep their minds, their humanity, making them safe again. No one has to die, ever again."

"Then why the chains?" I ask those burning eyes staring into mine.

Marigold wilts a little. "Not everyone agrees with me, yet. Sometimes the sickness overtakes them towards the end, but Ranya hasn't shown any signs of the aggression. I may even take her home, let them see what the future can hold."

"We can't stop the spread of it. There's too many already out there, but we can change the spread, making the sickness something we can coexist with instead of fear. The future infected won't be what we are used to running from. We won't have to lose our loved ones, anymore."

"You've clearly lost your mind," Genny whispers with her shock.

"No!" Marigold rushes to stand beside a male. "I'll prove it!"

The male watches her with eyes filled with a look of hesitation. His once pressed black suit shows the abuse of his death and his new life. The white dress shirt has yellowed, appearing stiff, where soft cotton once yielded a look of sophistication. He chose to dress for his death, unknowing that death for him would be never fully arriving.

He doesn't lunge for Marigold as I would expect him to do. He's watching her with the same appreciation a snake has for its prey. He watches, waiting to see what this woman is going to do while plotting his plan.

"This is Marco." Marigold points to the man. "His little girl got sick and was taking a turn for the worse over the winter. We all knew it was only a matter of time until she would pass away. I went to him; told him I could keep her alive. I told him she didn't have to die, and he agreed to let me take her to the barn. I saved her! I saved his little girl and she's there now.

When I tried to reunite them, she panicked and bit him. It was unfortunate, but the bite changed him, too. I thought I had lost him, but I haven't." Marigold smiles, waiting to reveal her final magic act. "Say hello, Marco."

"Hello," Marco says.

The words fall from his swollen lips like lead. The syllables are hard, almost two different words, but there is no denying what we heard. Nor can we deny the smile upon his face after saying it.

"Nope! Nope! Nope!" Aimes is already climbing the ladder, rushing to escape what new terrors Marigold has presented to us.

"They keep their minds!" Marigold is shouting at us. "Not just the adults, but the children, the children keep their minds! I can cure them! Death never has to take another person we love!"

I stare from Ranya, a broken doll spread across the floor with all of the emotions to match, to Marco, who still smiles at our shock. His eyes are filled with an understanding no creature of death should be able to hold. Just the sight of them is enough to turn bowels to something loose and flowing in fear. Their sounds were already enough to stir the deepest of dread, but hearing his voice form a word, a greeting, is a different kind of shock.

I'm the last to climb the ladder. I use every inch of sight allowed to me to watch Marco as I climb. As the height takes him from my view, I hear him again. I hear him and I know I will never be the same.

"Goodbye," Marco calls to me with a voice thicker than any human's I've ever heard. The words almost gurgle from his throat, spilling forth with a wet thickness.

Marigold's laughter follows us from the house. It clings to us, haunting us with the sound of what it really means. We haven't found a home. We have stumbled, yet again, into another hell. A hell which threatens to drag us into new depths of madness, deeper than the levels Travis had taught us. Travis had used the shots for damnation. Marigold is using them as salvation and damning her people in the process.

We don't speak to anyone when we arrive back to the safety of our hall. Our faces wear expressions of warnings, and no one is brave enough to try to change them. No one pauses to ask if we are okay or even offers to help us. For once, I am happy our stone-cold looks and tight lips spread apart those who would otherwise find themselves in our path.

As I lay upon my cot with my thoughts a haunted graveyard of my past, I ache for a mother I never knew. I ache to be something small and protected, someone sung to sleep and told that monsters aren't really real or under my bed. My heart beats in its denial. I know the monsters are real and they aren't under my bed. The monsters are in my head and the danger they now offer is very real. Closing my eyes to escape, I still see those small fingers waving goodbye and her smile to match the warning in my heart. The screams of my past begin their nightly lullaby. As their voices join into one, I wonder what my mother's voice sounded like as she was ripped apart in a rest area bathroom months ago.

Chapter 32

"You going to share where you three went last night?" Lawless sinks his body to the ground to sit next to me.

I can feel his brown eyes picking apart every inch of me, seeking some hint as to what has made the three of us so sullen and distant today. I've been watching the children play in their age-divided groups, as children do. I watch the parents, wondering if they know what their children they have handed over to Marigold have become. Do they lay awake at night thinking of those souls? Or, has Marigold convinced them with her distorted words that they are safe, enjoying themselves in their new life, with their new minds?

I cave to the feeling of needing to be fragile. I don't answer him. Instead, I lay my head on his lap. I can feel his body tense from my action. I don't blame him. We've been so touch-and-go as of late, with both of us lost in our constant mood swings, he's probably afraid of what my moment of weakness means. Softly his hand moves my hair from my face. He touches me with hesitation, waiting to see where this mood goes before becoming invested in it.

"What was it, Hells? Where did you go?" Lawless asks again. His voice is timid.

"We can't stay here," I tell him, trying to find the words to fully paint the picture of what happened last night. "She's turning them. She's infecting them to experiment, to keep them alive."

Lawless doesn't say anything. He isn't toying with my hair anymore, but his body is more tense upon hearing my words than he was before.

"You saw the house?"

His words pull my body upright. As my mouth becomes dry, my heart flutters in such a pattern my stomach answers it. My whole body becomes a war of shock and anxiety.

"You knew?" I whisper it, refusing to say the accusation too loud.

Lawless exhales a long breath, melting to the ground. He watches the clouds over us, delaying to find the right words or fighting against a memory my words cause him.

"Paula didn't understand why you weren't waking up," he begins. "She kept saying without some form of imaging she can't know if you've suffered internal damage she couldn't see. It was all a waiting game.

"Marigold came to me. She said there was something she wanted to show me. I played along, leaving Rhett to watch over you and Paula just in case the woman had some thoughts of still removing you.

"When we got to the house, she kept talking about a way to save you. If things were to get worse, she could save you. She took me downstairs and I saw what I imagine you saw. She told me we would never have to be without you. That I would never have to be without you.

"I didn't listen. I left. She told me if I told anyone, she would know and she would make sure I never saw you, again."

I don't answer right away after his revelation. I let it slide into the depths of my mind, lulling over what he's said before I say too much.

"And now that I'm awake you didn't think it would a good time to tell us what she really is?" My voice is still hushed, fighting to suppress the rage threatening to overtake me. "Let the others know what she's doing?"

He's still searching the sky overhead, casually saying, "I thought about it."

Exasperated by his aloofness, I punch his arm, trying to achieve any emotion from him. "And why didn't you?"

He rolls to his side to face me, asking, "If I had just told you what you saw last night, would you have believed me?"

"No," I honestly answer.

"You would have wanted to go see, like you did."

"Yes," I answer him, again. I have a feeling I already know where he is taking me with his logic.

"And then what would have happened?"

"We would have been outraged and shut it down."

"And then what would have happened?" he echoes.

"A fight."

"And then what would have happened?" He shows no delight in the tour-of-things-to-come he's taking me down. His eyes are almost sad.

"The high school all over again," I answer, ending the tour.

Lawless settles back on the ground, returning to his cloud watching. "I've thought about it over and over. Do I risk it? Do I just keep quiet? I keep asking myself, what would J.D. do? I don't like any of those answers, either."

"Earlier," I test my words, saying them gently, "when I asked you about how everything was falling apart? Is this why?"

Lawless inhales sharply, knowing a nerve has been exposed to the brisk air. "I felt like a piece of shit. Here I was telling them to just do it, just do what they ask, and this whole time this old woman was smiling at me, knowing she had me.

"They thought it was because of my worry over you, and part of it, yeah, it was. Mostly it was because I didn't know what to do. This wasn't the type of thing I could just pull one of them aside and talk about. It would have exploded. I couldn't risk it with you still being down and Paula waging her own war over your care.

"After a while, I couldn't tell them what to do anymore. It didn't sit well. I let them do what they wanted, go where they wanted. We fell apart because I couldn't hold us down like I should have; I couldn't keep them in line with anything other than the threat of what may happen to you. They took that, needed someone to blame, and poured that anger all over the other group. It was easy for them and I watched it all because it was easier than having to say the truth."

"So, what are we going to do?" I ask, still hushed and restrained.

"We are going on a supply run. Queen Bitch says we need things, and no one is better at doing what is needed than our crew," he mimics her words with a salty tone of insult before adding, "Maybe it will be a step back to where we once were." Lawless smiles. A genuine smile of excitement as he stands. "And then we will figure out what we are going to do about her."

"Or Marxx will finally explode and kill us all," I offer a second possibility.

"Or Marxx will finally explode and kill us all," he smirks.

"Be honest," I say, as he pulls me to my feet. "You just want to see your bike."

Lawless pulls me close. He wraps his arms around me, saying with a mischievous grin, "We had good times on that bike."

"We've had good times in my truck," I toss back, sharing his smile and remembering the nights we were on the run.

"Yeah. It was a little odd with your dad so close."

"Since when did that bother you?"

"Since there weren't any walls to hide behind." He chuckles.

"I think Peyton was more judgey than my dad. It seems my dad is used to me stepping out."

Lawless' smile slides from amusement to caution. "Do you ever wonder about her? How your life might have been different if she had raised you and not Carol?"

"No," I answer, fully aware my classic mood swing has ruined the moment. "I wonder more about her death. I wonder how my father could have not only left his kids alone, his wife alone, but also his lover alone to face their deaths."

He pulls my head to his chest. He refuses to let the storm of my turbulent thoughts spiral out of control, so he changes their route. "Are you really mad at him, or have you somehow figured out a way she's your fault, too?"

His question is like cold water to my building fire. The anger dissolves, melting my posture to relax into his embrace. "I hate when you do that," I tell him, with a pout of which I'm not proud.

He chuckles and I can feel the vibration through his chest. "We're both each other's kryptonite."

"Look carefully, Genny," I hear Aimes say in a mocking Australian accent. "Here we see the courtship dance of the passive-aggressive lovers' species. Knowing to only come out when the situation is either dire, or just finishing another round of drama-filled courtship, we can only speculate what has brought them out today from the dark hovels they live in."

"Speaking of kryptonite." I push from his arms, letting the still chilly air finish robbing me of his warmth. "What do you want, Aimes?"

"So rude," Aimes almost pouts. She's putting on a show to also recover from last night. "The other meat puppets said something about going on a run?"

Genny hasn't offered a single word into the conversation. She's pale, almost blueish with the many faint veins peeking through her distressed coloring. The sight of her pulls my mind back to the imagery of Ranya on the dirt floor. Closing my eyes against the memory, I force myself to return to the moment. Lawless hasn't missed my body buckle under the weight of the mental photograph. His fingers caress mine, letting me know he's here. I pull my hand away from his reach, crossing my arms to keep myself guarded.

"That's what Law said," I keep my distance in my voice, calm and uninterested in what she's asked.

Aimes almost smiles in relief. "Are the sidekicks invited, too?"

"Yup," I answer her before Lawless has the opportunity to say otherwise. Not that Aimes and I would listen to him, but it saves time from fighting over it.

"Oh, goodie." Aimes rubs her hands together. "You going to come?"

Aimes looks to the silent Genny. Genny shakes her head in a slow, dazed answer of a 'no'. Her eyes are too wide. Her skin too pale. I don't have to ask her to know she's stuck in the constant replay of last night. I don't have to ask because I was once where she is now - stuck, lamenting over it. Just like me, I know she's somehow tied it back to the day she lost her family. The two are in no way related, but our minds trick us, planting that seed and we are forced to watch the blood-streaked flowers grow.

"Genny," I call to her. Her eyes float to me, but her face doesn't change upon hearing her name. "Why don't you spend the day with Paula? Keep each other company." I suggest, firmly believing Genny is slipping into shock.

"Did you hear him?" Genny whispers to me, as if it's just her and I standing in this open field. "Did you?"

Genny is asking me, not because of scientific reasons, or even over the terror of what it means that they now talk. She's asking me to be sure she isn't insane. She wants to know that it really happened and wasn't just a lost moment of time she's embedded in the already thick tomes of torment she's been gifted.

I nod. I won't fray her fragile knots holding her together. I just nod, letting her know she's not alone. Yes, I heard him, and yes, I don't know what to do with the fact, either.

"I think I'll go see Paula," Genny whispers, again. "I think I'd like to see Paula."

The three of us watch her wander off towards Paula's self-established medical room. We each wear different faces with our thoughts taking us on different journeys of opinions.

"Should we leave her alone?" Aimes is watching her with a heavy heart.

"She's not alone." I walk past Aimes towards where the other 'meat puppets' should be waiting. "She has Paula. Paula most likely needs the company, too."

Aimes hears the words I don't say. She nods, understanding I haven't dismissed Genny, but sent her to a person who may also need someone right now. A person, just like us, who would never admit their need for someone, but yearns for the comfort.

We didn't have to travel far to find the rest of our family. Rhett's frame is hard to miss the sight of in these narrow, stone-built hallways as he leads the others towards us. We merge our groups, heading for the main entrance of this fort, turned tourist attraction.

Aimes isn't the only one to brighten with the fact we are escaping for the day. Rhett wears his smirk like one of the patches on his vest - wide, colorful, and hidden with meaning. Marxx's face is blank with boredom. It's a stark contrast to his counterpart. Even Dolph, a man of few words, seems bright and cheery standing next to Marxx. Which makes Marxx our pixie's first target.

"So gloomy, Marxx?" Aimes' voice is taunt filled. "Not excited to go see the only thing you've had between your legs in months?"

Rhett's smile blooms, and tossing a leather vest to Lawless, he responds to Aimes' remark. "At least the man has had something worth missing."

"What did you call Lawless and I earlier?" I ask her, when the men keep walking, avoiding any retort Aimes may pull forth from the depths of her sarcasm basement.

"This lake thing," Aimes skips over my question with one of her own. "Do you think Rhett would fit? We never really asked much about the lake itself."

"Cute," I tell her. "But we both know you'd jump in to haul him out if need be."

"Think so?" she asks. Her lips form a tight pout, pondering what I've said. "Maybe, but only after a few minutes and the bubbles stopped."

"Everyone knows this act you two put on is just part of your freakish idea of romance"—my eyes squint as they adjust to the sunlight bouncing off the metal boat docks—"and both of you would do whatever it took to save the other."

Aimes makes a noise of neither agreement nor disagreement. In fact, it's close to disgust. She does notice something I missed, per usual.

"It's just us," she states.

She's right. Peyton nor my father are here. It's just the six of us.

"Where is Peyton and Collin?" I ask the man helping Lawless untie the boat from the dock.

"I was told six. I take six," he answers. "If you want, I'll take five, maybe four." He stares at Aimes and me with the innuendo.

"Wait," Aimes steps on the man's fingers holding the slackened rope. She doesn't press her weight on them, but she has his attention. "What do you mean 'take'?"

The man isn't amused. Most aren't when being dick-checked by Aimes, but he answers her.

"Take," he begins. "As in, you get in boat. I drive it. I drive back. Take."

"Thanks for using small words. Would have hated for you to hurt yourself." Aimes removes her foot from his hand when he answers. "Just the same, I don't think so."

Marxx hasn't missed the reason for her concerns. He shares a look with Rhett, something practiced and perfected. If Lawless is aware, he doesn't act like it. He continues to help the man with the chores of the boat.

Dolph extends his hand to help Aimes and me into the rocking craft. Having before been on the receiving end of those well-timed, hidden glances, he too has caught their silent language.

"Get in," he mouths the words, extending his hand with more urgency.

Lawless watches us climb into the boat. He stares at us over the head of the kneeling man Marigold sent to escort us to shore and then leave us. His posture and expression are flat. Neither hold any tension, any hints as to what is about to happen.

"We ready?" the forced help asks.

He doesn't hide his annoyance with his task. Maybe if he had, they might have been nicer to him. Maybe.

Rhett smiles at the man. It's the type of smile J.D. taught him. A smile taught to unnerve someone, but not enough to make them suspicious, not completely.

"I guess that's a 'yes'?" the man asks, with a little less hate in his voice.

Marxx steadies the boat, holding into place. Once it's secure, Lawless pushes the man. He's tilted off-balance, and as he sways, Rhett finishes the job.

With both hands, Rhett heaves the man off the dock before climbing into the boat as if nothing had just happened. He stretches his long legs along the back bench-styled seat without a care for the man screaming for help in the water beside us. Securing his shoulder-length black hair in a slicked-back style, he winks, and I'm reminded of the man he was before a high school changed him.

"Tell Queen Bitch we'll get her supplies. We don't need an escort," Lawless shouts to the flailing man in the water.

Launching the boat from the dock, Dolph starts to laugh. It's a soft sound at first. So soft, it's almost hard to hear. It tests the air around us before building in sound. Soon, the whole boat is filled with it. Each man, in his own pitch, joins the laughter. It fills the space around us, trailing behind us over the roar of the motor.

For a moment, they forget the tension they have been drowning under for these past months. For a moment they are just boys, laughing over a prank they have pulled. For a moment, I almost forget everything we are leaving and everything we have left. It's just a moment, but I'll take it.

Chapter 33

Their bikes are exactly where we left them. Each one parked in their normal row, waiting as if time had stopped the day we ran from the beach. They didn't start as if time had stopped, but with verbal coaxing and cooing from their owners, they each roared to life.

"Just like a lady," Rhett shouts over his pipes. "Pout when you leave them, but hot to ride when you get back."

"You're disgusting." Aimes shakes her head, but no one missed the smile she gave him or the wink he sent to her.

"Where to?" I ask the general crowd. "I missed the directions she gave."

"Really?" Marxx is watching me, peering deeper into some part of me where he thinks he'll find some answer.

"Really..." I let the word hang, unsure of what he's suggesting.

Marxx's face forms the lines of suspicion before hiding his eyes behind his dark sunglasses.

"She said for us to go back to that daycare. The one where you were stabbed by the punk. She even asked to make sure you and Aimes were with us when we went." Marxx is still watching me, but his eyes are hidden as he talks to me. "Any reason why she'd want you to be there?"

"Other than trying to get us all on a boat to be dropped off and then picked back up at random?" Aimes inserts herself into Marxx's line of sight. "Or maybe, because she's bat shit crazy and has wanted Hells gone from the moment we arrived? Or maybe, she's just super jealous of all of Hells' new scars and figured why not add a few more? I don't know, Marxxie poos. What do you think?"

Marxx swings his leg over his black beast without another word. He doesn't spar with Aimes. Not because he's intimidated by her or of what she may say to him. He doesn't join in because he'd rather just punch you than talk to you. Marxx was never a man of many words. Aimes uses too many.

"Careful, Marxx," I say to him, when Aimes slides into the truck. "You remember what happened to the last man who tried it with me at the daycare?"

"Murder!" Aimes shouts gleefully from her seat.

"It was a lucky shot," Marxx tells me, but it earned me a small smile.

Lawless waits till I have the truck backed out and ready to follow them. He doesn't seem to be brave enough to ride behind me anymore. The memory brings a smile to my face when I turn the truck to follow them onto the road.

"What's the smile for?" My partner in crime asks.

"Just thinking of all the times I've scared them with my driving," I tell her, still wearing the smile.

Aimes whispers in a theatrical style, "Murder!"

It's the last words we share. We ride in silence. Each of us lost in our thoughts over what last night revealed and what Marigold is trying to reveal. More importantly, what's waiting for us at the daycare we left. We didn't dispose of the corpses. We didn't clean the sins created there – ours or his. They wait for us, now. The blood will be thicker. The scents will be heavier, and we will be made to pay, one way or another.

The driveway is exactly how I remember it. The large holes jar my shocks, despite my best effort to avoid them.

"It's fine. I don't need all my teeth." Aimes is grasping to the dash for support from being bounced around inside the cab of the truck.

"Your teeth are safe," I assure her, when we come to a stop.

We both sit in silence, staring at the building we thought was only a memory. We had hoped it was just a spot in time, locked behind the many doors we've invented to keep such places safely stored away. As the clowns return our stare, those doors start to rattle, rattling my courage with them.

"I really don't want to do this." Aimes has melted to the long bench seat, trying to hide from what is before us. Her fears are robbing her of even the smallest shred of bravery. "Why is it every time I think we have met the definition of crazy, life has to go and redefine it for us?"

"It shouldn't be as bad this time." I ease out of my battlewagon knowing she'll have to follow. "Everything should be dead."

"Since when has that stopped them from trying to eat us here, lately?" Aimes mutters, doing exactly what I knew she would do.

The only thing worse than being stuck in your fear is being stuck in it alone, in a truck, in the middle of nowhere.

"What are we doing here?" I ask the ones who are waiting for us.

No one looks excited to be back here. Dolph keeps his eyes on the area around us, searching for any movement our loud arrival may have caused. Rhett is pulling out the large vinyl bags we keep stashed in their saddle packs for supply raids. He also is doing anything he can to not directly look at the building.

"There's supposed to be a shed somewhere behind the place." Dolph offers. "Leigh said it's where they hide the things they can't carry so they can come and get them later."

"You and Leigh, now?" Aimes makes a clicking sound with her tongue when she asks, trying to shine her armor.

"Did Marigold send us or did Leigh?" I ask, skipping over Aimes' attempt to change the whole conversation.

"Marigold," Marxx interjects. "Leigh came later. Told us where to look to save us time."

"Well isn't Leigh just full of advice of where to look, these days," Aimes said it to the group, but it's me she's staring at when saying it.

"Let's just go." I stare into the windows watching us. "Anything to avoid going back in there, even if the suggestion came from Leigh."

There's a sound of agreement from those around me. We imagine there can't be anything worse than what we left in those rooms. We were wrong, again.

The white wooden fence runs the length of the property's space. It's decorated with the same tumbling clowns around large letters and numbers. The artist at the time had no idea how their vision of playful charm would be turned into sinister warnings, but it has, and we should have listened.

Lifting the handle, Rhett cautiously waits before we enter the yard. We are straining to hear even the faintest of sounds, any sound which may hint we aren't alone. Anything to give us a clue of what secrets these long, white boards are keeping from us.

Lawless braces himself, securing his gun with both hands and tilting his head to level the sights. He's waiting for Rhett to pull it open fully, exhaling the air in his lungs, Rhett does.

Nothing rushes us. There's no crescendo of growls or cries from beyond the grave. The scent the air whirled around us with the forced motion, we know that smell.

It was faint before now. I marked it to being from the building; the fragrance of past travesties clinging to the bricks with shame. It wasn't, but it belonged to travesties, just the same.

Lawless lowers his gun and his head with what he is seeing ahead of me. Rhett braces against the wooden gate for support, peering over his arm into the space I cannot see. Watching the two of them, it's enough for Marxx to step back, not eager to join his brothers. I'm a different type of calamity. I have to see.

Lawless doesn't try to stop me. Rhett, sensing my approach, slides to give me room to fit through the opening. I receive my wish.

The side yard contains the playground. It holds the normal swings, teeter-totters, and slides one would expect to find. What it also contains is someone's warped attempts to keep the place filled.

Children of various young ages fill the landscape with their jaws hung open, stuck in silent screams. Their bodies are tied and fastened to the structures with ropes and cords of different colors. Children, with their legs scattered below them from rotting, swing as the breeze moves what's left of their decayed bodies on the yellow plastic pieces. The slide is covered in birds feasting on the scraps of the flesh left on the children who were posed to climb its ladder. The slide itself has lost its playmate. Arms are all that remains, holding onto the metal sides with the wrists secured in place. The owner rests in a discarded pile at the base, having smeared the metal with dark colors upon their escape. A head has rolled away from the boy on the teeter-totter, resulting in its headless torso hoisting the slumped body of a girl into the air.

"I'm glad you shot him," I whisper to Aimes, who has come to stand beside me.

I'm unwilling to let my voice carry to these once cherished children. I'm unwilling to disturb whatever it is we are looking at with mixtures of anger and disgust.

"Me, too," she tells me. "Me, too."

Rhett points towards a small building across the yard. "Must be the spot."

"Of course, it's through the valley of death," Aimes sighs.

I take the lead, as always. Not out of bravery. It's pure habit at this point.

We don't speak as we pass the collection of broken dolls. I try not to even look at them, but as Aimes said, dead does not always mean safe. It's the same when we make it to the shed. Even as unsettling as the sight is, it's more unsettling to turn your back to it.

Dolph's mind doesn't only see the tragedy, he sees something else as he stares at them. "We should bury them," he whispers over the shame their story brings him.

"Nothing left to bury." Rhett casts a side glance to the monuments, but returns his gaze quickly to the door of the shed Marxx is trying to open. "If you moved them, they would fall apart on you. You'd have nothing but pieces to carry."

"So, we just leave them?" Dolph asks the other man.

"We just leave them," Rhett tells him. "You'll make it worse for yourself if you try. They are already dead. They don't care. But if you move them, that conscience of yours you're trying to settle, will be dealing with deeper issues when they fall apart on you."

"Not to mention what they may leave on you," Lawless offers, trying to settle Dolph's unease. "Some things you just don't need to know."

Dolph isn't settled. He looks to me for support. I have none. Shaking my head, I silently agree with the other two. I have enough dead children stored in my haunted heart. They already dance and play together in their groups. They don't need to make new friends.

"It's empty!" Marxx's voice pulls me back. "It's fucking empty!"

Marxx is roaring with his anger. He kicks the door of the shed closed, letting his wrath explode upon a solid surface. The reverberation of the wood sends the birds scattering from their feast.

"Why would she send us out here if there's nothing in here?" Marxx roars again, completely forgetting the dangers which could be near us.

"Because it was never about the shed," I whisper, not out of fear of what's around us, but the fear of what's in front of us. "It was never about the shed."

I watch as the many black birds begin to resettle around the corpses of the children. They perch on the secured bones of the children's shoulders, anchored in angles to the swings. They rest on exposed skulls tossed back on unsupported necks, pulling long strands of hair from what's left of their once delicate scalps. Black eyes watch us, waiting to see what we mean for them, but it's what they mean for us that has caused us to be sent here.

"What are you talking about?" Marxx demands from behind me.

I stand in the middle of it all. I stand exactly where Marigold pictured me standing when she stressed to Marxx to have Aimes and I present. I stand, seeing this scene, not as it stands, but as it stood the day it was constructed.

Pinky didn't do this. His insanity wasn't this deep, nor were his reasons centered around the toddlers. For him, it was all about his first love. This, this is about something darker. Something Marigold wanted me to see.

This isn't about the death she has framed, wilting to dust like the roses on a desk. This is about the life she thinks she can preserve.

"She thinks she could have saved them from this. She wanted us to see this could have been different. In her mind, these children, this is what *could* be happening; playing with their friends instead of dead and decaying."

"What?" Marxx asks, not sure he heard me.

Aimes did. "Oh, shit."

"What?!?" Marxx is practically raging at us, unclear of what we are talking about.

"Where did you leave April?" Aimes asks Rhett.

Rhett tenses upon hearing the little girl's name. "With Leigh," he answers with confusion. "She wasn't feeling well this morning so Leigh said she would take her, and she could play with Wren. Wren had something she wanted to show her while we were gone."

"Oh, shit," Aimes says, again.

I'm already running towards my truck before she can finish her thought. My feet match the pace of my heart as my lungs fight to keep up with the demand I have placed upon them. It was never about the shed. It was about teaching us a lesson and we walked right into her classroom without blinking.

The men don't ask about my panic. They don't question as Lawless starts his bike without a glance to spare them. They don't pause, but follow him out, fighting to stay faster than the grill of my large truck.

"Why won't they hurry?" Aimes demands, frustrated with our failure to see the bigger picture.

"It's gravel," I tell her, as if it's a thousand explanations and apologies at once. The sound of my pulse in my ears disagrees with both.

Everything seems painfully slow. Time feels to have almost stopped, reluctant to move us forward to save the ones we've left behind. The beat of my heart is mismatched to the tempo around me, it almost thuds with its heaving heaviness. My ribs threaten to break, letting the pressure of my chest escape from its cruelty.

"We aren't going to make it." Aimes' voice is fragile, breaking under the same strain my body is fighting against.

My eyes stare at the images in my rearview mirror. Through such a small opening of a gate, I can see so much. I can see the children with their hidden messages. I can see the monuments to madness they have become, when they should be resting at peace, free from the suffering they endured at the end of their lives. They were spared one fate to be a shrine to the fate of others.

Their bodies should be resting under marble headstones adorned with cherubs and angels welcoming them to some version of peace. Instead, they rot under the many seasons, falling, scattered, and dismembered to provide a testament for a woman whose madness will never know peace. Their fates are intertwined, these tiny victims and her, and when I am through with her, she too will never rest under poetic words or soft sobs from the ones who loved her.

"We'll never make it," Aimes says again. She's almost chanting to herself as her fears push her broken mind.

"We will," my voice is sharp, double-edged with anger and concern.

We will make it because we must. We aren't fighting to secure a home, this time. This isn't for a stone building, nor for the many people living inside it. This time, we are fighting to secure our family. We'll make it. We must.

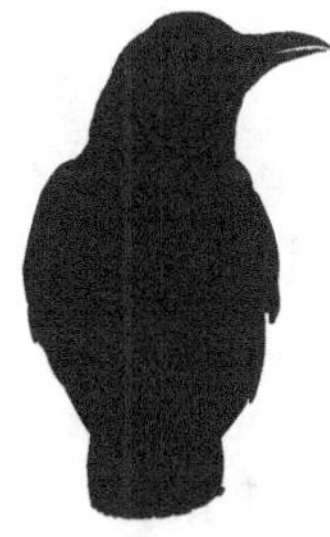

Chapter 34

Marigold isn't waiting for us on the dock like my mind pictured. It's Torri, her second in command. Her daughter, and the mother to the little girl being used as a pawn, Wren. She wears the smile of a slaughterhouse, luring the cattle in with false promises and soft words. We're the cattle, and she doesn't dim the wattage of her beaming face as we cut the engine of the boat.

"You made it back!" Torri exclaims, with a sticky sweet tone.

Her blonde hair holds thick ringlets of long curls. They bounce with her enthusiasm, adding to her false charm. It's her eyes, though. They leak the secret. They glow with a mischief unknown to honesty. A gleam which means only one thing, someone has done something terrible and she's waiting for us to discover it.

"Where is April?" Rhett asks her with a tone of boredom.

Torri makes a face of uncertainty, pursing her lips with her concentration. "Around. I'm sure."

Aimes places her hand over Dolph's when he tries to take the keys to the boat out. The man pauses, trying to read her face the way we often do when the unspoken words begin.

"Where's April?" Aimes asks, again, still holding Dolph's hand.

Torri just shrugs. Her shawl billows around her with her arms held out, mistakenly letting the grip of the gun show. Her motion was supposed to leave a thousand unanswered doubts. Her waistband answers them all.

Torri senses the change in our mood. Her brown eyebrow lifts, arching with the change around her. "Now, y'all aren't thinking of doing something stupid, are ya?" she asks us, still wearing her red lips in a curve.

"It's kind of our thing." I match my smile to hers, as I say the words.

Aimes taps Dolph's shoulder to change seats with her. She knows where my mind is headed. After all, as I just said, stupid is kind of my thing.

Torri reaches for her waistband. Before the men can answer like with like, the sound of a shot shatters the air around us. Tori's body bounces forward. Her once amused eyes now gleam with fear. Her knees buckle with gravity pulling her body to the dock. It's a slow fall and she's aware of every second. The shot wasn't fatal, but she'll die. She's already coughing thick, black blood onto the metal around her, smearing it the way the slide is stained from similar fluid.

Leigh steps into the boat's hull without a greeting or a word about what she's done. She doesn't put the gun she just used to kill Torri away. Crossing her legs, she silently stares at us over the sounds of Torri's labored breathing.

"Still want to take the gun from her, Marxx?" Aimes asks.

It's Lawless who puts his hand on Aimes' shoulder saying, "Let's go."

"We don't know where everyone is!" Aimes' pitch is close to hysterics.

"Yes, you do," Leigh tells her, with her flat voice sounding more ominous than the dread her words bring.

"All of them?" I ask her.

"All of them," Leigh repeats, not changing a single tone or placing any emphasis on any of her words.

Upon hearing what he feared, Rhett lifts Aimes from the seat she took from Dolph, dropping her on the back row. She doesn't fight him or make a single remark with Leigh's words still heavy around us. As each of us interpret what her words may mean, Aimes doesn't object at all when Lawless takes over the controls. Her mind is lost on the little girl her and Rhett have adopted to form their little trio.

Tori reaches her blood-covered hand out to the expanding space between her and us. She laughs with Leigh's revelation. She watches the blood drip from her fingers with a steady beat. When it spills from her lips with the effort to speak, she finds it all darkly amusing.

"She just wants to save them, but she hasn't figured out if yours are worth saving, yet," Torri tells us, taunting us, even as the dark blood flirts with the knowledge her death will be soon.

The sound of her laughter follows us from the docks, haunting us with what she knows and of that which we do not. Leigh doesn't react to the melody of Torri's death. Leigh already knew Torri would die and she already knows what's waiting for us.

As Lawless races the boat to the little island, her steel eyes watch me through her hair being tossed into black ribbons around her face. There's a heavy weight to them, warning of the battlefield waiting for us. We both understand we are the pawns rushing to fight the queen. Whereas she can move anywhere, at any time, on this field of her creating, our movements are small and measured. Leigh's asking me if I'm prepared for what is about to happen. I'm not. I never am. Stupid is kind of my thing.

"Anyone going to fill the rest of us in on what we are missing?" Dolph asks. His eyes bounce from the sullen Aimes to the finger-tapping Lawless, knowing something is about to happen, but unsure of which way he should prepare his emotions.

"Marigold took them," Leigh calmly explains. "She heard of what happened to the man she sent to leave you on the beach. She wanted to be prepared for when you made it back."

"Why, though?" Marxx joins the questioning.

"Because you know," Leigh exhales with her words.

She expects her answer to complete the circle of questioning, but it doesn't. They don't know. She's only looped more questions in the start of a downward spiral of Marigold's madness.

"Woman, I don't know shit!" Marxx shouts. "We did what she asked. We went where you told us to and there was nothing there. Now, you're telling us she has our people. Why?"

Leigh doesn't answer Marxx. She's watching me again, waiting to see what I will reveal, and what I won't.

The silence strains what is left of Marxx's nerves. "God damn it! Someone tell me what is going on!"

"Marigold is infecting people with the children she turns from other children she's already turned, because she thinks of this as a cure for death, but she's really just making these things to make them and now they can talk and shit. So, she's taken the rest of our people to the lake house to turn them which will keep us here forever under her thumb or drive us batshit crazy like her!" Aimes screams in one breath, each word overlapping the other as they fight to escape.

The same way I was stunned when Lawless admitted it, everyone in the boat is stunned, now. Everything from shock, confusion, and rage flow upon the faces of those around me. Sometimes all three, only to form the expressions all over again with their thoughts circling over what Aimes has said.

"How long have you known?" Rhett's voice is deadly. It's the hushed whisper of a man having his last will to live dangled in front of him.

"Last night," I tell him. "We learned last night."

Lawless still taps his fingers on the steering wheel, saying nothing. His face is blank with his brown eyes empty as they watch the island growing closer. I won't tell them he's known the whole time, but I won't forgive him for not telling them, either.

"So, you go, bust her little secret shack and in less than twenty-four hours she has us by the balls?" Rhett is leaning dangerously close to me. I can feel the heat of his words when they escape his mouth.

"She's very proactive," I hiss back, leaning into the rest of the space he has left between us.

"And now the bitch has April." Rhett holds his space, letting his words flow slowly with his anger.

"And she has Genny. Who is actually blood, not just a side piece to make me feel better about my life." I don't slow my words, nor do I even think about them, until after I've said them. Words are like that, poison-tipped and filled with regrets.

"Maybe she is. Maybe she isn't. But if she is, then it's because of a side piece who made someone feel better about their life." Rhett digs deeper with his poison, making sure it's secure in one of the four pumping champers of my heart.

"If you two are done dick checking each other's panic, we are here," Aimes shouts before I can form my next attack. "Just an idea, but maybe you two should save some of that for the woman who has our 'side pieces' and not each other? Just an idea. What do I know?"

As soon as the boat hit the compacted sand, I was out of it. I don't wait for back up, or a plan. I don't even know who I'm rushing to – Paula, Genny or April, maybe even the other men, but I do know I'm escaping the ghosts Rhett has stirred.

All my heart knows is that they need us, and we left them. We left them to become stakes in a battle they didn't start. Like a spoiled child not happy being told what to do, I started it, and she's threatening to break all my toys to teach me a lesson.

The trail seems twice as long this time. The mud has turned to dirt, dusting me as I run. I'm covered in more than just panic and sweat when I finally arrive at the house. Its doors are wide open. Like the arms of an enemy waiting to welcome you with false promises and deadly designs, I run right into them.

Stalling in the front room while my eyes adjust to the change of light, I listen, waiting for any noise to hint where they may be. This is a three-story house, four if you count the cellar. Picking the wrong floor may cost me time I cannot regain.

Marxx crashes through the same doors I just did, panting and just as dirt covered. I wave at him to be quiet and he flips me a middle finger response.

"Leigh says the barn," he fights to say between his breathing.

"Leigh also said the shed," I point out, still forcing myself to listen for any hints.

Marxx stands up from where he was resting on the doorway. "You don't trust her?"

"She shoots one person and suddenly I'm supposed to believe her? No, I don't trust her."

I can see him mentally chewing on what I've said. His jaw twitches as he weighs my words and her deeds. "They've all headed to the barn."

"Just you and me, again?" I ask him, pulling forth memories of the times we stood back-to-back against the world.

"That didn't end well," he reminds me, but he joins me as I listen. "You're going to get me killed one day."

"Death is inevitable. Isn't that how J.D. used to explain all his choices?"

"Yeah and he's dead."

"Guess he made his choice." I end the verbal game by taking the stairs as fast as I can.

I'm not ready to face Marco, again. Besides, the cellar is too small to fit them all. She would hold them somewhere where she could control them, turn them, or kill them as she wanted. The cellar doesn't provide her that comfort.

"Slow down!" Marxx is shouting in an attempt of a whisper.

I blew our cover a long time ago. I'm not worried about any of that, now.

Kicking open the first wooden door I come to, I blanche at the smell of piss and thicker things. An old man wearing stained pajamas lays chained to his metal bed frame. His mattress is bare, exposing where the springs have worn their way through. He stares at me with hope, a flashing minute of where he thinks I am here to help him. All around his bed trays are scattered with food having become nothing more than crust with its age spent on the floor. A woman of his same age sits in a rocking chair. A cotton housecoat hangs upon her frame. Her body is slumped in such a way to answer any concerns over her in life and death. She, too, has become nothing more than waste as she was left to rot in front of who I can only assume is her husband, but the chain loops around her arms hints there was no other fate planned for them.

Marxx almost slams into my back with his momentum. "What the ..."

"Welcome to Marigold's world."

"We don't have time for this," he says, placing his hand on my shoulder to pull me from the room. "We'll come back," he whispers into my ear, trying to pull me back to the hell we are facing and not the hell I am seeing.

The man begins to struggle against his chains when he sees us stepping away. The paper-thin skin splits from his actions causing fresh blood to seep and join the numerus stains around him. A garbled voice is calling out from this throat, but there's something wrong with his mouth. There are no words, just sounds, and I realize he has no tongue.

"We'll come back," I tell him, trying to calm him, but we both know it's a lie.

Looking at five more doors down a hallway, it seems to stretch beyond its capabilities. Five more possible scenes of deep human depravity for me to discover. Five more chances for Marigold to expose her darkest demeanors. Swallowing down the bile creeping along my mouth, I start towards to next round of Marigold's peepshow.

Marxx grabs my shoulder again, clamping his fingers around it to keep me in place. "This is going to take too long," he tells me.

"Hello??" I shout down the hallway. "Anyone in here?"

"Not exactly what I had in mind."

I start to argue with him when we both hear it. Several doors down, there's a thumping sound. It's methodic, patterned and clearly an answer to my call. Running towards the sound, I don't let myself think of the many things it could be answering me, waiting for me to open its prison. I can't let myself think Life would be that cruel, even as I know she's exactly that.

The sound never stops its thudding. It leads us right to the magic door holding either a hostage, our answers, or our doom. Lifting my foot to force it open, Marxx makes a sound, pushing my knee back to the ground.

"Depending on what's in there, we may need a door to close," he whispers, twisting the knob like a sane person would.

The door opens with restrained inches. With my impatience mounting, I almost tilt to cheat it from its secrets. The fragrance is so heavy I can almost taste it, feel it sliding down the back of my throat. My stomach lurches with it and I must take a step back. Marxx is trying to hold his stance, but he too is overcome with it, having to hide his face in the sleeve of his shirt. Even as our bodies threaten to betray us, our minds screaming to run, we stand waiting for the door to reveal whatever else it has lurking behind the wooden barrier.

The thudding sounds never stall. They keep the same pace as the door swings to expose her hidden mysteries. My eyes follow the pattern of the worn grey carpet with each inch she exposes until they land on the shoes of Peyton. Tied to a chair, he's kicking the ground underneath him, answering my call with a call of his own. Eyes wide with emotions over his gagged mouth, he doesn't stop kicking when I rush towards him, leaving Marxx to secure the room behind me in my haste.

"Anyone else in here?" Marxx asks, unwilling to believe the stench engulfing us doesn't have a form.

Peyton shakes his head 'no', making the effort to untie the knots holding the gag in place even harder.

"You have a knife." Watching me fight with the material, Marxx sounds only somewhat judgmental. "Use it."

I refuse to admit he's right, but I use my knife while glaring over Peyton's head to saw through the ropes, freeing not only his mouth, but him from the chair, as well.

"Where's the rest?" Marxx asks, still peering into the closet and under the shambles of a bed.

"They took Collin into another room. The girls they took with them," Peyton gasps in between the words, working the sore muscles of his jaw from where the rope was tied.

"Guess we did pick wrong." Marxx mutters his words with aggravation.

Petyon stands from the chair, stretching his once bound limbs. "I'm glad you did," he tells us, catching Marxx's concealed meaning. "Let's find Collin and get out of here."

Marxx has already retreated to the hallway where the air is not as thick. I can hear him kicking the doors open, knowing we have wasted time. His choice words let me know enough about what is hiding behind each set of splintered wood.

"Why did they do this," Peyton has latched onto my arm, pulling me back to him.

"You'll see," I tell him. "Hopefully before it's too late."

Dropping my arm as a reminder that the clock ticks against us, he follows me to the hallway Marxx has destroyed. He's dragging my stumbling father towards us. Collin is struggling to keep his numb legs underneath him and Marxx's speed isn't making the chore any easier.

"Let's go," Marxx drops the limp body of Collin in front of Peyton.

"Really?" Peyton's voice drips with annoyance, as he looks down to his discarded friend.

Marxx doesn't reply. He's already heading down the stairs to what he thinks will be an easy escape from this clapboard prison. He should know better by now, Life doesn't work that way.

Life is extending her other hand, the one covered in secrets and riddled with death. She let us find Peyton and Collin with little effort, but she's about to teach us why we thank her for small blessings. Big blessings come with a higher body count, more screaming and deeper nightmares than most can crawl free from, and she's just starting to tally the score.

Chapter 35

I take the stairs two at a time to keep up with the disgruntled Marxx. I am sure his mind has painted in the lines of everything we have risked, just as mine has done. I'm not brave enough to ask about the older man waiting for us to come back to be his salvation. Nor do I ask him to slow his steps so Peyton and Collin can keep up. I know, as well as he does, our choice may have cost us someone and that will be on our souls forever.

Marxx doesn't go out the front door. He turns to exit the door closest to our next target. The stomping of his boots silences any interjections from me. They keep pace with the blood pounding through my body, spurring me to move at his elongated gait. When I see what's in the room we are about to pass, everything inside me halts, locking my body with dread.

"Stop," I choke on the word, my fear robbing even my tongue from the ability to move. "Marxx, stop."

Marxx turns to me, annoyance clearly upon his face. "What?" he barks.

My eyes won't leave the opened floor. The rug is rumpled, pushed astray in a discarded style. It's creased, lumped shape whispers of being a result, and not a step of the door being opened. Someone opened the door from underneath it, not from the top, as Wren had done yesterday. Which means, something is here with us, watching us with the new tools hell has provided it.

Marxx loses some of his bite when he asks, again, "What?"

"Don't move," I whisper, more from stress than worry.

Holding up his hand, Marxx signals for the other two men to wait on the bottom step. Peyton is already glancing around, knowing something is gravely wrong for us to be frozen to this spot.

"Be ready to run," Marxx tells those behind me, still unsure of why I am afraid.

Like the boogey-man of childhood nightmares, Marco leans his tattered frame around the far doorway of the room which once held him. His eyes meet mine, discolored but still alive, knowing more than just run and catch, but also hide and seek. With a smile, he pulls himself back into hiding. A toss of red hair lets me know he's not hunting alone.

"It smiled?" Peyton's question is a vibration of uncertainty. Just as when we first saw it, we didn't believe it, either.

"Yeah. They do that now." I'm creeping away from the doorway, keeping sight of the room when I tell him this.

"Anything else I need to know?" Marxx's annoyance isn't with just this, but with being left out of so much, which may bite more than just our asses.

"It's a long list," I tell him.

My back is glued to the hallway wall. From what I know of the house, there's two paths the deadly duo can take. One path would lead them behind us to the hallway which connects the front of the house. The other, in front of us, waiting in the kitchen and blocking the exit. That's the best-case scenario. If they separated, they could be stalking us from both rooms, blocking our options completely.

Peyton has slipped from apprehension to the calmness of prepared. He's crouching low, bracing his body for when the threat should show itself. "Which way?" he whispers to me.

I'm locked between the many different scenarios. Self-doubt taunts me more than any school-yard bully, drowning my mind with the possible threats of picking the wrong option. Marxx is watching me, ready to make the choice for me when I use the one advantage I don't want to know about.

"Marco?" I shout into the house.

"Polo," that wet voice I remember calls back to me.

Marco steps from behind Peyton and Collin. He's edging his way towards the wide-open front door. His eyes are watching us with the same intensity of anticipation as ours holds him. He doesn't want us. He wants out.

"Ranya?" I ask, still refusing to admit mentally that this is possible.

"Polo," he says, his eyes casting to the direction to further down the hall beside him.

I wasn't aware I had pulled my knife. I don't know at which point I reached for my safety blanket but now I lift it into the air, showing him, I don't want him. I, too, just want out.

I look to Marxx to copy my motion and he holsters his handgun into its hiding spot of his vest. There isn't a doubt in how he looks at me, telling me he hates this decision. Peyton and Collin walk backward to where we stand, also with their hands open. I don't have the heart right now to point out Marco never acknowledged them as threats.

With the space we have created between our standoff, Marco reaches his hand out to the woman waiting for his sign. His knuckles are oozing, depositing a soft waterfall of fluid onto the wooden floor. The nails are gone, ripped from the soft flesh of his fingers, leaving jagged sores from the abuse. They weren't let out. He found a way out and took Ranya with him.

"The rest?" I ask him once he has the woman half-pushed through the door.

He turns and smiles a smile which robs my knees of strength. "Marco," he whispers, before following his new partner down the stairs and into the woods surrounding the house.

"Let's go!" I shout, unsure if Marco just told me his name or hinted a childhood game may be ready to turn deadly.

The men don't hesitate. We rush through the long hallway, exploding through the backdoor with images of what else maybe lurking in the rooms around us. My feet trip over themselves when I remember the old man above us, chained to his bed and the perfect sacrificial dinner for Marigold's newly invented family. I remember how I had told him I would be back for him. I left him with that hope. Now I leave him to die. I know it won't be the last time I see him. He'll be there tonight when I close my eyes. He'll be standing on a playground surrounded by children. He'll join them in their songs and J.D. will smile over my mistake.

The short space between the house and barn whispers of no hidden threats like the house displayed, but its doors are just as open. Marxx covers us as we run to them, spinning as he runs to keep the yard in site. He's the last into the barn, pulling the doors shut with hopes to keep it that way.

"They talk now?" Collin asks. His words are clipped with his panting and he's staring at me as if I hold all the answers.

I shrug, unwilling to keep rehashing the horrors of this place. Especially with what I know could be waiting below us. My father isn't the one to stand his ground and fight, but at the very least, I may need an extra body to recuse those she has hostage.

Marxx gives me a side-glace when he passes me. It's heavy with unsaid words, which only confirm what my thoughts already held.

"Less talk," Marxx barks. "We have to find the others."

"Don't have to look far," Lawless' voice calls from a far stall.

There's an edge of pain and darker emotions to his voice. Marxx and I don't wait for the other to move first. As if pulled at the same time, we rush towards where we heard him call out, racing Time herself to reach him.

He has propped himself up against the barn wall. His left shoulder is clutched tight in his hand, yet I can still see the red stained cloth he presses against it. His normally tanned skin holds a shade of pale and his eyes are dull with the pain he is fighting against to stay awake.

"Guess we really do suck without Paula," he jokes, trying to ease the dread on our faces.

"How?" I ask, falling to the dirty straw around him. I'm afraid to touch him, and afraid if I don't, I may never touch him again.

"Doesn't really matter," he tells me, reaching over my head to shake hands with Marxx. "Get down there before Rhett does something stupid."

I can't move. I know what my delay may be costing, but I can't leave him. I've left so many behind, I can't be asked to leave him.

"Go," he tells me. "I'm not going anywhere." He settles his eyes deeper than a look should be able to stir, telling me, "I promise."

Marxx pulls me from Lawless, following his new leader's command. The two brothers by choice lock eyes for a brief second before Marxx forces me to my feet.

"You heard him," Marxx sighs, his voice heavy with the decision left before us.

I don't look back. I'm looking at the handprints Marxx has left on my arms where he lifted me. I'm staring at the blood which belongs to Lawless; blood which now stains my arms from our goodbye. I remember a cold winter night when I counted headlights. I remember waltzing with Grief before dancing with Irony. The dark red marks hint there will be no celebrating when this is through, but I will be dancing, just the same.

"Let's go," Marxx says, again.

I look down the hole we are about to descend. Marxx has found it from following the clues Lawless' head motions has given him. Every part of me knows, this barn will keep some of us.

Some of us will add our bones to the secrets kept here. We are poised to fail and those of us who survive will be tormented, just as the children Marigold has kept as trophies to her insanity. We will hold ourselves in the cages of our failures. We will strap ourselves to swings which will never release us from the memories, as they sway from the winds of change. No matter the outcome, there is no doubt, Marigold will win today. Travis has taught me that. You don't truly ever defeat evil. You survive evil. You outrun its demons. You bury the dead and hide the scars, but defeating it? No matter how well you lock your doors, or how tight you pull the curtains, no, you never truly defeat evil.

I glance to the stall which cradles my past in her wooden arms and decayed straw. If I believed in Gods, or Goddesses, by any name at all, I would call to them now. I would offer what's left of my rotting soul in trade for his survival. I would pray, that when I climb back out of this pit, not only my past would she be cradling, but also my future, because I don't know if I have one without him.

"Let's go," Marxx calls to me, again.

Once again, it's just he and I standing together, and as he already has reminded me, that doesn't always play out well.

Chapter 36

The shouting hits my ears before I'm fully below ground. I can hear Rhett's angry voice bellowing, but I can't make out his words. All along the walls there is proof of a struggle. Handprinted smears of blacks and reds zigzag along the surfaces. Papers are tossed from the open rooms, littering the ground like dirty snow, tracked, and marred with footprints. Just as I had expected, Collin has taken to the back, letting his daughter and another man have the risks of going first.

"Plan?" I ask Marxx.

"Since when did you invest in those?" he returns, using me as the target of his anxiety.

"Since we keep finding ourselves in smaller and smaller spaces."

Despite our surroundings, stalking the sound of Rhett's voice, it brings me hope. If he's yelling, then there is something to still fight for, something still left of our family to cause him distress.

"How much ammo do you have?" My mind is blank for a plan. It's a small room, and without seeing where and who, there's no option left for us, but walking right into the storm.

"Full." Marxx is watching me, waiting for me to finish my line of thought.

I don't tell him I don't have a line of thought or even a plan. He's right. I don't invest much in either. I do what I do best. I walk right into the last room and face the devil inside of it.

Rhett has forced Marigold into the far corner. It's a standoff with her holding April's arm near a cage and Rhett holding his gun pointed at her head. The child inside the cage holds her gaze for Rhett, the louder of the two. I know this cage. I remember this little girl. She's the one who waved those small fingers with a grin, boasting of the things we didn't know, at the time; things we still yearn to be in the dark over.

Paula kneels with her back towards us, as Dolph stands over her, shielding her so she can do whatever it is she is doing to the color-stricken Genny. Her hands are placed over a spot on Genny's arm and my mind already races with the worst of what it may mean. Aimes has followed Rhett's lead. She's blocked the aisle made from the cages, leaving Marigold with no exit and even less options. I thought I had the room mapped, but I forgot one. The one who is always so easy to forget.

Leigh stands in such a manner projecting she hasn't taken a side, yet. She fidgets with the latch on the cage closest to her, tormenting the child inside of it by clunking its large lock against the metal bars. The key to the prison is in her hand at her waist. She flips it back and forth, its metal catching the light ominously with her hidden agenda. She isn't watching the room. She's watching us. She's waiting to see how the scales tip and if she wants to release the army Marigold has made to unbalance the scales all over again. Leigh smiles at me, and it's one of the few times I've seen an expression on her face. It's almost as unsettling as the child behind her petting her long black hair.

"Go to Genny," I tell Collin, who struggles to find somewhere to be in the chaos.

The sound of my voice pulls Marigold's awareness to me. Her face droops for a moment, trying to figure out a way to retake control. Her delaying is the clue. She doesn't really want to turn April. She wants control. She, just like Marco, is only thinking of an escape.

"You don't have to do this," I tell her, walking to Aimes' side and keeping clear of Rhett's barrel. I keep Marigold's and my eyes locked. "We will go. We will leave tonight, and you'll never have to worry about any of us, again."

I can see Marigold tossing my words around in her mind, measuring the cause and effect of what I have suggested.

Leigh has stopped her toying, pushing the room into a deep silence. Not even Rhett, who we heard from the ladder, makes a sound. The demonic cherubs are waiting, watching with eyes holding a deep interest in what is going on around them.

"We've returned Leigh to you," my voice is hushed, keeping the room at an uneasy energy. "Now return April to us."

April is tossing her eyes from me to Rhett. Her fear is easily seen upon her face, twisting her child-like features into worry and fright. She doesn't want to see the monster to which she's being offered. She doesn't want to look. She's searching for anyone to look at to help her hide the facts of what is happening to her.

Aimes has crouched down beside me. The second a motion is given, she is ready to steal away the little girl who has been stolen from us. Aimes isn't hiding in a back room this time. She's here, ready to fight. I almost fear for Marigold if her and Rhett should get their chance.

"You'll ruin everything!" Marigold stretches April's arm closer to the cage with her rage. "If she's bitten, they will see! They will understand!"

"We saw your playground." Marxx has joined Rhett's side, lending his brother his strength and support. He's also lending him another gun. Marigold now stares at two barrels as Marxx tells her, "We understand."

"That's your fault! You, and people like you, who would rather have children die than be saved!" Marigold is shaking with her anger and April's little arm dangles in front of the open cage.

"Lady, we just cleaned up a daycare. They were already dead." Marxx's voice is calm. He's ready for whatever comes next, he just wasn't watching the real threat.

The rocking motion pulls the child's eyes to April's small arm. Everyone is watching Marigold for a sign to rush her. I'm watching the child who has found her signal to eat.

The little girl crawls towards the dangling treat. She doesn't make a sound of warning. There are no growls of conquest with her foreseen victory. Like the silent killer she has been groomed to be, she lunges towards the tender flesh as my scream tears the space around us.

I didn't know where the shot came from, at first. My vision was only for the little girl with her exposed teeth and murder covered clothes until Dolph acted. The shot exploded her head, sending pieces of her to coat Marigold and the wall behind her. April was baptized in fluids thick and visceral, holding colors darker than a living body would hold.

Each group cradles their child. Rhett and Aimes rush to pull April to them, checking over her to be sure the blood running down her is not hers. Marigold is wailing in her attempts to pick up the headless body of the child whose blood she is wearing.

Marigold is lost in her mental anguish. She caresses the broken doll, staring at what is left of her creation while staring at the blood covering her from the action. Thick pieces of the child cling to her silver hair to only fall freely with her rocking body as she begins to wail.

Aimes has already escorted April behind me to the doorway. There's nothing to protect Marigold now from Rhett. She has no shield to keep her hidden and safe from his wrath.

"It's over." I pull on Rhett to keep the man from doing exactly what Lawless was afraid he would do. "Let's just get April to safety."

I use the girl's name like a holy word. I use it to try to pull him back from the cliff he's about to plunge, but Rhett has already dove deep into his rage. His body is relaxed, ready to spring. Only those burning eyes hold life. There's not a priest in this world who will be able to abolish the sins he is about to create, but once again, we forgot about the silent one who has no stones to cast when it comes to murder.

"Don't," Leigh's voice slices through my attention.

"Hells!" Aimes screams, turning the two men who were ready to even the score.

Leigh didn't stop toying with the lock. She opened them and not just the single cage. Every cage in her reach has its locks popped. It's only a matter of time before the creatures inside those metal bars figure out their freedom is a simple push.

Marigold has stopped her banshee screams. She's inching her way towards Leigh while her eyes watch those around her, but her destruction isn't over yet. I should have stopped her. I should have reached out and ended the woman who has lived for the deaths of those who thought she was keeping them safe, curing them. I was too busy keeping Rhett from stirring the watching demons who were waiting for their own signal to attack. I was too focused on talking down the man who held me when I thought my world was over. I forgot the depths grief can drag you to and the actions that can be made rational when pain is the only feeling left to someone. Marigold is about to remind me.

Somewhere along Marigold's timeline of dementia, she had the thought process of a fail-safe. There was a time when Marigold saw her little pets as something dangerous, when she viewed her experiments as just that, experiments and not the precious adopted children her mind has made them.

"I'll start, again," I hear her say, torment and regret coloring her words. "I can build, again."

Aimes has already scooped up April, clinging to her when she hears Marigold. Aimes is standing next to an air vent, staring at it in confusion while the rest of us watch Leigh and Marigold calmly leave the room. They, too, don't want to start the frenzy which will happen should the children be prompted to attack.

"We're just letting them leave?" Rhett asks, between his clenched teeth. "After what she's done, we are just going to watch her walk out?"

Dozens of sets of eyes swing towards him. Some of the children retreat to the darker corners of their prisons. Some inch towards the light, ready to defend themselves, or just ready for whatever comes next.

"For now," I tell him in a sing-song style, trying to edge back the beasts watching us.

"Hey guys," Aimes calls to us. "I think we should get out, like now."

Rhett storms towards Aimes and the group waiting by the door. He holds open what is left of it watching the two women retreat down the hallway with eyes so hate-filled it scares me. No one says a thing, as we sneak past the open cages, grateful they haven't tried to test the metal doors swaying as we pass them.

I'm the last one in the room when I catch the smell in the air Aimes had noticed. It's faint, barely there until I moved towards it, but it's there, hovering around me like a thick cloud. There's a moment when I place the smell. My mind travels to the old stove my grandmother had in her home. The little blue flame dances in my memory with a warning, but it's too late. The last sight I see of Leigh before she finishes ascending the ladder is a matchbook, roaring with life, she throws into the vent beside her.

The heat is instant, knocking me onto my back and scattered those around me like abandoned toys with the explosion. Flames climb the walls, fed by the gas being pumped around them. Pieces of paper dance in the air like fireflies at a summer cookout. My dazed mind finds it all fascinating as it buzzes in tune with the summertime bugs.

Those around me begin to move, shuffling and testing their bodies. Moaning softly, I echo the sounds around me when I try to stand. My legs are weak, fighting against my commands to move and check on those still laying around me.

Paula has pulled herself to her knees, but that's as far as her body will move. I can see the blood in her hairline, flowing down her ashen face. She blinks through it, asking me something, but I can't hear her. Peyton crawls to her, using his strength to lift not only himself, but also her to their feet. Collin has already stood, carrying the weight of the limp body of Genny in his arms towards the hallway. Peyton is motioning to me. Something behind me has him frantic.

My body is moving too slow. The stiches on my shoulder have ripped, torn the flesh they were meant to hold together. The whole arm hangs limply, slapping against my side as I try to move towards them. It should hurt. It doesn't. Nothing hurts.

I almost giggle watching it swing loosely in my dark blue sweatshirt, but as I'm watching my fingers, little feet come into my vision. Someone is standing directly beside me, shadowed by my body. My altered mind thinks it's April for a moment, but I know she has shoes, little boots so like my own which Aimes found for her. This isn't April's foot standing so close to me.

Petyon is shouting again, a slow slur of excitement as my brain tries to catch up to my surroundings. I want to calm him, assure him it's not April. April is safe. As he hands the wounded Paula off to Dolph, he rushes towards me and I make the mistake I knew was coming when I said 'goodbye' to Lawless.

I promised my soul for his. I prayed, if someone was listening, to save him. Turns out, you never really know who is listening, but someone was, and the deal was accepted.

Chapter 37

I stumble backwards, tripping, startled by Peyton rushing towards me. His hands are outstretched, screaming my name, but I fall into the waiting arms of Marigold's trinkets before my fingers can reach his.

The explosion had rocked the room, casting the cages from their secure perches. With their cells broken, the ones who survive crawl free, not feeling the damage it has caused their small frames. Some of the children have caught fire. The flames dance along their numb bodies, following the trail of their clothing and hair. Some were thrown free, shattering their skulls so their bones are uneven, taking the soft flesh of their faces with the impact. Eyes swing free from their once tight sockets, hanging on with the cord of muscles fighting to keep them attached. I'm staring up at a collection of nightmares who stare at me with eyes of a starved hostage.

They descend upon me without a sound. There was no reason for their sudden flurry of attacks. As if of one mind, they move at once latching their teeth through my thick sweatshirt, trying to find the soft meat they crave. Raising my only arm which works, I try to fend them off, pushing their faces from my neck. There's so many of them, as I fight off one, others fall into the space.

My lungs fill with the scent of their deaths and the deaths they wear. I gasp against it, fighting for the air to scream from their assaults. They are sitting on me, pulling along the clothing I wear to expose my flesh. Their small hands flutter along my stomach and I know soon the still healing flesh will be their easy access, their gateway into my core of sticky sweet treats.

Peyton is still screaming my name over their howls of frustration. Strong hands clamp around my ankles. I kick at them in my panic, but they don't relent. Instead, they pull me towards them, sliding me along the floor and out from under the enraged descendants of Marigold's madness.

"Stop!" Peyton barks at me, yanking me to my feet.

He's pulling me, shoving me, anything to get me moving before the children form a second plan. There's no door to seal them behind. There's nothing to trap them, nowhere to hide from them, or escape them.

Peyton and I are walking backwards, watching them mimic our slow steps amid the burning room. Their broken bodies are starting to betray them. Their frail bones may be broken, but their distorted minds don't feel the legs they are dragging. They don't register the broken backs which have them dragging their torsos to keep up with their class. Having been locked in those cages for so long, the only thing their minds care about is the scent of blood twirling around us.

I try to turn my head to see who is in the hallway where we are leading this macabre parade. My neck is stiff, screaming from the pain shooting along my spine. Marxx's arm is extend from above, hauling the people Rhett helps to climb the ladder. Rhett is blistered, almost raw from where he was caught in the crossfire of the rooms when the flames burst through. He winces, crying out with every movement, but he presses through the pain.

"Hurry," I call to him, leading this dance of death with a slow pace to buy them more time.

I'm almost to them when I hear a small voice call to me.

"Please don't leave me!" Wren calls from the corner of the room beside me.

She's trapped behind a metal cabinet. Mimicking a deep wound, it has fallen, pouring the many papers it once held along the floor. The papers smoke with their edges flickering to life from where the fire has consumed them. Any moment, those scattered stacks will catch, sending everything in that room into flames.

"You have to be fucking kidding me," are the words I hear myself mutter. "Get out here." I'm whispering my urgency with a smile, trying to lull the monsters plotting against me.

"I can't." Wren is crying in her fear. Tears are suspended on her pointed chin before being released to her clothes. "My ankle hurts."

"You've got to be fucking kidding me," Peyton mimics my earlier statement.

Despite the circumstances, I laugh quietly upon hearing him say such a word. Peyton has always kept a tight grasp on his anger, letting petty be our ride. The children flash faces of confusion hearing my sound. It resets their minds, and their bodies hesitate with the new information they have sent it.

"Get her," I hiss at Peyton with the small army no longer creeping towards us. "Be quick!"

Peyton doesn't argue with me. Even he has learned it's pointless, or maybe he's just happy to no longer be in the direct line of a potential massacre. Either way, I'm left alone now to keep the gaze of fifteen cannibals.

Their eyes, with their unsettling colors, watch Peyton's disappearance. A few even try to tilt their bodies to watch him, keeping track of their meal. Most just swing those deadly eyes back to me, waiting to see what I am going to do, bracing what they can of their body in either defense or attack for what is happening.

Peyton isn't discreet with his rescue. Metal clangs, rolling their eyes to the sounds and back again. Their concerns over losing their first live meal is causing them to grow anxious. Soft sounds of protest bubble from their throats, growing louder as each of them join the chorus. We are running out of time.

"Peyton," I whisper to him, urgency rocking each syllable of his name.

"I'm here." Peyton stands beside me, looking lost at what to do next.

Wren is hiccupping with her sobs. She clings to Peyton's neck like it's the last thing to keep her from drowning. She's right because the sight of her has triggered their programmed minds. Wren means it's time to eat.

Their focus is completely on Peyton and he knows it. Time slows again when he looks to me. His face is settled, peaceful with the decisions he is about to make, and I can feel my heart start to break.

There is barely enough time for me to run to where Marxx and Rhett have lifted the last to safety. Sliding along the stone floor, I turn my body to take Wren from Peyton, to add her to the strong arms of Rhett to lift to the waiting Marxx. Peyton never made it.

With Wren secure in my one working arm, they overtook him, pulling him under their waves of manslaughter. Long nails are used as talons, securing into the meat of his back. I can hear the ripping of his shirt blending with the tearing of thicker things. Faces dive into the red widths of his body they have created, chewing and slurping with pure abandonment, pure joy. Their eyes close with their meal, rejoicing in what his screams mean, having been starved and forsaken for so long.

"Helena!" Rhett is holding his hand out to me, trying to guide me away from the same ledge he was standing on moments ago.

I should run from this damned place. I should look away and just be thankful it's not me, like so many others would right now. I'm not others. I'm Helena Hawthorn, and I know exactly what that means now.

Rhett's gun is hanging from the waistband where he keeps it tucked. The black metal winks at me, ready to follow me down into the self-destruction I've branded as my own. Rhett figures out what I am about to do, and he doesn't bother to talk me out of it. He climbs the ladder halfway, tossing me his gun and waiting for me to chase away my demons, to purge myself of the ghosts who dance around me.

I turned my back on a little girl in hallway once before. I left her to their feast with my fears and shaking mind, lost in what was happening at that time. I tossed a little boy into a closet, deluding myself he would be safe. I left a man who only wanted to save me, time and time again, to their sharp teeth and bone crushing hunger. I'm not doing it, again.

I've gotten better since that day in the rest center. The recoil doesn't shock me anymore, bouncing my shots wide. The weight doesn't feel heavy, pulling my aim off to one side or the other. The trigger is smooth, easy as death.

I don't aim for the carnage-covered children. They aren't the ones suffering. Being children, their buffet will take hours to kill Peyton. He won't even bleed out, escaping into shock before they reach their desired prizes. I tell myself, the last part of my sane self, I'm doing him a favor. My breath catches with the shot, ending his screaming and hopefully freeing him from the hell we've been plunged into. His blue eyes fade, and I pray for his forgiveness.

The children are unmoved by his death. They are so absorbed in the red-black warmth on their fingers and faces, they never look up. They never see the first one of them fall. The little boy slumps into the small cavity he and another have dug from Peyton's shoulder. His partner in excavation simply pushes him to the side, exposing the still seeping red meat they have worked to find. He doesn't enjoy it long. He, too, falls sideways as the bullet pierces a forehead a mother must have laid a thousand kisses on once upon a time.

It takes four deaths before the other eleven notice something is happening. Pieces of Peyton dangle from their mouths and hands when their bodies freeze, mocking the beautiful angels they were meant to be with the image. Their eyes slowly swing towards me, so slowly it's almost maddening, making me the target of their attention, once more.

They stand to their full height, keeping their arms locked in their feeding positions. Turning like robots, programed for one mission, they start their march towards me. There will be no stopping them this time.

"I'd shoot faster," Rhett chimes in his useful advice.

"Thanks," I mutter, and do as he suggests.

There was a time when watching these small victims fall would have shredded my worn-thin heart. As I finally lay these tortured toys to rest, I only see Peyton. I stare into his cold blue eyes which held such a warmth for life. I see what they have done to him, and whereas a part of me knows they aren't fully to blame, I have no shame in hating them.

The clip clicks empty as the last two children smile. The girl's brown hair is tinted where the ends have become black with blood, painting her pink shirt as if they were brushes of an abstract artist. The little boy was once the very picture of a father's joy. He even still wears his baseball jersey with the number proudly flaunted in the corner. They should be chasing each other on a playground, not rushing towards me, breaking the frail bones of those they have lived beside for who knows how long in metal cages of a decaying zoo.

With only one arm of use, I slide up the ladder, pressing my back to it for gravity. Spinning the gun to use it as a blunt weapon, I wait for these two. I wait for them to reach me, calming my racing mind from the panic which swells inside me.

When the girl trips, lodging her ruined tennis shoe into the ribcage of girl her own age, she is slowed. She screams with her rage and impatience when the boy arrives to the ladder first.

He reaches for me. His mouth is as open as his hands, both eager to feel my blood upon them. His ruby-stained lips pull back to expose his tiny teeth, and still I wait. I wait until his hands secure themselves in the tight denim fabric of my jeans. His fists squeeze tight, making the skin scream with the bruises I am sure he is leaving upon my calves, and I still wait.

Leaning his head down to my legs, he exposes the back of his auburn hair covered scalp. I finally bring the weight of the black gun down upon him. The first swing stuns him, fracturing the bones protecting him. My rage provides enough strength for the second to break them, but it's my third swing which sends the broken pieces into the soft matter underneath them. Drowning in rage and desperation, I don't count the rest of the swings, melting his skull to something soft and spoiled like rotten fruit.

Marigold was correct in some regards. Her little projects have achieved her goals of humanity and this one must have been one of the three Wren warned us about. The little girl isn't screaming, anymore. She's almost transformed into a face of something innocent when she realizes she's the only one left. Her slowed mind has her looking around, trying to form an answer for what has happened. She's lost, like a child waking up from a nightmare. She turns to me with sad eyes. A tear falls, cleaning away a path of murder along her jawline. I watch as that tear cleans her sins away.

"Mommy?" her torn voice asks, and then I watch as her body bounces from Marxx's gun.

Her pink shirt blooms in shades of dark flowers, a deeper pastel covers her torso when her body goes limp. She floats to the floor, bouncing one last time when she lands amid the rest of her ruined friends and the still bleeding body of Peyton, and I scream.

I scream with my grief. I scream with my rage. I scream with the sounds of a little girl crying for her mother in my mind. I think back to Margaret and the pile of bodies I had left there; all those little children, just like this girl, who in their final moments, just wanted their parents.

"You done?" Rhett asks. He's gentle with his words, but harsh with his question.

We are all screaming in some way. Our bodies beg us for rest. Our souls are overloaded with grief, and I get to tell Genny, she's lost another. It never gets easier, I had told her. I wish I had lied.

Chapter 38

Lawless is pale. His skin ashen with a grey cast to his color, but he is alive. Marigold had forgotten about him in her escape with Leigh. It was Lawless who crawled over to unlock the hatch, letting Marxx out when he began to bang on the rough wood.

While I cleaned the mess Marigold left for us, Paula had recovered enough to tend to his shoulder. She's tied a sling around his arm, forcing him to keep the shoulder immobile with the many layers of packed cloth she's stuck in the hole. She joked it would be refreshing to be stitching someone else for a change. Until she saw me. Now, she's mentally counting how many supplies she has left available at the fort.

The white house still stands. What it may or may not still hold, we didn't go in to find out.

"We'll send someone for them." Marxx is watching me, hoping I'm done with my heroics for the day.

"We won't," I tell him. "We can't risk it."

Marxx still doesn't know Marigold has made it contagious. He doesn't know the risks of bringing anyone she has left chained in the house back to the fort. Marigold made their graves the moment she brought them to this island. She knew they would never return.

The path to the boat is silent. We listen for any sound, any motion signaling of what may be around, and for the two we know are around. My fear is more of how many of Marigold's backup we don't know may be around, waiting to rescue her or finish us.

"I need to reset that arm." Paula is gripping my numb hand, testing it and the rest of the arm with some examination which makes perfect sense to her.

"It can wait." Since the arm isn't listening to any of my demands, I jerk my whole torso to escape her. I can only imagine how ridiculous it must look.

"We don't even know if there is a boat still. You may need it to swim back." Paula turns to my favorite tormenter. "Hold her steady, Marxx."

Marxx does so with a smile. He wraps his arm around me from behind, holding me close to him. "This is going to hurt," he whispers into my hair.

"Traitor," I whisper back.

Paula doesn't count to warn me. She lifts it, lining up the socket, testing the range once or twice with soft sounds of preparation. When I relax, thinking I have some time, she shoves the joint in place.

I don't scream. I simply half-faint in Marxx's embrace. I can feel him hold me tighter, cradling me tenderly until I fully recover.

"I warned you," Marxx says, with a tinge of amusement.

"Try not to use it too much." Paula has already moved on to her next victim and Rhett is protesting just a loudly as I had.

I follow the stumbling shambles of our group down the dirt path. My whole body has begun to ache. A molten heat is traveling the length of it, burning a path to my brain. I preferred the threat of shock to this suffering.

I fight through my blurring vision to see the boat is still there. Sitting at its helm, is the raven-haired shadow who tried to kill us all. She's been waiting for us and the smile she beams gives not a measure of relief to anyone around me.

With a sigh of his acceptance, Lawless hands his gun to Rhett. We know there will be no stopping him now. Watching him storm towards the boat, for a second, I almost feel sorry for what is about to happen to her. Almost.

"Don't shoot the boat, you big dummy!" Aimes shouts at his back. She, too, knows he has become rage over sense.

Leigh never stops smiling. She watches his approach as if he's merely joining her for a chat, not her possible death. Rhett, lost in his emotions, doesn't stop to think maybe it's not her death she has her mind on, but his.

We are tired, beaten and even broken. We let our guard down, thinking Rhett will close this chapter so we may turn the page to a better ending. We have forgotten it's not over. We have taken everything from Marigold. She plans to do the same.

Aimes' scream rings out the same time the shot echoes in the trees around us, sending the hiding birds scattering in the sky. Rhett's knees fold, and as his body collapses to the sand, I tear my eyes to the many birds above taking to flight. I refuse to see Rhett fall. I won't watch what I never thought could happen. His body stranded on the beach and not beside his family, rails against everything he's fought for to this point. Our demi-god of destruction has been brought down. For once, I don't want to see.

"Do something," Aimes is screaming.

Paula is doing her best to restrain her, to keep her hidden in the trees. Lawless has crouched down, trying to see where the shot came from, or who is watching us. Using the large scope of his rifle, Dolph copies him, scanning the opposite side. All I can see is Leigh with that daring smile, mocking us, once again.

"There's a second boat." Dolph points down the long beach. "I can't see how many are on it, but that has to be who did it."

"What do we do? We can't stay here pinned like this." Collin has kneeled, rocking the still unconscious Genny in his arms.

My mind is shattered, refusing to live in this moment, or any of the moments today has held for me. I watch Collin rocking Genny, her hair so like my own, and in my state, I wonder what my life may have been like if he ever held me. There's a rage bubbling inside me that I don't understand. Peyton is dead. Rhett is dead. Here, all I can focus on is my daddy issues and an inferno in my veins.

"Helena?" Lawless is tugging on my uninjured arm, trying to pull me down.

I'm the only one still standing, making a beacon of myself in my lunacy. Even this doesn't fully register. The heat of his skin does, because despite the fire wandering along my veins, I'm so cold.

"I'll go get him," I say, as if Rhett's just taking a long nap.

Lawless looks at me, wondering what secret plan I've made in my mind. Marxx doesn't stop me, so used to my lone ranger antics. Paula stares at me. There's something in her warm eyes which should have let me know that something is dangerously wrong.

Leigh's face melts as I come to the edge of the trees. I almost feel offended. I've watched her go from her beaming smile to a cold neutral face in mere seconds.

"Where's *my* smile?" I shout to the woman. "All this time, I thought we had something."

Leigh doesn't answer me, but the way her eyes dart to her right, I know where Marigold is hiding.

"Do you remember the porch of the house we squatted at?" I ask her. I can see her trying to figure out where my story telling is leading us. "You just walked around the right corner of the house, disappearing without a word."

Her mouth twitches, thinking she has the clues she needs. "Yes. I knew the right side would be more interesting."

"How many of those things did you kill that day?"

Leigh's smile spreads again, saying, "I didn't keep a good count."

I shrug, wincing with the pain it causes me. "Guess?"

"Three maybe four. You took the left side, I heard, killing another five, maybe?"

I can hear the men behind me spreading out. Leigh gave us the answers we needed.

"Nothing compared to the fifteen I had to clean up in the basement," I tell her, knowing who else is listening.

My comment hit its target. Marigold stands from behind the cover of the rotten boat hull. Her aim is wide, consumed with the grief of her loss. The sand around me erupts as the result of her rage, but none are close enough to stir my dulled nerves to a point of panic.

Shots ring out from all around me. Some from the trees. Some from the shoreline. Shouting follows the sounds, inciting pure chaos along the still waters of the shore. All of this, in my mind, means it's the perfect time to save Rhett.

Leigh stands, swaying the boat with her movement, when she sees me coming towards her. "Get down," she shouts at me.

I flip her off, coming to stand where Rhett is laying. The water around him is flowing red, tainting the color of the water with each wave that crashes over him. His face is covered by his uncut black hair. It washes along his jaw line, pulled with the ebb and flow of the water around him. Even in his deepest of sleeps, I've never seen him so defenseless, so broken.

I can feel the cold water soaking through the knees of my jeans where I've knelt to lift his head. Sweeping the hair from his face, he blinks at me, moaning as he comes awake. It's a sound that makes me weep with joy. I don't hide my tears, as I once did. Chapel never saw what his loss meant to me; I don't want the same for Rhett.

"You're going to have to wake up, now," I tell him, looking into his hazed eyes.

He doesn't answer me. His eyes flutter close before I can convince him of the danger around us.

"Get him in the boat," Leigh has come to stand beside me, lifting half of Rhett's heavy body to help me move him.

It isn't easy to drag the unconscious man to the boat. The waves push against us, stealing a step for every three we take. There is nothing gentle about how we toss Rhett onto the boat, rolling his long legs with a heave of a motion. I've turned my back to the shoreline, concentrating on saving my demon of protection. In that slip, I have completely forgotten about the civil war unfolding behind me. I had, until its General appears with the sound of the chambering revolver to my head.

"What did you do to them?" Marigold's shaky voice asks me.

I don't lift my hands in surrender. If she's going to shoot me, my hand position will not detour her. "That's odd coming from someone who tried to blow them up."

"What did you do to them?" Marigold screams, destroying the image of the revered mother she worked so hard to project at the fort.

"Which ones? The adults? The children? Or your daughter?" I hear myself ask.

"I should just kill you now. I knew the moment you arrived you would ruin it all. The way they turned to them instead of me and Torri. The way we kept bending rules to keep them out of sight just to have control again. I knew you would ruin everything." Marigold is rambling now, biting off her sentences with her heavy thoughts.

I have no idea what she's talking about, but I listen, trying to figure it out. With one who keeps flipping sides and the other who thinks psychopaths are trainable, listening for a hint of how to understand her may be my only way out of this mess. I can't help but think it would be nice if Rhett were to wake up, right now.

"Ranya is going to be the answer. She is going to be the first adult to be a carrier and not just a host. Everything you've done, it's for nothing. She is going to allow me to save more than just the children!"

"The children were the only carriers?" I had never put that together, until now.

All the bites on Ranya's arm were small, children's teeth and Marco met his end when going to meet his child. Marigold had the children turn their parents, hoping the same bloodline would transmute, morphing it to be sustainable in adult hosts. Now, she's out there, somewhere, passing it along with her very need to survive.

"They were, but I changed that."

Marigold sounds proud of herself. I guess I'll have to fix that.

"Too bad she escaped." I don't even shy away from the joy I feel telling her the little fact she's missed. "Her and Marco are long gone, making little undead babies of their own. Maybe. I don't really know how your voodoo works."

"Why do you have to be so defiant?" I hear Marigold ask me.

She's seething now over what I've done to her and how little I'm scared of her. It only brings me more joy.

"Like I told Torri – doing stupid things is kind of my thing."

I've watched enough bar fights to know when someone is serious in their threats, or just threatening to bolster their nerves. If Marigold was going to shoot me, I would already be dead. But I don't want to wait around until she's ready to kill me, either.

Planting my feet, as well as I can in the thick mud of the water, I spin my upper body, letting my elbow connect with her face. It rocks her, flailing her body backwards with the force of my strike and the pull of the waves. She fires a single shot into the air as the current takes her under. Even as I prepare myself to find her, to finish what should have ended in the barn, it's Leigh who beings to fire into the water where we last saw Marigold.

She continues to pull the trigger of her gun until it clicks empty, and still she pulls it, refusing to accept what the sound means. It's several seconds before Marigold appears, crawling onto the shore. She's spitting more than just the salty water onto the sand. She claws herself out of the water, raking the compacted sand into long furrows. Waves crash around her, trying to steal back their treasure. Her silver hair is dark now. Its thick mats soaking in the water, discoloring it with salty stains. Leigh and I watch her struggle until she doesn't anymore. We watch as Marigold melts, falling limply back into the water, despite her best efforts to free herself.

I had promised myself she would have no stone monuments in her name. I had vowed that there would be no tears cried for her. As we watch her float by, I know no one will.

"Do I want to know?" I watch Leigh as Marigold sinks from our vision, tossing in the deeper waves.

"She was my mother," Leigh says this, as if it should make her murder completely understandable. Living my life, it does. "I didn't know what she was doing down there until she had me go find Patrick. When I did, I tried to stop him. He caught me trying to burn the building. That's when he put me in the closet. He knew he couldn't kill me because my mother would cut him off, but she never came for me, either. She let me sit there, more invested in her creatures than her daughter. Wren was supposed to be her next subject." Leigh turns to me so what she says next will fully sink in. "Her own granddaughter."

"And that's why you killed Torri?"

"Someone had to stop them."

Leigh says this in a complete monotone voice. She doesn't expect me to understand or argue with her. She's not looking for awards or thanks. She simply did what she knew in her heart had to be done. No fame or glory needed.

The island has sunk back into the silence of seclusion again. I can hear Aimes and Paula shouting the little girls' names from beyond the trees. Whatever happened with the rest of Marigold's people, I'll ask later, but right now I'm so very tired.

With the last of the adrenaline leaving me, I can feel my body caught in a wildfire of conflagration. Even the cold water up to my waistline does nothing to quench the heat. My whole body is screaming, splitting my head with the pain it's causing me. I just want to rest, to close my eyes and let someone else worry about things.

"Do you have April?" Aimes' voice startles me, bringing me back.

"Yes, I always drag small children into my fights."

"I'm serious! We can't find her or Wren." Aimes is staring at the shoreline, trying to spot anything of resemblance to the little girls. "We left them by the trees. I told them to sit together, to not move, and I'd come get them when it was safe."

Lawless and Marxx emerge from the thick trees with the rest falling in behind them. Paula is walking backwards with her hands covering her eyes from the late afternoon sun. She, too, is searching for the little girls, but she too is also having no luck.

Lawless checks the pulse on Rhett when he arrives beside me. His shirt is stained in irregular patterns of splotches and swirls. The many shades speak to it being more than just his blood he is wearing, but neither of us make a comment about it.

"You look like shit," I tell him, earning me a smirk. "Still carry two guns, I see."

"People keep taking my main." His voice is as defeated as mine.

"We have to go," Marxx whispers it to Lawless, pressing him on the urgency, despite the two missing girls.

The shock of what he said must have shown on my face before my words escape my lips. "You can't be serious?"

"Rhett is bleeding out. Lawless is bleeding out. You look like you're going to fall over any moment. Who exactly do you think is going to go into those woods and find the girls?" Marxx asks.

It's a hushed conversation about the little girls' fate. Rhett will never forgive us if we leave her out there, but Rhett may not live to forsake us if we don't head back. It's a coin toss of morality, outweighed by necessity.

"Wren knows the island." Leigh is trying to sound assuring, but she too is watching the shoreline with a prayer on her lips. "She'll keep them safe until we can come back tomorrow morning."

"We're leaving?" Aimes is close to a full mental break. Her voice trembles, cracking under the pressure of what is about to happen.

Everyone is watching Lawless, waiting for him to make the call. His knuckles are white, grasping the metal railings to keep himself standing. Brown eyes stare into the bottom of the boat where Rhett lays, covering the floor in pink-tinted water. Shaking his head, he makes the choice he hopes won't come back to haunt him.

"We're leaving," Lawless says, hoisting himself into the boat.

It's not a suggestion. He doesn't leave room for anyone to argue or try to change his mind. He watches me, waiting for me to try both. I give him neither.

Marxx has already grabbed Aimes, also discouraging her from trying to argue. Instead, she cries. Soft sobs escape from her with her eyes only for the tree line where she left the children. She will forever tell herself this was her fault. She was supposed to protect them, keep them safe, but she abandoned them. She will hear their cries tonight. She will hear their cries every night until we find them.

Marxx and Dolph help load what is left of our family into the vessel. We rushed to this beach filled with eagerness to save those upon it. We pull away drenched in blood, tears, and defeat. When this started on a snow-covered road by a high school, there were fourteen of us. When we arrived at the fort, there were eleven. Now, as the sun starts to set on a long-forgotten island, there are nine. With the amount of bleeding people rocking with the waves, that number may also change.

Paula has already started working on Rhett. She assures us his wounds are superficial and that he'll be fine. Yet, not a single one of us tries to wake him. We let the sleeping beast lie, because when he does wake, every single one of his demons will demand payment for what we have done. Aimes holds his hand, stroking his damp hair. Even her gentle touch won't be enough to quell his rage once it starts.

"Let me see that arm." Paula nudges me awake, pulling the neck of my sweatshirt to examine what's left of my stiches.

Whatever she sees, sends her face to a neutral mask even Leigh couldn't match. She doesn't ask me any more questions. There's no long list of verbal check points, as she held with the men. She just watches me with eyes betraying her flat expression.

This should worry me. Somewhere, in some small rational part of my mind left to me, I know this should worry me, but it doesn't. I surrender to the pain, letting it wash over me and pull me into the blackness of oblivion. I can hear her say something to Dolph sitting beside me, but I can't make out the words.

I let it all slip away to escape the fire eating me internally. I don't even cringe when Margaret begins to sing her damning song, but when her new playmate calls out for her mother from a dark corner of the cage I've invented, it shatters the last piece of my soul.

Chapter 39

My body is shivering, sweating as the flames threaten to engulf me. I cry out with the pain, begging Paula for help, but she just watches, as she tries to hide her tears. It comes in waves, pushing me to the breaking point and then dragging me further each time. It's unrelenting and I don't understand what is happening.

Collin is sitting beside me, holding my hand. He's the last person I want to see, yet at the same time, he's the only person I want to see.

"I think I should tell you about your mother." Collin's voice cracks when he says the words we have both been avoiding.

I chuckle, amused by his horrible timing. "Now?" I look to him, asking again. "Really? Now?"

I don't miss the image his eyes hold. Those blue eyes, so like the ones who had damned me long ago, stare at me with a sadness I didn't know he could hold for me. He stares at me as if this may be the last time he sees me.

"I think so," he whispers.

Sighing, I breathe through the lull the pain has allowed me. He takes this for an invitation, beginning a story I have both dreaded and craved.

"Her name was Alicia Helen Clark. I named you after her," he says this with a smile of a soft memory. "She had the most amazing green eyes. All I ever had to do was look into those eyes to warn me of her mood before her sharp tongue could."

"It's why she hated my eyes." I don't ask it, but he nods to confirm it. He knows which 'she' I am referring.

"Alicia and I..." He pauses, trying to find the right words for his indiscretion.

I wave him off, avoiding having to listen to his past romances. "I get the idea."

"No. You don't. She loved you, Helena. I snuck her pictures of you behind Carol's back. I wasn't supposed to have contact with her after your birth, but I did. We would meet and all she wanted to know, all she wanted to talk about, was you. I failed you both. Too afraid of upsetting Carol and too afraid of being found out, I never picked a side. I never fought for you."

His confession doesn't move me. Once, it may have been everything I wanted to hear, but now, it falls flat with a past constructed of too many mistakes and too much anger.

"She came for you. That day it all started she came to the house looking for you. It's how we found each other. We both walked out of that house not knowing where our children were. She held that against me until the day I lost her, too."

Turning to him, he pushes away the hair matted to my face from the salty water and thick layers of my sweat.

"She would have been so proud of you," Collin tells me, cooing with his statement. "You are so incredibly like her – strong, resilient and as defiant as they come. When I hear you laugh, it's like she's standing beside me, again. You both have that 'I dare you' attitude which makes you unbreakable."

I don't want him to see me cry. Not over this. Not over a woman I never knew. Not over the gaping holes my childhood left in my heart.

"Genny is so like you both" Collin's words are fading as the pain begins to climb. "Helena, rest now. I promise you, I won't fail, again. Just let go, Helena. I'll stay right here until you let go. I won't leave you again."

I don't understand what he's saying. I scream with the pain. I can't control the convulsions, snapping my body rapidly on the bed. My head slams against the cot, and I'm terrified my neck will snap from the force of it.

"Helena, listen to my voice," Paula whispers, trying to calm me through the red haze of pain. "You were bitten, Helena. There's no reason to fight this. I can't save you, but I can stop it, or you can hang on for a few more days until your body burns itself out. Just tell me what you want. I'll do whatever you want."

I can't speak through the cresting wave of agony. I can only scream disjointed syllables. I don't want to die, but I don't want this suffering, either.

Looking to my father, I see that he's kept his promise. He holds my hand to his lips, not looking away as my body rips itself apart, but it's who is over his shoulder which breaks my heart.

Ashley, in her soft pink pajamas and white socks smiles at me. She's holding hands with Conroy who still wears his cowboys and dancing horses. Lilly is standing beside them, twirling in her white night gown around the room. They smile at me, silently beckoning me.

"Stop being a douche, Helena," Conroy tells me, with a wide grin of a shared secret. "Come play."

"Won't you come play with us?" Lilly asks me, her voice twinkling with her soft bell of a pitch that only innocence can gift someone.

There is no sinister motive behind their smiles. They are as they were before all of this. Three perfect angels left to an imperfect protector. I've tried so hard to make up for my sins since that day, hoping they would forgive me for how tragically I failed them.

"I left them alone." I struggle through the pain to say. "I didn't know where else to take them. I just wanted to take them somewhere they would be safe, somewhere that they knew and could keep them safe until you were found. I didn't want the responsibility. I had just killed Carol. I didn't know what to do." The pain has me panting, struggling to stop the confession of my soul and struggling to keep it going. "I left them, and I went to the bar to hide. I just left them."

My tears are as hot as the fire inside me, streaming freely along my face. Collin thinks I'm searching for redemption, some pardon for my sins, but I just want them to understand. I never meant for any of this to happen.

"It's okay, Helena," Collin whispers into my hair. "I should have been there. You never should have had that burden. There's nothing to apologize for."

"I've killed so many."

"You've saved so many more."

"I left them behind."

"It was never your fault."

Collin repeats the words Chapel once told me before I scream as the wave reaches its full strength, but I never take my eyes from my angels.

Ashley leans so close to me, for a moment I don't understand why he doesn't see her. She tells me, "They don't need you, anymore. We do."

"Helena," Paula shouts over my brutal screams. "Tell me what you want me to do!"

"Do it," I hear Lawless from the corner of the room.

He comes to stand on the other side of me, my lighthouse, but he can't guide me home from this. Not anymore.

I don't know what the command was he told Paula. I don't feel the needle slip into my arm, or the deadly cocktail she pressed into my veins. My breathing becomes slowed, less painful, and heavy. My body loses its tension, letting me rest mutely on the stiff fabric. The fire recedes to nothing more than a warm blanket wrapped around me. I feel featherlight, floating even as Lawless cradles me.

"You should go," Paula whispers, her voice hoarse with emotions. "I'll finish it."

Neither men show any signs of listening to her, and I'm so happy to be pain-free, I'm not following the conversation.

Paula clears her throat, fighting down the sadness which coats it. "There will be a few seconds before it happens. She won't wake up. I'll make it fast."

My vision begins to blur. The room fades into shades of greys before becoming total darkness. I can hear Lawless moaning, such a tormented sound to come from a man, but it doesn't reach me. Nothing does. I'm floating in a warm bath, fading deeper into the darkness.

"Helena!" Conroy is shouting for me, skipping ahead of me as if riding an imaginary horse. Upon his feet are bright red sneakers with yellow markings. "Can't catch me, Helena."

I follow him into a memory of a time long ago. A time before scents became dank and smothered in loneliness. When hope was more than just a rope we clung to, but a memory of times long forgotten. I smile at him knowing we will never again endure nights too dark or dawns which come too soon. We are no longer surrounded by fragile things and our nightmares no longer walk among us. I guess you could say, I've always had a hatred for the dawn.

Epilogue

Dear Journal,

I don't know what will happen to us, now. There are ghosts in their eyes, only Helena could chase away. I may be her cousin, but I'm not equipped to cleanse such damage. She held them together when she thought she tore them apart, and now, they are hanging by a rope; a rope which resembles a noose more and more every day.

It's been three weeks since her death and we still haven't found the girls. Rhett and Marxx go every day, but they always come back without them. Rhett finds comfort in the fact there's no trace of them. I know what he's saying without having it explained to me. It brings me comfort, too, but we are leaving now despite Rhett's many objections. He doesn't want to admit it, but he knows if they haven't been found by now, we won't find them.

Lawless doesn't talk much, anymore. He's stepped down as our leader and handed the reins to Marxx. Marxx wasn't happy about it, but he accepted. We're all worried Lawless will try to follow my cousin, but there's nothing we can really do about it to stop him. He sits by her grave every morning, talking to her about his regrets. I wonder if she ever really knew how much she meant to him.

Aimes is trying to hold everything together. She keeps her banter on the lighter side, less of her harsh wit, but I see her when she thinks no one is watching her. She hides her tears well, but I see them. Her and Rhett haven't been the same since that day. They try, but there's too many unsaid things between them.

Collin hovers over me. I can't breathe without him asking me if I'm okay. I know he's just trying to take care of me since we are all that we have now, but the man really needs a hobby. He keeps saying how he won't fail again, but I have no clue what the man is talking about.

Dolph and Paula keep to themselves. The scars the island gave them are still healing and they are both afraid to have them picked at. All-in-all, they are suffering like the rest of us, but just want to do it alone.

I worry about all of them, but I'm not sure what I can do.

My cousin taught me that defiance is sometimes loud, like an unsettled crowd, jeering each other into a frenzy over imagined injustice. Defiance is sometimes silent, like the lost souls standing wordlessly in their suffering, united against the world. Sometimes, defiance is an act, bold and unnerving as you stare into Death's dark eyes and tell her, "Yes. I see you." with nothing more than a smile and blood-soaked hands. My cousin was a hero, despite how she saw herself. Collin says I have her spirit. I can only hope he's right.

"What are you doing?" Aimes asks me, as I close the thick book I have begun keeping.

"Something my mother taught me," I tell her with a smile.

"What is it with you Clarks and your mothers?" Aimes smiles with her question, but I know what it cost her to ask.

I shrug, packing the book into a purple book bag she had found for me in one of the rooms of the fort. I told her we should have asked before we took it, telling her it might make someone angry. She had said, "Good, I hope it does."

"They ready to leave?" I ask her, figuring that's why she's come to find me.

"Yeah." Aimes is staring at the makeshift marker my cousin's memory now represents. "I guess we are."

Lawless comes to stand beside us, watching the same spot as we are.

"You really coming with us?" he asks me with his eyes still for my cousin's memory.

Nodding with my words, I tell him, "Yeah. You really going to play nice with Collin?"

Lawless half smirks, turning just the corners of his lips. "Just keep him in the truck."

He turns to lead us towards the boats, but after a few steps he stops, telling me without turning towards me, "Put it on. It's yours now."

Looking to Aimes, she nods, approving of what I'm about to do.

With shaking hands, I unzip the purple bag slung over my shoulder. I stare at it before I pull it out. I've come to know their scent like a comfort, something I've used to chase the nightmares away, and I smile at the skull who stares up at me.

Dropping the bag to the ground, I pull out the leather vest. The weight always shocks me. Heavy enough to hold a life of its own, I slip the leather over my shoulders like a taboo ritual. It settles on me, as holding a hug from a long lost relative. The long, double-edged blade with its leather holder I tuck into the safety of my boot. It caresses my ankle, and I feel safer just knowing it's there, that it was hers.

Lawless is watching me now. There's a sadness to his brown eyes, but he smiles at me over it. "Looks good," he tells me, but I know a part of him is breaking seeing her items. "She would have wanted you to have them."

I don't argue with him. I didn't argue with him the day he handed them to me. I'm happy to have them, to be immersed in her memories. I know I can never replace her. I only hope I can live up to her reputation. I hear she had a thing for doing stupid things.

Extras

THE SIREN SERIES BOOK ONE
CROWN OF BETRAYAL
Daggers will kill you,
but the cloaks will
destroy you.
MARIE F CROW

Verona has lived in the safety and bliss of the palace and the luxury of what being a Siren means. Content to live her life in the shadows of her beautiful mother, Ostila, and the enchanting, dark beauty of her aunt, Morlena, Verona never thought about what life would be like should they be taken from her. At her mother's coronation, these once impossible thoughts become shockingly real.

Corander has lived his life in the shadows of his father, Kurt. At the head of the Empradar bloodline, Kurt holds no mercy for those who fail him and even less for those he distrusts. When the palace falls to madness, it will be Corander who is tested by his father's desires and torn by his own.

Together, Corander and Verona must discover who they really are, and who they are truly meant to become, before all is lost to hidden plots and crowns of betrayal.

Continue Verona and Corander's story here!

About the Author

Marie F Crow weaves her stories around the human element of the horror verses the 'monsters' themselves. She believes that the real horror of life does not come from the expected, but from the unexpected responses of the human nature and what depths of trauma a person must survive in certain situations. She began writing The Risen series when feeling that the popular genre was slipping too deep into the realm of pure 'slasher' and forgetting what the horror of zombies can mean for a story.

Now, with her children's series launched, Marie hopes to use her favorite 'monster' as a teaching tool to inspire children to understand that not everything that looks scary, is scary. With

Abigail and Her Pet Zombie series, Marie hopes to further spread her love for all things "that go bump in the night" with small children showing them that it's okay to be different and to embrace those same differences in those around them.

Social Media Links
Facebook: @MarieFCrow.Author
Instagram: @authormariefcrow
Twitter: @MarieFCrow

Additional titles by Marie F Crow:

The Risen Series
Dawning
Margaret
Remnants
Courage
Defiance

A Risen Series Novel
Genny (Coming Soon)
Lost Doves (Coming Soon)

The Siren Series
Crown of Betrayal
Crown of Remorse (Coming Soon)

The Abigail and her Pet Zombie Series
Illustrated Children's Books
Abigail and her Pet Zombie
Zoo Day
Spring
Summer
Halloween

The Abigail and her Pet Zombie Series
Beginner Chapter Books
Abigail and her Pet Zombie

The Great HEXpectation Series
The Little Lies (Coming Soon)

About the Publisher

Kingston Publishing offers an affordable way for you to turn your dream into a reality. We offer every service you will ever need to take an idea and publish a story. We are here to help authors make it in the industry. We've been hurt by publishers in the past and we want to provide a positive experience that will keep you coming back to us.

Whether you want a traditional publisher who offers all the amenities a publishing company should or an author who prefers to self-publish, but needs additional help - we are here for you.

Now Accepting Manuscripts!
Please send query letter and manuscript to:
submissions@kingstonpublishing.com
Visit our website at www.kingstonpublishing.com

www.ingramcontent.com/pod-product-compliance
Lightning Source LLC
Chambersburg PA
CBHW070619100726
47907CB00007B/1799